THE ANTUNITE CHRONICLES: BOOK 2

TERRY BIRDGENAW

Copyright © 2022 by Terry Birdgenaw

All rights reserved. No part of this publication may be reproduced, distributed, or transmitted in any form or by any means without the author's prior written permission, except with brief quotations within critical articles and reviews permitted by copyright law.

While reading this book, you will meet historical arthropod fictional figures whose names, words, or actions may resemble people here on Earth, either from the present or past. The resemblance is only implied for humoristic purposes and is not meant to reflect literal, thematic, or chronologic historical accuracy, as the novel epitomizes political satire or parody. Except for public or famous historical figures whose statements appeared in the public domain, any resemblance of the insect and insectoid characters to persons living or dead is coincidental. The views and opinions expressed by these rhyming insects, or the insectoid historian narrator, are their own and should not be attributed to the author.

ISBN: 978-1-778-1516-5-1 (paperback)

ISBN: 978-1-7781516-6-8 (ebook)

Legal deposit, Library and Archives Canada, July 2022

CHARACTER CONNECTIONS IN EPOCHS I-II

(Underline: Anthiery and Antianna's classmates; Italics: Renaissant's cabinet; Asterisks: studied with Renaissant* or Innovant **; # Antilla's father; + also fallen hero)

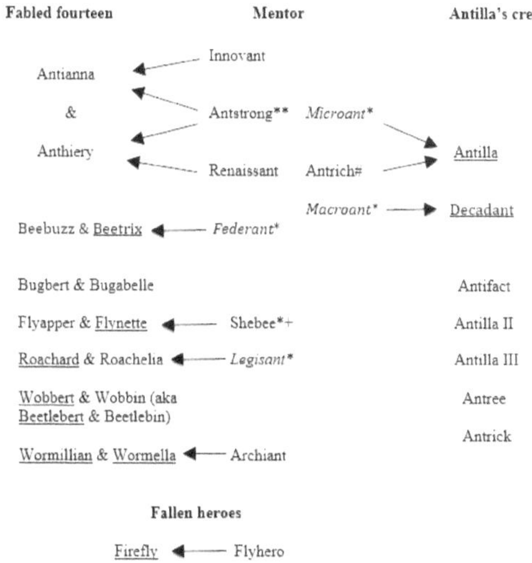

Epoch II heroes: Gretant, Roachman, Heroach, Thunbug

Additional UNIT professors: Antland, Antoria, Antrain, Beefarm, Beetree, Truant

Lesser characters: Beeanna, Spyfly, Wiseant, Prudant, Wobbella

CHARACTERS BY HEXURY ON BILALUNA IN EPOCH III

First & Second Hexury

Fabled Fourteen: Antianna, Anthiery, Beebuzz, Beetrix, Bugabelle, Bugbert, Flyapper, Flynette, Roachard, Roachelia, Wobbert, Wobbin, Wormella, Wormillian

Fifth & Sixth Hexury

Congress & Queen: Senant, Threebee
New Refugees: Antoria, Gretant, Thunbug

Ninth & Tenth Hexury

Queen & Congress: Beewise, Roachboss
BITE Scientists: Beemajor, Natbug
Alien Scouts: Antwell, Gofly, Roachian
Earth Visitors: Celeste, Hawk, Matt

Fourteenth & Fifteenth Hexury

Queen: Beehappy

OPENING PODCAST [TRANSCRIPT]

Narrant: Like the moth that fluttered too close to the fire, [static] the roach underfoot, the fly engulfed in the smokestack draft—it did not end well. Either scorched to ash, spiracles and tracheae compressed, dioxide poisoned, [pause, loud static] whatever the means—it did not end well. It took an instant to smother an eternal fire. It spanned ages, yet was over in an infernal gasp. Some survived, but millions did not. [loud static, inaudible 00:32]… took a few to damn the many, and many were taken by those now damned by a few. I know the story, the complete story, from start to finish and beyond. Now I must tell the story. [loud static, inaudible 00:51]… had it not been for those few that endured, I could not tell the story. [pause, static] Our history would have vanished. [01:00] [*Narrant's pheromonal secretions were electronically translated and broadcast in a crackly transmission*].

Vive: This is Vive McDougall with my weekly Astro-science read-u-mentary podcast—*What's Out There?* It's January 7, 2051, and this is our first podcast of the new year. Those of you who followed our podcast in September and October last year will remember our interstellar author Narrant from the moon of our sister planet, Poo-ponic. And folks, this is the day! I talked about it all last Fall, and finally, we're going to read volume II of Narrant's story. Yes, we'll be reading *The Complete History of Poo-ponic and Bilaluna: Volume II—From Boom to Doom and Back Again*. [02:32] [brief pause] Welcome, Narrant. I think that's how you like to be addressed.

Narrant: Like before, Narrant is good.

Vive: Narrant, I wanted to launch the podcast with the prologue of your second volume, because it's so powerful [03:01]. We know that your insect and cyborg insect societies went through rough times, but that opening brought it home. Or should I say, down to Earth? But for those who missed volume I, tell our listeners a little about you.

Narrant: Yes, I am a cyborg insect or insectoid known as an ANT, for allied noble tripod, the first cyborg insect phylogenetic family created on Poo-ponic. I live along with 999 other insectoids on Bilaluna, Poo-ponic's moon. [03:32]

Vive: I remember last time you said you were a descendant of the first colonists that came to Bilaluna from Poo-ponic 15,000 hexs ago. I think most of our listeners know what a hex is now. It's the time for the orbit of Poo-ponic around your solar star.

Narrant: Yes, as you know, our time reflects the heximal counting system we use because we have six limbs.

Vive: The heximal system applied to shorter and longer time units, with words like hexonds and hexades, and each step goes up or down by times 6, not times 10. [03:56]

Narrant: Yes, I used the decimal system for most numbers in the book, but as a historian, I wanted to keep our own system for time units.

Vive: For those that missed our Fall programing, could you give a little more background about your engaging society, how you evolved, and why you wrote your book?

Narrant: Vive, our first colonists, were refugees from Poo-ponic, where our small biological insect ancestors first constructed cyborg insects. [04:29] To avoid the cultural and environmental mistakes of our past and to provide a caution to our new friends on Earth, the All-insect Historical Society or AHS charged me with documenting the complete history of the demise of Poo-ponic.

Vive: And Narrant, you did it, and the story is remarkable, even vaulting from your planet to your moon. Could you tell our listeners what period of your history this volume covers? [06:01]

Narrant: The story follows the history of the last generation of insects on Poo-ponic to the final three survivors of the plague. It also provides an account of our time on the moon Bilaluna from the first fourteen settlers.

Vive: I see the story is about insects and insectoids and how they coped with perilous times thrust upon them by draconian leaders.

Narrant: Yes, the treatise follows the tales of great and infamous insects and cyborg insects, [06:29] including the notorious Antilla-the-One and his clones, the Fabled Fourteen, and the courageous Gretant and her partner Thunbug. I was also lucky to acquire various diaries of what you might call ordinary insects and insectoids, which allowed me to write this history more like a story. As you might say, it goes into the common den, as well as palaces and houses of government. [06:58]

Vive: And your history is so rich, [08:01] it seems your society went through an incredible evolution, one that you might say parallels human history.

Narrant: Yes, Vive, my book records momentous events throughout our past, including cyborg creation, the Great Small Insect War, Poo-Ponic's atmospheric collapse, and Bilaluna's recovery.

Vive: Indeed, Narrant, your account seems like a roller-coaster ride of highs and lows. Your book title reflects it well, and it also appears to be a cautionary tale. [08:29] Your society went through so much, especially on Poo-ponic.

Narrant: Well, it was not all gloom and doom. Some parts were heartening, some were humorous, and there was hope. But as times got bad, the signs were there. They just did not heed them.

     Terry Birdgenaw

Vive: I assume you know too about the troubles we've had—the hurricanes, wildfires, and the submersion of many of our island nations. Disasters have displaced many people from their original lands [08:56], and tropical diseases are now universal.

Narrant: Yes, that compelled me to translate my book, so humans could learn from our calamities and try to reverse their trajectory. I not only translated the book, but I targeted it to you—insectoids would not understand many references.

Vive: As before, you have a delicate balance of tragedy and comedy. There was such devastation, but I sometimes laughed aloud while reading about it. And again, you have poetry before every chapter, and some are very provocative. [09:25]

Narrant: As a historian, my account was as accurate as possible, describing the destruction of our planet and its inhabitants, as well as the near destruction of our moon. Like in the first volume, the poetic preludes are a tribute to my rhyming ancestors.

Vive: Yes, I remember your elites often speak in rhymes, following in the footsteps of your early poet, Antspeare. But there's not only poetry but plenty of humor.

Narrant: [laughs] Having read my earlier essays on the subject, my superiors complained that my prose was too comical occasionally. But I find the sheer horror of what happened to our society needs some counterbalancing humor. Anyway, my ancestors, and their fellow insects, were an amusing bunch before ignorance, [10:59] greed, and their leaders led them spiraling to the lowest depths.

Vive: I see you broke your book up into epochs. Why is that?

Narrant: Each of the three epochs covers a vital part of our history, with as much as hexuries separating them. In between, not much of great significance occurred.

Vive: And what would you say to our listeners about why they should read this book? I assume you wish to highlight environmental issues and political tyranny. [11:26]

Narrant: Yes, [in a severe tone] other civilizations should learn from the error of our ways, lest they be doomed to suffer a similar fate if conditions so dictate.

Vive: Yes, some of our leaders have steered us down the wrong path, and our world is worse off for it. And with that, we should start with the first chapters.

Narrant: Yes, I am excited that humans will hear our story.

Vive: Okay, listeners, we shall begin. Each week we will read two chapters—each one starting with Narrant's lovely poems. [11:59] This will go on week-by-week until we finish the twelve chapters. After we finish reading the book, Narrant will join us, and he has again agreed to answer questions from our listeners.

Narrant: Yes, I am happy to join you and answer more questions.

Vive: Oh, and by the way, listeners, as with all our podcasts, you can either listen each week on Saturday or read the clean verbatim transcripts uploaded by Sunday morning. And for these broadcasts, with the feedback of the syntax generator, we had our professional audiobook reader take over. We also dubbed over Narrant's voice during our interview to reduce the noise. [12:31]

Narrant: Yes, Vive, and he does an excellent job. And your listeners will get much more out of it than with me using pheromonal ant-speak.

Vive: [laughs] That's right, it's hard to smell online. Here goes—chapters one and two from Epoch I of *The Complete History of Poo-ponic and Bilaluna: Volume II—From Boom to Doom and Back Again* by our guest Narrant. [12:50]

EPOCH I: FROM ROBOTS TO CYBORGS TO CHAOS

CHAPTER 1

GROWING PAINS

It's an orb of unmatched beauty with folk of mighty brain.

Yet a land afire with averse and unrivaled beastly brawn.

And ne'er is power so combustible as that based on ego.

*When one flames their id by mindless
deeds that none would see as super.*

ABOUT FOUR HUNDRED and fifty mega-hexs after Antuna's death, the combination of thousands of plants and insects multiplying and living in unfettered harmony resulted in a healthy, dense forest extending throughout the planet. With an oxygen-rich atmosphere and thick clouds, daily rains over hex-uries helped create beautiful rainforests of lush tall leafy trees and jungles with tropical plants and flowers. Crystal clear streams and brooks fed cascading silvery waterfalls that begot turbulent rivu-lets and sparkling rivers, dividing rich green groves of forests and jungles. A canopy of majestic conifers, with cypress, kauri, and sequoia, offset an assortment of coconut, date, triangular, and fan palms. Various deciduous trees, including maple, red oak, apple, and sweet gum, umbrella'd multi-shade green sprinklings of ferns, mosses, and vines. Particularly breath-taking were the groves of flowering magnolias, lilacs, and rhododendrons, with their diverse hues of pink, purple, blue, yellow, and red blossoms. This myriad-colored foliage complemented a blend of herbaceous flowering shrubs and plants, including ruby columbine, wild pink roses, orange hexay-lilies, green chrysanthemums, wild blue indigo, and purple coneflowers. This flora generated an intense rainbow of vibrant hues any avid gardener would envy.

The colony capital Queen Bee, young Beeanna, described it well, "There is no more lovely a place in the universe, with leafy green plants to feed us, and crystal-clear water to quench our thirst. With the flora's bright colors and the waterfall's roar, this land is our homeland with wonders galore."

Beeanna loved her gardens, but also had a strong interest in history. Eager to learn about the planet's early colonists, she hired a young Antunite, Anthiery, as an attendant.

She asked Anthiery, "What do you think is the biggest difference in our society compared with Antuna's time?"

Anthiery answered thoughtfully, "Many things changed, but the greatest alteration was domestic life."

"In what ways did relations differ?" asked Beeanna.

"Families in Antuna's time were like those on Earth. Queens were the only mothers, and they sterilized other ants and bees."

Beeanna walked towards Anthiery. "How did they do that?"

Anthiery released a stifling scent. "Queens released pheromones that suppressed the sex hormones of the workers."

Beeanna wilted a little. "So only the Queen could lay eggs? And she had to mate with all the drones?"

Anthiery replied. "That's correct."

"I can't even imagine that. And so many larvae and pupae to clean up after. That is a big transformation," exclaimed Beeanna.

Anthiery turned to survey his surroundings. "Yes, and the central hive was also the home for everyone, and they didn't have satellite hives and nests as we have now."

Beeanna considered it for a long moment. "Why did they change things?"

"Nobody knows for certain, but it's likely because we lived much longer," responded Anthiery. "Some say my ancestor Antuna started it by having offspring, even though she wasn't a queen ant." *The first in my line on Poo-ponic, she was a trailblazer.*

Beeanna scanned the hive. "There's no way a queen would let her offspring hang around for hexades. And later, queens probably thanked Antuna because she broke the mold."

"Exactly," concluded Anthiery.

Beeanna looked hard at him. "You didn't learn all this from Antuna's stories, did you?"

"No, Queen, some facts I learned in my classes."

"This is your final hex, isn't it?" asked Beeanna.

"Yes, I graduate next hexth," said Anthiery with pride. "I know you always pick a student as your attendant, so I will need to leave your employment in a few hexeks." *I will miss it and you.*

"Indeed, but I will miss you dearly," said Beeanna warmly. "I hope I can find another Antunite. So, what are your plans after high school?"

"I have thought little about it," replied Anthiery honestly, "but I'll miss school." *I don't know what I'd do without it.*

"I assume you'll settle down and raise a family," noted

Beeanna. "You're such a handsome young ant. You must have plenty of girlfriends."

"I like this girl Antianna, but I'm not sure whether she's interested in me as more than a friend." Anthiery frowned. "She's dating Antilla. His father is one of the richest ants in the colony." *He's such a jerk.*

"You have a brilliant head on your thorax, Anthiery. I'm sure Antianna will be attracted to the smart ant," consoled Beeanna. "And keep learning your whole life, and you'll never get bored."

Over the hexs, many societal norms transformed, and the insects became more like civilized humans on Earth. The insects had freedom of choice and increased technological advancements, and they established businesses to supply the demand. The insect phylogenetic families no longer fought each other, so they did not need large armies, except in extraordinary cases. And since most insects ate either fungi or honey, the insects foraged less for other food sources. Except for bees that were quite busy collecting nectar and making honey, workers became a more diverse group with more employment choices than foraging or fighting. As the insects lived longer lives, the young spent more time at school and studied for hexs at both low and high schools, and they continued to get smarter.

Although Poo-ponic ants mastered the principles of chemistry that helped the entire colony in the Spider-Termite War, their newfound scientific strength lay in biology, physics, and especially engineering. The brightest of the ants studied biomechanics and robotics. One might say all robotic clubs around the planet were crawling with ants. Using their telekinetic powers to move objects for manufacturing over many hexuries, clever ants such as Innovant and Renaissant developed specialized robots to help them complete various tasks.

Renaissant was a multi-talented ant who dabbled in history, science, and politics. His scientific endeavors led to many inventions that sparked technological revolutions in insect society. He was an ambitious ant who expounded, "An ounce of good measure spares a pound of displeasure."

Innovant was also a renowned inventor-ant whose motto was, "If there's a way to do it better—find it—do not quit till you can say you designed it."

Several of the robots the two invented looked like bugs and performed many of the insects' work-related tasks. These innovations afforded insects more leisure time, which many used for thinking and experimentation.

Innovant avowed, "Automation can provide little treasures to expand your mind and increase your *leisures!*"

Renaissant added, "You may delay, but time will not. Turn back your clock with a robot."

❧ ❧ ❧

Both Renaissant and Innovant were also advocates for education. Each had several apprentices, and both encouraged the society to maintain free education for low and high school. They took on high school students for their senior hex projects. Two of their most accomplished students were Anthiery and Antianna, principled ants that influenced society as they matured. Antianna was among the elites in society, and with all the benefits of wealth, she was one of the brightest students in the school. But her family taught her to be generous and caring for those in need. Anthiery's family was not so well off, but they valued education and raised him to take advantage of his schooling. He worked hard and excelled at everything he studied. Anthiery and Antianna had a friendly competition and alternated being at the top of the class.

One afternoon, Anthiery shyly approached Antianna outside their classroom and questioned her, "Who are you planning to ask as a mentor for your big senior project?"

Anthiery had liked Antianna for hexs, but they had always been good friends. He wasn't sure if she aspired to be more than friends, although sometimes he felt she wanted to be closer. And she was dating someone else right now.

Antianna stared into his eyes. "I asked Innovant, and he agreed."

Anthiery thrust his forelimbs upward. "You got Innovant to be your mentor? He's amazing. How did you manage that?" *You are incredible.*

Antianna turned away and blushed. "He was reluctant to mentor a girl, but he asked about my family. When I told him who my parents were, he couldn't refuse me."

Anthiery patted Antianna on the back with his antennae. "That is so cool. You have Innovant as a mentor. Wow!"

Antianna continued with a prideful smile, "Did you ask anyone yet?"

Anthiery shrugged. "No, not yet." *Who'll want a poor schmuck like me?*

Antianna raised her brow. "You should ask Renaissant."

Anthiery shrunk down. "No way. He's even more of a catch than Innovant."

"When I spoke with Innovant, I told him I had a friend with a great idea for an invention. He said he couldn't take on any more students, but he'd recommend you to Renaissant."

Anthiery reared up and was about to initiate a hug, but stopped short. *I'd better watch it. She'll push me away.* "Antianna, I can't believe you did that for me. How can I ever thank you?"

Anthiery had a growing crush on Antianna, but was too shy to make the first move. He cherished her friendship, but feared rejection if he pushed it further. After all, she was a princess, and his family was not as well-to-do. He imagined she would settle down with a prosperous business ant, and she'd have no trouble attracting one. He knew their wealthy classmate, Antilla, was interested in her, and Antianna dated him.

"Well, don't stand around gushing. Go ask Renaissant before someone else does," Antianna pushed.

As Anthiery headed out, two other students from their class, Antilla and Decadant, approached him.

Antilla jumped in front of Anthiery to prevent him from leaving. "Did I hear you two talking about senior project mentors?"

"Yes, I was just leaving to go ask ..." started Anthiery. He oozed a soggy scent. *Not this scumbag again. I don't have time for this.*

Impervious to Anthiery's essence, Antilla interrupted, "Well, my dad got the famous economist Microant to be my mentor. They're both members of the same country club."

"That's great. Did you ask someone yet, Decadant?" enquired Anthiery, ignoring Antilla's boast.

Antilla interjected, "My dad arranged for Macroant to mentor my good bud here."

Decadant added, "Yeah, I am so ...."

Antilla interrupted again, "My dad said it would be fitting that the slim guy gets Microant, and the fat guy gets Macroant. Haha! Funny, huh?"

"Well, it's great that you both found a mentor already. Sorry, but I gotta run." Anthiery slipped around Antilla and left the school.

Anthiery was not only in a hurry to ask Renaissant about his senior project, but he also wanted to end the conversation with Antilla. They were best friends in the lower grades since they wanted something from each other. The young Antilla admired Anthiery's inventive mind and loved to follow along in his imaginative games. His family was wealthy and gave him anything he wanted, but they never instilled a desire for learning. Antilla's father was strict and cheerless and only appreciated business and amassing wealth and encouraged him in those two endeavors only.

Anthiery, with his high curiosity, befriended Antilla only to see how the other half lived. His lower-middle-class family gave him much love, joy, and intellectual encouragement, but few extras. When Anthiery went to Antilla's nest, he was like a bee in a massive wildflower garden. But as they grew to be teenagers, their friendship waned. Anthiery was tired of entertaining Antilla like he was babysitting a pupa. He also could not bear Antilla's growing selfishness and egotism. Because Antilla's father bought him everything, he felt better than everyone else. Anthiery also knew he was too poor to move in Antilla's circles. Still, he could see Antilla had a strong desire to show off to him. This annoyed Anthiery even more because his ideas were quite pathetic. Most of all, Anthiery feared he was lagging Antilla in vying for Antianna's affections.

⁕ ⁕ ⁕

The architect Archiant designed the high school building with a beautiful atrium and large glass skylights that flooded the entrance with hexay-light. Antilla hung around in the school's foyer the next afternoon to see who else he could brag about his senior project. He overheard some of his male classmates talking about the subject. Antilla jeered, releasing a swollen stench, "I thought you no-brain, worker-types would take the general tract and skip the senior project." Antilla had an insatiable desire to put down most of his classmates, especially insects he considered lower on the evolutionary scale.

Roachard, Beetlebert, and Wormillian were close friends and hardworking, ambitious types. However, they were less academically inclined than their ant classmates and came from more impoverished families, typical of roaches, beetles, and worms. Roachard crouched low and spoke softly, "What a jerk. He and his rich dad. He doesn't understand what it takes to eke out a living."

Catching Roachard's wispy whiff, Wormillian slid close and added, "Yeah, I bet he's never even had a school-break job."

"Have you ever seen his claws?" interjected Beetlebert. "They look like he never uses them." Then he joked, "I bet his mother still feeds him."

Roachard stood up, laughing. "Forget him. Are you doing the senior project, Bert?"

Beetlebert shrugged. "I don't know. I already got turned down by three mentors."

"What about you, Mill?" Roachard continued.

Wormillian curled himself up and raised his head. "I have to do the general track. My dad has a big contract, and I am helping him dig out a new burrow. I won't have the time, but what about you?"

Roachard raised himself into a stilt stance. "Yeah, me too. I have a little business transporting fertilizer poo from the nests to the fungi farm and bringing back fungi for the ants. Ants hate doing the work, and they pay me well to do it for them."

Next, Antilla passed a group of Antianna's girlfriends, discussing their senior projects. Once again, he shunned his classmates, throwing out an insult while slipping by. For Antilla, all females, even ants, were lower on the evolutionary scale.

As he drifted by, his mocking words slipped out rather spitefully. "Do they even let girls do the senior project?"

Antianna had good friends from all walks of insect life, including bees, flies, and worms. But she had to leave early that afternoon to help her mother, so she missed the conversation with her friends.

Antianna's BBF (best bee friend) Beetrix ranted out loud to the other girls, "Don't listen to that rich hindgut hole. He can't even write, and I bet he pays someone to do his report."

Her fly friend Firefly flapped her wings rapidly. "Yeah, I can't believe he's even in the advanced program. He's so brainless."

"I heard he cheats on his tests," added her other fly friend, Flynette.

Wormella slithered up close to the other girls and squirted a stinging scent. "Forget about him. He's a racist, misogynist creep."

"Misogynist! Oh, Ella, you always come up with the best words," exclaimed Beetrix. "I bet Antilla doesn't even know what that means. I can't believe he's wooing Antianna, and she's playing along. We have to make sure she drops him."

Firefly flapped her wings in agreement. "Yeah, Antilla's so two-faced. He would never have insulted us if Antianna had been here. Let's hope his rich dad doesn't get him into politics. We don't want him leading anyone."

"So, other than Antianna, who scored Innovant, has anyone got a mentor?" questioned Wormella.

Beetrix puffed herself up. "I got this young guy, Federant, who's into politics. You may not have heard of him, but he will be a burrow-hold name soon. He surprised me when he accepted a female bee."

Wormella interjected, "I asked Federant's friend Legisant to be my mentor, and he said no because he took a girl from another school, Roachelia. It's okay, though, because the architect Archiant agreed to be my mentor."

"That's amazing, Mella," chimed in Firefly. "He's fantastic. And you've always had a knack for designing and building things."

Flynette buzzed her wings briefly to get the other girls' attention. "I got this up-and-coming journalist, Shebee, who studied politics with Renaissant. She told me Renaissant was the one who trained Federant and Legisant."

"What about you, Firefly?" queried Beetrix.

Firefly spread her wings and tilted herself as if gliding, then said, "I'm going to ask the flyboy, Flyhero. He's into aeronautics and speed-flying."

"Wow, looks like we're off to the races," joked Wormella, raising herself like a cobra.

Antilla passed the girls again as they were about to break up, and Beetrix gave him a nasty upward left claw sign.

Firefly, who had her back to Antilla, belted out to the other girls, "I know Beetrix and Antianna have some high society event to attend. But who of the rest of you girls is up for a party on Satur-hexay? I found a good batch of strong sap. We can meet at the hollowed-out log on the far side of the sequoia forest for a pre-senior project bash."

There was a chorus of "I'm in!" and "You bet!" from the gaggle of girls. As always, strong sap had a powerful draw for high school students.

***

Two of the mentors, Renaissant and Innovant, were also planning to start up an institution of higher education. Innovant and Renaissant met a couple of hexays later to discuss the opening of the University of Noble Insect Technology, or the UNIT.

Innovant looked at the old flying hall, imagining everything he could do with the open space. "Yes, this structure will work well for a few hexs while building the new campuses."

The be-speckled, long-haired Renaissant nodded in agreement. "We should have no trouble filling the classrooms; high school students are getting smarter every hex. And with little physical labor required lately, they are craving more learning."

"I expect things will start slow. So, this building will suffice. We can erect dividers so the ant and bee students can have their own space," surmised the balding Innovant.

Renaissant gazed over at the empty lot and the forest beyond, scattering a sparkling scent. "Yes, and when the construction is complete, ant students will populate the main campus over here, and bees will study at the adjacent satellite campus."

A few hexeks later, the two unveiled the carving of the UNIT label over the doors of the old flying hall and erected signs to show the building site of the new ant and bee campuses.

Innovant announced the plans to the public, "In the coming school hex, we will begin classes leading to elementary 'Larva' and advanced 'Pupa' degrees in science or engineering.

Later, as we hire more staff, we'll allow students to study for a Larva or Pupa of Arts."

Renaissant added, "The initial teachers will be our apprentices that have studied with Innovant and me for hexs. In time, we hope that all professors at the UNIT will have obtained their primary and secondary Larva, followed by a Pupa of Arts, Engineering, or Science."

～ ～ ～

Antianna ran up to Anthiery as he came out of class that afternoon. "Did you hear the big news? We haven't even begun our senior projects yet, and our mentors are starting up a university in time for our graduating class. We have to apply soon."

Anthiery jumped up, joining her excitement until the thoughts of the expense shattered his chipper mood. "I don't know. It might cost too much to attend." *My folks can't afford it.*

"I'm sure if you do your project with Renaissant, he'll be able to get you in," Antianna reassured him.

Anthiery shrugged and looked down at the ground, unable to bury his disappointment. "I doubt it works like that, but I'll do my best."

Antianna was still bouncing at the thought when she asked, "By the way, aren't you going to the 'Science for Teens' conference this hexek?"

Anthiery perked up and smiled. "Yes, I leave tonight, right after my first session with Renaissant. Thanks again for setting me up with him." *Things are finally working out for me.*

Antianna glanced toward the new flying hall, then turned to look Anthiery straight in the eyes. "I wanted to go to that conference, but Beetrix and I have the rehearsal tomorrow night for our coming-out party. You'll be back on Satur-hexay night, so you're coming to the party, right?"

Anthiery stared into Antianna's eyes, then blushed a little. "Did you invite Antilla too?" *I'll skip it if Antilla comes as your date.*

Still in a world all her own, she said, "We discussed it, but Antilla said he's been to so many before that he'd rather just come by at the end and pick me up after. I think he said he had something planned earlier that evening."

Anthiery turned away and asked, "Are you going to meet him?" *I'm steamed she would even consider it. He's such a letch.*

"I don't think so. Antilla asked me out tonight," Antianna replied. "I don't want him to think we're going steady."

That's good, but I need to test her further. "You could do worse. His family is very wealthy." *But all of them are pigs!*

"Wealth isn't everything, but he has given me some nice things."

So, I'm glad you're not after his money. But why did you invite him in the first place? "I'm not sure about Satur-hexay night since I might get back late." A stroppy smell lingered as he spoke. *I don't care! You can have Antilla if you want him.*

"I gave you a ticket, so I hope you won't waste it," retorted Antianna with a biting bouquet.

Anthiery picked up on her subtle sarcasm and considered throwing back a barb, but thought better of it. "I'll try to make it. I haven't been to one before." *Dang it, I can't give up on her.*

❧ ❧ ❧

Later, Antilla, followed by his ever-present sidekick, Decadant, approached Anthiery and said, "I heard some girls are heading out to the sequoia forest to party on Satur-hexay night."

"Yeah, Antilla and I are going to play a trick on them," sneered Decadant.

Antilla rubbed his claws together and laughed. "We're gonna light a small fire at the narrow end of the log and smoke 'em out."

"Why would you do that?" barked Anthiery. "It's cruel. And someone could get hurt."

"Don't worry, Antianna won't be there. And I will take good care of her later that night."

Imagining Antianna with this guy rips me apart. "She won't join you if I have anything to do with it. And you better drop this smoke-out idea, or I'll tell the teachers," insisted Anthiery, releasing a steely stink. *I can't believe this guy!*

Antilla backed away a little. "Okay, okay, I'll come up with a better prank." He thought for a moment. "I know. We'll drip honey on them from the top!"

I still have some sway with this guy. I was his idol when we were young. If I'm assertive, he'll be intimidated. "That's still kind of mean," said Anthiery with a dismissive shake of his head. "Why don't you leave the girls alone?" *It's crazy we were ever friends.*

As Antilla backed away with Decadant at his side, he added, "Okay, Anthiery, whatever you say. You know I always listen to you."

Anthiery turned to walk away. "Well, you'd better." *He's lying just to get me off his case.*

Antilla threw a departing shot. "As for Antianna, she'll never pick a poor boy like you over me."

As Anthiery stormed off, Decadant leaned in and muttered, "Are we going to let that geek tell us what to do?"

Antilla snickered. "No way! I only said that to get him off our backs."

⁂

Anthiery returned early Satur-hexay excited to attend Antianna's social at the new flying hall. He built up his courage and convinced himself this was his opportunity to ask Antianna to be his steady girlfriend and win her affection from Antilla. The event was a coming-out party for Beetrix, Antianna, and other bees and ants from theirs and other high schools in the colony. They were in the flying hall because those coming out were young princess bees and ants still with wings.

As part of the ceremony, it was a tradition for the young female bees and ants to show off the flight moves they learned to attract the most mates. Since the colony insects lived much longer now, there was less pressure to mate right away, compete for mates, or even have more than one mate. Still, the traditional flying dance was a popular part of the coming-out party.

Antianna and Beetrix walked together back toward their seats when they finished their dance.

Antianna said, "I liked your routine, especially when you buzzed the crowd."

"You got some brilliant moves too," complimented Beetrix. "You were trying to impress Anthiery, weren't you?"

Antianna scanned the hall to find Anthiery. "Do you think it worked?" *What must I do to get him to like me that way?*

Beetrix cracked a big smile. "His eyes never left you."

"Are you sure?" questioned Antianna. "I like Anthiery, but I always feel he only wants to be friends. He isn't chasing me like Antilla." *I hope she's right.*

Beetrix frowned in response, uncovering the distaste with

her expression. "Please don't go on about Antilla. You know how I feel about him. You should stay away from that snake. He insulted our friends and me at school the other hexay."

I respect your feelings, but you're wrong about Antilla. "He's always nice to me, and he's given me some delightful gifts. He fawns over me and makes me feel special." *Yet, he creeps me out sometimes.*

"Antianna, try to remember how you felt about him before he started dating you. He's still that same guy." Beetrix puffed an intense perfume. "He knows you're coming out tonight, and I heard that every hex he picks a debutant to date. He goes to her party, uses her, and drops her a few hexeks later."

"But he didn't come tonight," responded Antianna. *He wouldn't do that to me.*

"Yeah, but didn't you say he invited you to go out with him after the party? He wants dessert, even though he didn't come to the dinner."

Antianna sighed and looked again through the crowd to catch sight of Anthiery. *Anthiery would never treat me that way, but does he even want me?*

🐜 🐜 🐜

Meanwhile, Antilla and Decadant crept through the forest and approached the log where Antianna's worm and fly friends were partying. There had been no rain for a couple of hexeks, and the forest timbers were as parched as molted worm skins left in the sun. The girls were getting tipsy as the party had been going for a while. Antilla and Decadant started a small fire on the narrow end of the log to produce fumes to smoke the girls out. They didn't notice a large amount of sawdust blocking the passage from the thin to the wide end of the log.

As Firefly leaned over to offer her some more strong sap, Flynette said in a panic. "Do you smell smoke?"

Firefly put down the strong sap and sniffed the air. "No, I think the wood just smells like that when it's old and dry." *She always worries too much.*

"I don't know. It doesn't seem normal," added Flynette. "I'm going to look around outside."

Just then, smoke billowed through the sawdust toward the wide end of the log. And the girls!

Firefly screamed, flying out of the log after Flynette, "It's on fire! Everybody, get out of the log!" From the corner of her eye, she saw Flynette pointing at Decadant, who scurried as fast as he could away from the scene. *I organized this party! I must make sure everyone is safe.*

A beetle and roach friend of Firefly pursued her out of the log, coughing and overcome with smoke. "Where's Mella? Oh no, she's on fire! Get her out of there." *I can't believe this is happening.*

Her friends were too stunned and overcome by the fumes, so Firefly summoned all her telepathic power to levitate Wormella and drag her out.

Flynette came close, radiating a rumpled reek. "She's still on fire! Roll her over."

Wormella was still conscious but in shock as Firefly and Flynette rolled her along the ground to smother the flames. The flames extinguished, but not before Wormella had sustained severe burn injuries.

The girls sobered up promptly. Not knowing what else to do, they carried Wormella to the social event that Antianna and Beetrix were attending in the Great Flying Hall, desperate for help.

Antianna and Beetrix ran over to them when their uninvited girlfriends crashed the party with the injured Wormella.

Antianna shrieked. "Oh no, what happened to Wormella? Was there a fire?"

A soot-faced Firefly who had organized the party cried, "Y-yes, we were celebrating before senior projects at the hollow log outside the sequoia forest, and it caught fire." *It's all my fault! I brought the girls together tonight.*

Flynette added, "Antilla and Decadant were playing a trick on us. They tried to smoke us out!"

Beetrix flew closer to hold Wormella's head up. "Why do you think that?"

Firefly, who was second out of the log, stood tall and added, "She saw Decadant running away, and so did I. It was dark, and neither of us saw Antilla." *Yet, I know he was there.*

Antianna's mother, a healer, took Wormella outside, scraped up a few aloe leaves, and placed them over Wormella's burns, packing mud to hold them down. Then, in a soothing voice, she said, "That should help, but she'll need plenty of time to recover. She'll molt her skin, but the burns are more than skin deep. These are serious burns. I'll send Antianna over daily with more aloe leaves, and she can change her dressing."

Archiant was in attendance because his grandniece was coming out, and it was the first major event at the new flying hall he had designed. Although an architect, he was also a justice of the peace.

He angrily announced, "We need to sort out this foolish prank. I'd like to interview the girls and any student at the school who might know of this transgression. Wormella is an outstanding young worm who was about to start her senior project with me, and now it looks like she'll be fighting for her life instead."

The tragic news dampened the enthusiasm at the coming-out party, and many left to go home. Antianna tended to Wormella, trying to comfort her as she placed her on a makeshift stretcher to bring her home.

"Antianna, let me help you carry Wormella," offered Anthiery.

"Oh, thank you, Thiery. You must be disappointed the party is over." *And if Beetrix was right, I'm sorry you lost any chance to make a move.*

Anthiery looked deeply into Antianna's eyes with a warm smile. "Your dance was the most beautiful thing I've ever seen. And I'll be honored to be your dance partner whenever you want me."

"Oh, Anthiery, I thought you'd never ask!" Antianna seeped a silky scent and gave him a close hug. *I never wanted to dance with anyone but you.*

Anthiery told her what Antilla had said about planning the smoke-out caper and that he was going to tell Archiant. Antilla arrived just as Antianna and Anthiery were leaving the hall with Wormella. If Antianna's glare could burn, she would have injured Antilla worse than Wormella. Although Antianna did not speak to him, he got the message that he would not be getting any further with her that night or any other. Instead, she cast an adoring look at Anthiery.

Terrified to be accused of the crime, Antilla sought Anthiery the next hexay before Archiant started debriefing the girls and other students.

He pleaded with Anthiery not to incriminate him. "You

just have to say that you never talked to me, and I'll pay you more than you've ever had. They'll expel me from school, and I'll never get into the UNIT." *I know he'll help me. We were best friends when young, after all.*

Standing erect, Anthiery turned away from Antilla, unmoved by his state of panic and desperation. "You should have thought of that before you pulled your stupid trick and burned Wormella. She might die."

Antilla approached Anthiery with heavy eyes. "She's just a worm! And she'll get better, anyway. They crawl out of their slimy skins whenever they want." *Like my dad always says, they're disgusting.*

Anthiery reared and barked, "I'd like to rip the skin off of you."

Antilla reared fully at the threat. "I'd think twice about that. My father is powerful, and he could destroy you and your family. He already told me he'd crush your father if I go to prison because of you." *You don't want to be my enemy!*

"It won't be because of me. It'll be because of your stupidity. I'm telling Archiant what I know." Anthiery turned and began marching away.

Antilla trembled and wailed, "Well, tell him Deca went alone. Because he did, and if you don't, you'll regret it forever. I won't be your friend ever again."

Anthiery turned toward Antilla and shot a searing scent, pulling the words from his glands that had perhaps been there, waiting for this moment. "I was only ever your friend because I was too young to know better. Once I understood your selfish ways, I wanted nothing to do with you. And now I'd love to see you rot in prison."

Anthiery didn't mean the last line but wanted to drive home that he never wanted to hear from Antilla again. Anthiery stormed off and told Archiant about his conversation with Antilla and Decadant before the fire. He didn't mention the second conversation because he never believed Antilla's story that Decadant went alone.

⁂

When he heard Anthiery had met with Archiant, Antilla pleaded with Decadant, "You have to tell them you did it alone. If you do, my father and I will take care of you for the rest of your life, and you'll have everything you ever dreamed of." *This is my last chance!*

Decadant cowered and shook. "But I'll go to jail!"

Antilla reached out to Decadant with his antennae. "You're going, anyway. Some eyewitnesses saw you. Why should we both go to prison?" *Do this, or I'll ….*

Decadant stood erect, trying not to gape. "But it was your idea!"

Antilla sidled up to Decadant and put his left forelimb on his shoulder. "But nobody needs to know that. And if I go to the slammer with you, my father will find an excruciating way to shorten your sentence. He knows many guys who know guys in prison, and they'll take you out before you could even say the word parole." *Do it, or I'll get him on it.*

Decadant pointed at the cold ground. "So, you're giving me a choice between over six figures or six inches under?"

Antilla edged close to Decadant again, putting his right forelimb on his other shoulder. "Yes, and if you cover for me, my dad will make sure you have a short sentence and an easy time. He has lots of friends and can be very persuasive." He pleaded, "Come on, Deca, you're my right-claw man." A smarmy scent fogged the area.

Decadant chose riches over burial, and Antilla coached him on what to say. Decadant met with Archiant and confessed, but he insisted Antilla did not come with him. One of the few times Antilla was ever faithful to his word in his entire life, all of his promises to Decadant came to be. Decadant served only half a hex in a prison burrow where he had all the conveniences of home. After that, Antilla and his father took care of him for life. Decadant rode on Antilla's coattails, and the two did everything together to the very end. And Antilla did everything in his power to punish Anthiery. Because Antilla didn't go to prison, his father did not destroy those in Anthiery's family. But he never considered Anthiery's family for contracts, financial aid, or employment within his many businesses.

❧ ❧ ❧

Beetrix accompanied Antianna one morning on her way to Wormella's burrow to tend to her wounds. "Antianna, you know Antilla cooked up the plan that injured Wormella. Decadant would never think up such a thing. He's just Antilla's leech-follower."

"I know. That's why Antilla couldn't come to the party. Anthiery told me Antilla had planned it all, and I am furious with that rich hindgut hole." *I'm done with him.*

"He couldn't turn down the chance to prank several girls, just to please one," jabbed Beetrix.

"Beetrix, I should have listened to you. I was naïve to think he'd changed and truly liked me," rued Antianna. "I realize now he was only interested in me, for one thing." *I figured it out at long last.*

"Something you should save for Anthiery," teased Beetrix.

Antianna cracked a wide smile. "Yes, and I respect him even

more for how he stood up to Antilla and spoke to Archiant."
And finally, Anthiery's after me.

"I'd say it's time to show Anthiery how you feel about him and turf that Antilla out the door."

"Yes, Beetrix, I have done both. I've learned my lesson not to be fooled by that disingenuous rogue Antilla. Never again will I let anyone blind me when I know what is right."

Beetrix dispersed a breezy bouquet. "And you've chosen the best, Mr. Right."

"Yes, and Anthiery finally expressed how he felt about me, and I'm so happy," said Antianna. "Now, let's go take care of Wormella." She lifted her wing over Beetrix's shoulder while they walked on.

Antianna realized it is essential to look at an insect's complete personality and not just their recent interactions with her. She appreciated that although Anthiery could be shy, he was a genuine friend that cared deeply about her and others on all levels. Antilla might have been outgoing and demonstrative, but his general nature was selfish, and he lacked empathy.

CHAPTER 2

Cyborg Emergence

*As need sails windily into greed, a lust for
industry, education, and avidity,*

may list with gentry, stratification, and cupidity.

*And careless tacks jibe assiduity to asinine,
as one luffs all perspicuity.*

SINCE ANTILLA EVADED charges in the burning incident, he continued to go to the same school as Anthiery, although they avoided each other. Antilla completed his senior project with Microant, despite showing up only half the time because he found economics too dull or didn't understand the concepts. Despite Microant's reporting of his inadequate efforts, Antilla passed the project because he paid one of Microant's former students to write up a stellar draft of the required report. On the other claw, Anthiery impressed Renaissant immensely, especially when he explained the plans for his invention.

Anthiery approached Renaissant with deference. "Renaissant,

sir, I hope you could help me prepare a patent for my invention. I know you have written many."

Renaissant gave Anthiery an authoritative glance. "Anthiery, that's your project, and it's great. But you should write your own patent."

"But I could learn so much from you about patents." *I need your help.*

"Anthiery, you have a brilliant mind. So, let's together create an invention. You'll learn about patents when we prepare one together."

Anthiery streamed a sunny scent. "Okay, sir, that sounds perfect." *And I hope it works.*

The senior project went well, but Renaissant was so busy opening the UNIT that they didn't finish their invention and never wrote a patent.

~ ~ ~

A few hexeks later, Antianna and Anthiery took a walk together to check out the UNIT sign at the old flying hall. They had been busy with their projects and had seen little of each other since Antianna's coming out party.

Antianna asked Anthiery about his project. "So, how did your study with Renaissant go?"

In response, Anthiery's eyes lit up. "I learned so much, and we almost finished developing a new product. My teacher thought the ideas were great, and I got an excellent grade." *I loved it.*

"What about the invention and patenting it?" enquired Antianna.

Anthiery shook his head. "Renaissant told me that we'll finish it together when he has more time. But he told my teacher that most of the ideas were mine." *Yet my invention still has no patent.*

Antianna moved in close to Anthiery. "He was busy readying the UNIT, I suspect?"

"Yes, how did you know?" Anthiery puzzled. *We never finished or wrote the patent, so I didn't learn how to submit mine.*

Antianna raised her forelimbs. "Because the same thing happened to me with Innovant."

"But you learned stuff and passed, right?" buoyed Anthiery.

"Yes, lots, and I got an A," beamed Antianna.

"That should go a long way for our plans to get into the UNIT. Did you apply already?"

Pleased when Anthiery used the word *our*, Antianna turned and grinned at him, staring intensely into his eyes. "Yes, I applied to the engineering program."

Anthiery cracked a big smile and matched Antianna's gaze. "So did I." *It's great we can study together.*

Antianna smiled back, flapped her wings, and radiated a steamy scent. "I'd really like that dance you promised me now."

🐜 🐜 🐜

Although Anthiery's relationship with Antianna attained a new high, his relationship with Antilla reached a new low. On the very last hexay of high school classes, Antilla hid at the back of the library and watched Anthiery studying for the entrance exam that followed his application to the UNIT. He noticed Anthiery wrote everything in a papyrus note-roll that he carried with him everywhere. Antilla never took notes and wanted to steal the note-roll to help him pass the entrance exam himself. When the librarian asked Anthiery if he could help her by bringing a couple of boxes of large papyrus rolls to the storage area, Anthiery, always helpful, said he'd be glad to do it. He left his things at the table, and when no one was looking, Antilla slipped forward and snatched Anthiery's note-roll.

❊ ❊ ❊

Later, Antianna questioned the frantic Anthiery, "How do you know it was Antilla who stole it?"

Anthiery's antennae trembled. "I don't know for certain, but I expect he's the only one who would." *He's such a greedy pig. I'm sure he did it.*

Antianna wrapped her antennae around Anthiery's. "Don't worry, Thiery, you have a pheromono-graphic memory. I know you'll pass the exam, and you can use my notes too."

Anthiery stepped back and pulled his antennae away, then shuddered with panic. "But Anna, my invention! It was in my note-roll too. He has it now, and he could patent it." A shabby stink permeated the air.

"Thiery, I'm sure you could reconstruct the plans in no time and patent it yourself first. And Antilla barely reads, so he won't even know what it is."

Anthiery re-entwined his antennae with Antianna's. "You might be right, but I wish I had patented it with Renaissant." *I've lost it forever.*

"Hey, talk to Renaissant," suggested Antianna. "Didn't you tell him about your plans?"

"Good idea," responded Anthiery. *I must try something.*

Anthiery met with Renaissant, who told him that since he couldn't prove that Antilla stole the plans for the patent, there was nothing he could do. Renaissant also mentioned that patents go to whoever applies first. There were very few patents on

Poo-ponic, but most of them were by Renaissant and Innovant. So, he knew the system well.

~ ~ ~

At the same time Anthiery met Renaissant, Antilla asked to talk with his father.

Antilla crept into his dad's home office. "Father," Antilla said, "Anthiery came to me yester-hexay and told me he wanted to be friends again," he lied. *I hope he buys this.*

Antrich looked up from his work and acknowledged his son's arrival. "Is that so?"

Antilla continued his deceit, but hid his syrupy smell. "Yes, and he said that he wanted our help. He wants you to help him patent his invention." *Maybe he'll see it's me that needs his help.*

Antrich scratched his head. "I thought you wanted nothing to do with him and asked me never to help him."

"Well, I don't *really* want to help him," Antilla confessed. *I might as well come clean.*

"So, what's this about?" puzzled Antrich.

Antilla returned to his fabricated story. "Well, I pretended we could be friends again so I could see the plans for his invention and to see if they were any good." *Still, I don't want Dad to know I stole it.*

"And?" Antrich probed.

"He showed them to me, and they're amazing," explained Antilla with wide eyes. *I'm sure he'll trust me.*

Antrich still found the entire thing puzzling. "So, you still want to work with him after what he did to you?"

Antilla continued, "No, it's more that while the plans are amazing, they are quite simple. And I could remember them, so I scribbled them down." *He's got to believe me.*

Antilla's dad felt a tear forming in his eye when the realization dawned on him. Was he asking him what he thought he was asking him? "Oh, Antilla, don't tell me you're thinking of stealing them and patenting them yourself. And you want my help?"

A foul fragrance polluted the room. "Father, are you upset with me?" *Oh no! He won't help me. He's disappointed.*

Antrich stood up, walked over to Antilla, and hugged him. "No, son, I am just so proud of you. Show me the plans."

❦ ❦ ❦

Antianna's family spent a few hexeks at their country nest during the school break, and she was excited to see Anthiery and catch up with him when she returned.

Antianna ran up to him. "Anthiery, I missed you so much."

He stretched out his forelimbs for a hug. "I missed you too, and I'm glad you're back."

She looked up into Anthiery's eyes. "What's going on with your patent application? I've been worried the whole time."

"Renaissant and I worked hard, and we finished it," said Anthiery with a blank look.

"You don't seem very enthusiastic about it. What happened?"

Antianna was very perceptive at reading non-pheromonal communication, and the closer she and Anthiery became, she understood his emotions better than anyone.

Anthiery looked across the square towards his mentor's office. "Renaissant was so busy getting the UNIT going that it took hexeks to finish it." *Again, he has priorities higher than my issues.*

"But it's done, and you submitted it, right?"

"Yes, I handed it in, and the patent officer looked it over," explained Anthiery. *But there's no use.*

"Was he interested in it?" Antianna asked.

"He said that he'd received a similar patent only hexays before." *I'm doomed.*

Antianna rubbed Anthiery's forelimbs with her antennae, sensing his heartbreak over losing control of his invention. "Oh, Anthiery, that's not good."

Anthiery lowered his head. "I know. Antilla must have submitted first." *He's a jerk and a thief. He stole my invention.*

"Cheer up, Thiery, with Renaissant helping you, yours will be better, and they'll accept it." She tried her best to raise his spirits, but in some sense, shared his heartbreak.

"I'm sure it only matters whose came first." *I should kill that jerk.*

"I guess we'll find out soon," Antianna concluded with a deep sigh.

"At least I had some other good news," Anthiery added. *Enough about that rogue. I've had it with Antilla.*

Antianna jumped up and down. "Oh, did you get in? I have my letter here. I wanted to read it in front of you."

"Yes, I got accepted into the UNIT. I'm sure you will too. Open it!" *At least something in my life is going right.*

Antianna handed him the sealed scroll. "Can you read it to me? I am too nervous."

He broke the seal and unraveled the scroll. "Okay, are you ready?"

She bounced up and down, releasing a rickety reek. "Yes, read it!"

Anthiery tilted his head upward. "It says: 'Princess Antianna, we have accepted you into the engineering program at the University of Noble Insect Technology.'" *Super, we'll go on together.*

Antianna jumped into Anthiery's widespread forelimbs. "Oh Anthiery, I am so happy. You said you got in too. But did you get a scholarship?"

"Yes, and it will cover my tuition, and the letter said the scholarship is renewable every hex, as long as I keep my grades up," explained Anthiery. *You were right! I can't believe it.*

Antianna did a celebratory pirouette. "That's great. You won't have to worry about whether you can afford it. I knew having Renaissant as your mentor would help."

Anthiery grinned from antenna to antenna. "He delivered the letter to me himself, and he had a big smile when he presented it. The only thing that could make me happier right now would be to see you dance again." He winked and took Antianna's claw.

Antianna oozed an alluring aroma. "We're going to take the UNIT together by storm."

🐜 🐜 🐜

As Antianna predicted, Renaissant pushed hard for a scholarship program to be up and running when the UNIT opened and insisted that Anthiery be the first recipient. It pained Anthiery to discover that Antilla had received a patent for his invention and produced a production technology that all the hives used. Antilla had unlimited income from the automated honey extractor. His father insisted the beehives pay Antilla 3% of the honey produced as a rental fee for the new machines. Although his father was so wealthy that Antilla would receive a large inheritance, the extra income from the hives meant he never had to work a hexay in his life if he so chose. As the expression goes, he was an ant hatched with a honey-filled straw in his mouth, and that straw never emptied. Antilla's father, Antrich, made a significant donation to the UNIT, and Antilla got in. However, there were rumors he paid the same student who wrote his senior project report to take the entrance exam on his behalf. Ironically, Antrich's donation to the UNIT made Anthiery's scholarship possible, but Renaissant was careful to keep that to himself. Still, realizing that Antilla got rich off his invention enraged Anthiery.

❦ ❦ ❦

Antianna and Anthiery spent much time together over the last few hexeks of the school break, becoming very close. It was clear to both that they would have a shared future, and their encounters since Antianna's coming-out party were not just a two-night wing fling. Although their relationship was strong, Antianna worried about Anthiery because he brooded after Antilla stole his invention. She tried to convince him to let it go, but Anthiery remained bothered. Then, one hexay, Antianna noticed Anthiery carrying a package to the fly-mail office.

"What do you have there, Anthiery?" questioned Antianna.

"It's a present for Antilla," responded Anthiery.

She shrugged. "Why do you want to give Antilla a present?" *I thought you hated him.*

Anthiery raised his voice, "Because he deserves it. He deserves to burn."

"What does that mean?" puzzled Antianna. *This doesn't sound like you. I'm worried.*

Anthiery grinned and whispered with a shifty smell, "It's white phosphorus from my father's factory. When he opens the package, the water will leak out, and poof, he'll catch fire. I want him to burn like Wormella did."

Antianna had never seen such raw anger from him, and she trembled with fear. *What is happening to him? How can I stop him?* "Anthiery, you can't do that. You'll go to prison."

Anthiery turned and walked away. "It'll be worth it."

"What about your scholarship, your studies, our future?" Antianna pleaded. *My worst worries about Anthiery's obsession are coming true.*

Anthiery stopped and turned back, seething a scorching stench. "He's getting wealthy off my invention. I've been poor forever, and this was my chance to get rich."

Antianna attempted an antennae entanglement. "You're brilliant, and you'll have others," she consoled him. "Remember, you are an Antunite. Don't do it," she pleaded desperately.

Anthiery pulled his antennae back with a fiery rage. "But I hate him, and he asked for it."

Antianna rushed towards Anthiery. "No, I won't let you throw it all away. But *I will.*" *I choose love over hate.*

Antianna snatched the package from Anthiery and hurled it at a boulder across the square. The parcel smashed and burst into flames, igniting the night sky. She gazed at the fire. *Burn my antennae to their roots. What would that have done to Antilla?*

"Antianna, that stuff is expensive," Anthiery grumbled.

Antianna smiled and chirped, "It was worth it. I imagined the rock was Antilla." *I hope he finally lets this go.*

"Funny, so did I." Anthiery's scowl turned into a grin. "I don't think I would have mailed it. It's not the Antunite way." Anthiery approached Antianna for an embrace. "I'll think of another way to get back at him."

※　※　※

Anthiery's classmates, Roachard, Beetlebert, and Wormillian, opted for the general program and didn't complete a senior project. Since the UNIT only accepted ants and bees, it was just as well. But they still did well for themselves. Roachard's poo and fungi transporting business took off after he graduated high school, and he managed several other roaches in his expanding business. His operation was so successful that he could help his best friend Beetlebert start a strong sap bottling company, which also flourished. They developed a partnership and, as prosperous entrepreneurs, became business males that were pillars of society. Their friend Wormillian matched this success. Roachard bumped into him in the central square one hexay.

"Hey Mill, what have you been up to?" asked Roachard.

"Lots of work. I'm getting as strong as a grasshopper's thigh," joked Wormillian.

"Yeah, I heard all the ant contractors want you for their projects," Roachard said.

"Well, I work twice as fast as other worms." Wormillian writhed rhythmically. "And I got a knack for loosening large rocks with my secret wriggling technique."

"You always loved the physical work." laughed Roachard.

"It's been very profitable since I started my own company. I cut out the middle ant." Wormillian spouted a stuffy scent.

"That was a smart decision," concluded Roachard.

"You bet. I may need to shake off after work every hexay, but I am becoming a top business guy like you and Bert. I'll be hiring a crew soon," said Wormillian.

Roachard crawled up close to Wormillian. "Bert and I have started up a club. We call it the New Honey Guild. It's an exclusive group of successful business types among roaches, beetles, worms, and flies. All our members can rival ants and bees in amassing honey through their hard work. I spoke to Bert, and he agreed we want you to join."

"That sounds fantastic. I'd love to join. Could my new staff members join too?"

"No, Bert wants the cream of the working class, and only business leaders can join," explained Roachard.

Wormillian added, "That makes sense."

🐜 🐜 🐜

Over the next several hexths, Antianna and Anthiery excelled in their engineering programs. The UNIT also accepted Beetrix into a general program as she waited to study a Larva of Arts. After her first hex, Beetrix was excited to enter political science in the Arts program.

Beetrix bubbled with excitement. "I am so lucky that the Arts program is starting on schedule. I can take the classes in political science that I want. Some other courses like philosophy, geography, and history will come on board next hex when they train the professors. After that, the sky's the limit." *I love university life.*

"That's great, Beetrix. But how did the UNIT get the political science program up and running so fast?" queried Antianna.

"Federant and Legisant had studied with Renaissant for hexs. So, they just needed to complete a thesis to get their Pupa degrees. They each finished their thesis in one hex, and they're both professors now," described Beetrix. *That's not for me, but I can see myself as a highly educated queen bee.*

"Didn't you do your senior project with Federant?" questioned Anthiery.

"Yes, he's a bit of an ant snob. But he took me on because I was a princess." Beetrix tilted her head back, wiped her brow, and spread a shining scent. *I guess that almost makes me an ant in his eyes.*

Antianna smiled at Beatrix's antics. "What was his thesis about?"

"It was on a subject he studied when I worked with him," answered Beetrix. "It was something about a new central government, where all insects get to vote." *They called it a democracy, but I don't understand why they assumed only ants would run for office.*

"What about Legisant?" asked Anthiery.

"I'm not sure, but when he came to see Federant, he kept talking about his ideas for forming a Declaration of Constitution," replied Beetrix. "I expect it's about that, and I didn't understand it all." *Their thinking is way ahead of the curve, yet I believe it also lacks something.*

"But wasn't your senior project on that stuff?" probed Antianna.

"Yes, but I was more interested in what they called a Bill of Rights. So, I helped them with parts of that, trying to convince them that every insect deserves the same rights and privileges.".

"I'm guessing that was a hard sell?" interjected Anthiery.

"Yeah, but they listened to my case and considered it. I expect to read each thesis during my new classes," Beetrix replied. "I signed up for two classes with them and one with Renaissant." *I hope they took my ideas.*

"He's great too," gushed Anthiery. "I studied engineering with Renaissant. He has a great political mind as well."

"If I am ever a queen, I need to know this stuff." Beetrix pretended to wrap herself up in a cloak and put on airs. "I want to make sure these central government plans don't step on royal claws too much. And we don't want them to oppress ordinary insects." *I'm convinced powerful ants need bees to keep them in line.*

Antianna enjoyed Beetrix's capers. "Well, they won't get any tricks past you, Trix."

⁂

After Beetrix left, Anthiery and Antianna discussed his classes.

"Antianna, I'm taking a class with Professor Antstrong in mechanical design." Anthiery continued, "It made me realize there's a slight flaw in my design for the honey extractor."

"Really? I thought it was perfect. What's the issue?" *I don't understand why he is bringing this up.*

"The working mechanisms are too exposed," explained Anthiery.

Antianna scratched her head. "Well, it's no longer your worry. Antilla will have to deal with it." *I think he's up to something.*

"Exactly, that's what I'm getting at."

Antianna perked up. "What are you planning?" *I know him too well.*

He cracked a wide grin. "Remember how we learned in low school the farmers had to stop growing sugar cane because too many insects got addicted and repeatedly broke into the stores to get it?"

"Yes, but what does that have to do with your extractors?" Antianna puzzled. *I wish he'd just come out with it.*

"I found some wild sugar cane and determined that you can make honey using sugar instead of nectar."

Antianna fidgeted. *Where is he going with this?* "I still don't get it."

"I asked Wobbert and Roachard to go to the honey bar that

Antilla frequents." Anthiery licked his mandibles and oozed a viscid vapor. "I told them to sit in the booth next to Antilla and talk about my great idea for making sugar-honey. So, they described where I found the wild sugar cane and how it will make me rich."

Antianna stood up from her chair with a laugh. "Oh, you are devious. I love it! You get to 'sticky' it to him after all." *You can burn him without setting him on fire!*

A short while later, Antianna heard from Beetrix that several of Antilla's honey extractors were out of commission. Beetrix learned from her BEE contacts Antilla became enraged when he found his extractors gummed up with insects' feces and smashed them all beyond repair. She said Antilla would lose considerable income while constructing new extractors. He also ordered the bees to stop making sugar-honey.

🐜 🐜 🐜

In time, the UNIT excelled. With brilliant professors and students, it became a staple of the insect community, at least for ants and bees. Within three hexs after it opened, Renaissant and Innovant built and staffed both the ant and bee campuses. As a joke, students at the ant campus became known as *alphas*, 'ants learning physics, hydraulics, and stuff.' This clique of ant scholars named the bee students at the other campus—*betas*, for 'bees entertaining themselves academically, supposedly.'

Beetrix flew up to greet Anthiery in the quadrangle between the two campuses. "Did you hear ant students call themselves alphas and bees—betas?" She spewed a seething stink. "This labeling is the thing I wanted the Bill of Rights to prevent. I hope Federant and Legisant come out with it soon and don't water it down too much." *Why are some ants such jerks?*

"Yes, I'm embarrassed, as an ant, by those terms," said Anthiery. "We should stop it."

Beetrix huffed, "What can we do?" *My convictions are strong, but I need Anthiery's help to get things done.*

"You should talk to Federant right now," suggested Anthiery, snapping his pincers, "and I'll get my social activism group together." He continued, "I'm an Antunite, and as descendants of Antuna, many in my family support insectism."

"Insectism? I learned about that in class," declared Beetrix with bright eyes. "Most bees would go for that." *Anthiery will help me fight the causes I cherish.*

Insectism stressed the principles of understanding, empathy, and caring for fellow insects, regardless of their family. It was a movement that Antunites, compassionate bees, and justice-craving flies were all behind.

Anthiery raised a forelimb. "All those who support insectism will want to fight this. We'll organize a protest. Talk to Antianna too. I think many of her girlfriends would be interested."

The student titles stuck over time, despite the protests. Eventually, all ants became alphas, and bees were betas, regardless of whether they were students. Then the ants dubbed the other insect phylogenetic families, those not eligible to attend university, as chi for 'class-C helper insects.' Flies, roaches, beetles, and worms, who were neither stupid nor accepting of nicknames, detested the term chi. Yet, they accepted their status since the inventive ants had provided them with robots to lessen their loads and allowed them more rewarding and leisure-filled lives. Thus, what started as a joke among young scholars became a noticeable insect class system. It had become a society with ants and bees in the top two tiers and other insects below them.

As the insect class system permeated society, it was no surprise that the ants took over as leaders in economic and political realms. After Renaissant determined the UNIT was solid, he turned his attention to politics. He pushed his colleagues in the political science department, Federant, and Legisant, to finish what they started with their Pupas and apply the ideas to governing the colony. The civil government should become centralized as society learns more, he thought. He preferred a central government to the tribal system, with hundreds of queen bees and strong ants ruling their clans. Federant and Legisant finally completed documents taking the positions they each developed for their Pupa theses, including Beetrix's ideas for the Bill of Rights. Together, they created a political system resembling a democracy with Renaissant as president. Federant and Legisant were in the cabinet, and the three followed the rules dictated by their published Declaration of Constitution and Bill of Rights.

Most insects cherished Renaissant for his accomplishments, and ants loved the idea of a centralized ant-led government. Beetrix, Federant, and Legisant pushed bees to support the new central government. Beetrix wished the Bill of Rights was less ant-centric, but it was better than nothing. She convinced Queen Beeanna and most queens, then the other insect families joined in. They elected Renaissant president in a landslide, and he selected his learned academic colleagues for his cabinet. They stressed that government should be *of insects, for insects, and by insects,* and that there should be *one insect, one vote.* Yet, the system they devised was not so much a democracy, but more an *antocracy*. Although all insects chose them, the government members were only ants. Legisant's Declaration began with the phrase: *That all insects are equal is self-evident, but denying ants their due is improvident.*

❋ ❋ ❋

The power dynamic in the economic arena was no different. Even before insects established the central government, ants ruled! This insect society promoted capitalism, free markets, and the opportunity for any insect to get ahead. Yet ants always seemed to have a head start. Renaissant met with his newly formed cabinet, including Microant and Macroant, to discuss the economy.

"Welcome, colleagues. It was a monumental accomplishment having all insects agree to a central government," started Renaissant. "We must honor the trust our fellow insects have placed in us, and treat everyone fairly."

Federant shook his antennae. "Yes, that's why I wrote the Bill of Rights."

"But of course, the masses will rely on us ants to provide the guidance they need," added Legisant.

"All insects must have a chance to achieve their financial goals and pursue happiness," noted Renaissant, reveling in the shining smells.

"I agree," chimed in Microant. "I was happy that Federant used some of Macroant's and my ideas about equal economic opportunities in the Bill of Rights."

"Legisant's Declaration of Constitution is also based on sound economic principles," Renaissant concluded. "Since insects have traded honey for hexennia, it will continue to be the currency for our capitalist system," he added.

"Of course," agreed Microant. "You know my favorite

saying: Nectar is our sustenance, we're told, but don't forget honey is gold!"

Macroant added, "Indeed, plants may keep us fed and sound, but *honey* makes the world go round."

⁂

Ever since the colony's first queen bee, Beefirst, promoted the idea of bees sharing their honey with other insects, ants always wanted more. Bees traded the honey they produced for other goods they needed. Ants, in contrast, stockpiled as much honey as they could. The ants amassed so much honey wealth and greed for more that their desires far outpaced the bee's ability to produce it. Some chi went hungry.

After the new government thrived, Antilla's father, Antrich, arranged a meeting with Innovant, now the Principal of the UNIT, Antstrong, the Dean of Engineering, and Beefarm, the Dean of Agriculture.

One of the wealthiest ants around, Antrich, implored the UNIT academics, "We must increase honey production. The bees cannot keep up with demand."

"I'm pleased you came to us," responded Innovant. "I'm sure my colleagues Professors Antstrong and Beefarm can develop innovative ways to enhance honey stocks."

Antrich stated, "To the scientist who can make honey production double. Your weight in honey you'll get for your trouble." *I must get these scientists to buy into my goals.*

Antstrong scoffed. "That wouldn't amount to very much, given our small size?"

Beefarm emitted an eased essence towards Antstrong. "Typical of a wealthy ant that is no whiz, who'd rather put honey in his mouth than honey where his mouth is."

"I'm sure that if we fund the program well, the scientists at the UNIT can come up with miracles," declared Innovant. "And Professors Antstrong and Beefarm are the leaders that will get it done."

"Yes, I believe they will," replied Antrich. "I was joking about the honey reward. You know I have powerful connections in business and government, and I will lobby for the resources you need." *My ant business partners would give anything to get their hands on a better way to produce honey. It might require significant investments, but the rewards outweigh the costs.*

"Get us the funds, and you won't be disappointed," assured Innovant.

"If we can build a robot that makes honey, we'll do it so fast it's not funny," exclaimed Antstrong.

Not to be outdone by ants, Professor Beefarm added, "A bee's place is surely in the hive. So, more honey is ours to contrive."

As the funds came in, research networks blossomed at the alpha campus, using biomechanics and robotics to do the task. The alpha campus had already developed an expertise in biology and robotics, interests that were innate to telekinetic ants. After Anthiery completed a Larva honor's thesis with Renaissant, Antstrong agreed to supervise his Pupa thesis research. Antianna did her honor's thesis with Innovant and worked with a metallurgist colleague of Innovant for her Pupa degree. Both became involved in the project to create honey-making robots.

Core groups of bee scientists at the beta campus also formed hive minds of researchers collaborating on the best ways to improve honey manufacture from nectar. Agriculture and food production were already the mainstay of inquiry and teaching at the beta campus, so applied study in this area was natural for its faculty and students.

As the applied grants were lucrative, most campus investigations adhered to the two research goals. Academic freedom suffered, but supportive funds in these areas skyrocketed. Each institution developed more significant expertise and specialization in these two academic fields, led by Antstrong and Beefarm. The two campuses became known as the Alpha Institute for Advanced Robotics and the Beta Institute for Innovative Honey Production Techniques.

🐜 🐜 🐜

Soon after the grant funds started flowing, each institute devised state-of-the-art solutions to the goals of the research calls. Beefarm and her team came up with original means to enhance honey production. They produced fortified nectar after extracting phloem sap or 'essence' from flowering plants and trees. They pressed the sap's sugars and amino acids into syrupy nectar and transformed it into honey. Sap from trees was also heat-condensed and added to thicken the nectar, producing even larger quantities of honey.

Ants in the alpha campus perfected telekinetic abilities and developed biomechanical techniques. These advancements allowed individual insects to control massive robotic body parts to increase work productivity. They added large bionic parts to tiny insects to create human-sized insectoids. This cyborg technology was possible as the insects used their telekinetic skills to control the massive mechanical body parts. Their ever-increasing telekinetic skills allowed them to keep the mechanical parts from crushing them and allowed them to operate the bionic limbs. Antstrong's engineers designed the limbs with intricate, electronically controlled levers and pulleys so they could use them to manipulate massive objects. This innovation put insects and machines together as unified organic and robotic super-insectoids. Although the cyborgs were human-sized, they had physical strength far surpassing even the most muscular men.

Biologists from the alpha and beta campuses at the UNIT also worked together to produce anti-aging drugs. They discovered miraculous age-extending antioxidants and hi-tech protein-stabilizing biologics that allowed the host insect's lives to match the longevity of their bionic parts or over two hexuries. Ant biomechanical engineers and cellular neurobiologists discovered novel growth factors and protein-building cellular processes. These tissue growth enhancers allowed the insect's exoskeleton to grow over their mechanical parts so that the insectoids looked like enormous versions of their original tiny selves.

～ ～ ～

Antrich, Innovant, Antstrong, and Beefarm held a news conference to announce the discoveries to the public.

Innovant began, "With the generous support of the business community and Renaissant's government, UNIT scientists have developed unparalleled, innovative ways to enhance honey production." He continued, "With the leadership of Deans Antstrong and Beefarm, we have devised ways to extract, fortify and transport more nectar, and ways to enhance the production of honey and dramatically strengthen our insect species." *I took an enormous gamble using all the UNIT's intellectual resources on this project, but I find reporting its astounding success exhilarating.*

Innovant introduced Beefarm, who added, "Yes, we can

press nectar from the essence of plants and enrich it with tree sap. This discovery will increase honey production exponentially."

Antstrong stepped up to the podium on Innovant's beckoning. "And to keep up with the greater supply, we have devised robotic techniques that enhance insects' ability to process nectar. One small step for cyborg insects is a giant leap for insect-kind."

"Our team helped Antstrong increase the cyborg insects' lifespan," Beefarm added. "They are not only vast, but so built to last!"

Innovant exuded a bulged bouquet. "I cannot praise enough the work of Antstrong, Beefarm, and their colleagues at the UNIT." *The program is such a grand success.*

Antrich next took the dais. "I'd like to thank the scientists and the ant business community for their support." He boasted, "Many ants we had to dissect to improve life for each insect."

Antstrong corrected him, saying, "We harmed no ants. So, no need for apology, in the development of this advanced technology."

"We give thanks to Renaissant's government," added Innovant. "And to Antrich, the largest supporter among the business ants." *He may be an arrogant son of an ant, but he generously contributes to projects that boost his bottom line.*

"Happy to chip in and pleased Renaissant's crew helped too," added Antrich, keen to get the last word.

The first cyborgs were ANTs or allied noble tripods. The acronym differentiated ANTs from their smaller ancestors. They were tripods because the engineers built them with three mechanical forelimbs and hindlimbs instead of their natural three sets of two legs. This rearrangement allowed ANTs to walk upright like humans and manipulate objects better with their forelimbs, now arms. Antstrong and his team created these ANTs a thousand times their regular size. Being oversized and endowed with telekinesis, ANTs moved objects hundreds of times their size.

Antstrong pushed for Anthiery and Antianna to become the first two cyborg ANTs. Antianna's prestigious status as a princess from a well-to-do family supported her case, as did Anthiery being an Antunite and keeping his scholarship throughout his Larva and Pupa degrees. In addition, Antstrong liked they were a happily mated couple and rising stars in the engineering world. They selected Antilla and Decadant because Antilla's father, Antrich, had put so much financial support into the program and knew how to pull strings. Decadant also benefited from the general philosophy insects had to forgive earlier crimes for those who did their time, especially if they confessed.

Antianna and Anthiery met with Antstrong after receiving their bionic parts.

"Our cyborg robotic parts are so adept." Antianna stretched, then flexed her three arms. "We ANTs have incredible flexibility and motor control."

Antstrong looked Antianna and Anthiery over like a sculptor admiring his latest work. "If you two weren't so big, no one would know you were insectoids." *I am proud of my team's accomplishments, including these two young stars.*

Anthiery kicked out his middle leg. "Yeah, it's like we hopped into a magnifying machine and expanded to a thousand times our original size."

"But inside, only your brains and internal and reproductive organs are insectoid sizes," explained Antstrong. *We pulled out all the stops.*

"Why is that?" probed Antianna.

Antstrong reared and spread his two forelimbs as wide as he could. "Increased reproductive organ size ensures procreation, and your inflated stomachs, hearts, and tracheae supply your large brains." *I'm relieved that everything worked out according to our plans.*

"That's amazing. But what will we be doing to enhance honey production?" queried Anthiery.

"ANTs will be the supervisors of all advanced honey production activities," explained Antstrong. "They will also coordinate the production of all insect cyborgs. You two will be key players, Antianna with her metallurgy training and you as a creative inventor."

"When are you scheduled to get your bionic parts?" enquired Antianna.

Antstrong continued to stare at Anthiery, marveling at his flawless creation. "I'm too busy right now, but soon." *You guys are amazing.*

Anthiery picked up a large boulder and juggled it from arm to arm to arm, showing them off to his colleague. "Don't put it off too long. You don't want to be left behind."

Antstrong wafted a bloated bouquet. "The program wanted us to think big with a plus. Soon, you big brothers and sisters will take care of all of us."

CHAPTER 3

POWER GRAB!

In family trees, we find contention.

The turning leaf attracts attention,

be it the end of the season or an era.

Find a solution, promote evolution,
and defend the Constitution.

It's a new direction, new deception, new ereption.

Climb or fell that verdant giant,

resist or flee the reign of terra.

AFTER CONSTRUCTING ROBOTIC ANTs, the scientists realized they needed to create cyborgs from all insect families to enhance honey production maximally. Other insects needed to perfect telekinesis to the level accomplished by ants for this to occur. First, working with Beefarm, Antstrong opened classes in telekinetic arts to the brightest of the bee students and staff at the beta campus. They met with the first bees selected for the program, Beetrix, Shebee, and Beebuzz.

Beefarm addressed the group. "We selected you to be cyborgs because you perfected telekinesis to an outstanding level, and you will become bi-winged essence extractors or BEEs." *Given our campus' significant intellectual investment in the program, I am relieved to see it working so well.*

Beetrix diffused a strong fragrance, "I had no difficulty adapting to telekinesis." She joked, referring to her political exploits, "It's simpler to make an inanimate advance than deter head-strong belligerent ants."

"We also selected you and Beebuzz as UNIT graduates because we wanted leaders in the community," said Antstrong. "I appreciate your wit, Beetrix. And you're lucky I take insults well on behalf of my ant colleagues," he added, roaring.

"Obviously, as a UNIT professor, Shebee, you were at the top of our list," declared Beefarm. *As I always say, no one can beat the beta campus.*

"As a scholar and journalist, I am keen to be here to keep track of fresh developments," responded Shebee. "But how will us BEEs contribute to enhanced honey production?" she asked.

"As BEEs, you will be responsible for both the first and final steps of the process," replied Beefarm. "You first collect the essence from flowering plants and sap from trees and later convert the fortified nectar into honey in your underground hives." *I am proud of the stellar contribution BEEs will make to the program.*

Antstrong added, "With your great size, you can accumulate much more essence and sap than hundreds of bees."

Shebee frowned. "But won't our extracting essence harm the plants?"

"We don't think so, and we'll be able to produce much more honey," replied Beefarm. *Let's not fixate on potential negatives when the positives are so clear.*

"Since ants take so much honey, it makes sense to make more," added Beebuzz.

BEEs, who shared a strong interest in politics while training as cyborgs, Beetrix and Shebee, became fast friends. They also got to know Beebuzz well.

⁂

Antstrong and his cyborg team next established a Chi College of Telekinesis, enrolling fly, roach, beetle, and worm students with the highest CAT scores, reflecting excellent Chi Aptitude for Telekinesis.

Principal Innovant met with Antstrong and Beefarm to discuss the progress of their programs. "Professor Antstrong, how are the chi telekinesis classes going?" *Please tell me the system works well. I need to justify the program and report its accomplishments to investors.*

"I am quite amazed that each insect family developed high telekinetic skills," replied Antstrong. "It's been uplifting to see progress so clever in this joint beta-chi endeavor."

Innovant addressed Beefarm, hoping to hear more good news. "I hear flies are just as talented as the bees." *I'm delighted the beta campus held its own.*

"I couldn't be happier with their performance," said Beefarm with a swollen smell. "Ants thought they were the only masters of telekinetics, but it's clear bees and flies easily control their new prosthetics."

Innovant looked up at the sky. "Great! Now we just need to teach them all to fly."

An elite group of professors and students at the beta campus collaborated with accomplished ant engineers and the top fly graduates of Chi College to establish an advanced program in aeronautics. Firefly applied for the program, as did her mentor Flyhero, who was older but still the fastest flyer in the colony. They joined the bees, already selected to be cyborgs. The new program developed the aerodynamic robotic biomechanics necessary to allow cyborg bees and flies to take flight.

～ ～ ～

It pleased Firefly to meet Flyhero, her former mentor, following their selection to be FLY cyborgs.

"Flyhero, I can't thank you enough for your training that helped get me into the cyborg program," she professed.

Flyhero stretched out his massive wings, inspecting them for any bits of dust or dirt that might increase drag. "Well, sometimes hard works beat out brains. I no go to the UNIT, and I didn't do too good in school. But I flew fast and gots smart by competin' hard and learnin' from my failures." *I work hard all my life.*

Firefly instinctively gave her wings two quick flaps, a trick Flyhero taught her to flick off any dust before takeoff. "I taught Flynette some of your flying techniques, and she got into the program, too."

"I no Pupa, but nobody work harder or fly faster than me," Flyhero concluded as an inflated incense infiltrated the ether. *I don't need to be no UNIT professor to teach you a thing or two.*

"I heard some flies will transport cut trees from the forest to the essence presses," noted Firefly. "They're calling us flap levitating yeomen or FLYs."

"Antstrong saw that we not only flying experts, but we gots

strong telekinetic powers," responded Flyhero. "So, he wants FLYs to carry cut trees to furnaces. Burning 'em makes the power for runnin' the presses." *I so proud of all flies. We are the tops among insect families.*

"Won't us cutting down all those trees deplete our beautiful forests?" worried Firefly.

"They replant the trees," said Flyhero. *I think that should be good enough.*

"But they told me I'd be a messenger," added Firefly.

Flyhero outstretched his wings. "Yeah, me too. They want the fastest flyers to deliver messages to and from da ANTs." *I know ANTs always want the best.*

Firefly looked over at Flyhero's massive wings with stunned surprise. "Gosh, I thought you were fast as an insect, but you must be three times as fast as a cyborg. I bet there's nothing on Poo-ponic that moves quicker than you."

Flyhero spat on and polished his new bionic left wing. "Well, you no slow-poke yourself. But if there a faster one out there, I love to take 'im on." *I may be proud, but I would do anything fer Firefly, or any friend, FLY or not.*

The cyborg program challenged the scientists and students to produce bionic aircraft controlled by small bees and flies living within their larger flying cyborg bodies. The imagery was more straightforward for BEEs and FLYs than for ANTs, since their body parts were proportional to the original ones. There were no rearrangements of their limbs, but their bodies were a thousand times grander. So large, they looked like single-engine ultralight airplanes.

※ ※ ※

Not long later, Antstrong showed off the three other insectoid groups to his colleagues. "The development of these insectoid families was simple and needed only scaling up the size of existing robots and integrating them with organic masters." *Innovant is so inventive. I'm thrilled to impress him.*

"I see, and you built them at vastly different sizes," noted Beefarm.

"Yes, the large ones are robotic armored champs or RoAChs," said Antstrong. "They will transport nectar from the essence presses to the hives and honey from the hives to the vaults." *I designed these babies myself.*

"They seem to have armor over their storage compartments," noted Innovant.

"Yes, we protected them so no one can attack them and steal the nectar or honey," answered Antstrong. *We should prepare for the worst.*

"And what are those little guys over there?" asked Beefarm.

"Those are wood-boring buddies or WoBBs," replied Antstrong. "The bigger WoBBs drill through trees to cut them down, and the little ones bore holes to tap the tree sap or lop off the branches." *Working claw-in-claw with Beefarm, I learned to respect her almost as much as Innovant.*

"With those choppers, the trees don't stand a chance," shuddered Innovant.

"ANT supervisors will calculate the correct number and angles of boreholes to take them down efficiently and safely," Antstrong continued. "You can see the ANTs directing a WoBB tree extraction operation over there. See how they take down an entire line of trees in just hexonds?" *We have perfected everything down to the last spec of sawdust.*

"I know the burning of tapped-out trees is a critical step in converting essence and sap into fortified nectar," said Innovant.

"Yes, the industrial level pressing of essence into nectar and the condensing of sap into syrup require high heat, generated by burning trees in large furnaces," explained Beefarm. "The furnaces provide the heat necessary to steam excess water from tree sap, and the steam runs turbines that power the presses which crush essence into nectar."

"We'll have to replant trees, so we don't run out," suggested Innovant.

"We are planning for that, but the forests are so plentiful it's not a concern now," responded Antstrong. *Let's focus on the here and now. We'll deal with problems when they present themselves.*

"I assume those long ones are worms," noted Beefarm.

"Yes, they're wriggling rock movers or WoRMs," responded Antstrong. "We need them to dig burrows, nests, and hives since everything needs to be larger now." *We've thought of everything.*

"Seems we've made all these large insectoids to produce more honey, but won't they consume considerably more honey to feed their massive bodies?" asked Innovant, effusing a sticky scent.

"I wouldn't worry about that," responded Beefarm. "The BEEs are so efficient, and by taking essence instead of nectar and adding sap, we'll have tons of honey before you know it."

"RoAChs, WoBBs, and WoRMs also contribute to the operation and are equally efficient," Antstrong professed. "These cyborgs are so deft and strong to the core. We will not need tiny insects anymore!"

Not only were the BEEs large and capable, but the engineers dramatically expanded small roaches, beetles, and worms. They efficiently wielded their large bionic body parts with telekinesis. They converted tiny bugs and worms into construction-sized trucks, pneumatic drills, and excavators that performed thousands of times more work than their original small selves. The ANTs and WoBBs didn't need to fly, so they left the wings off.

∙∙∙ ∙∙∙ ∙∙∙

Anthiery's friends Roachard, Wormillian, and Beetlebert became cyborgs because of their excellent CAT scores and esteemed positions in the business world. Beetlebert even swayed the selection team when he and his mate, Beetlebin, changed their names to Wobbert and Wobbin to show how keen they were. Wormillian and Wormella were high school sweethearts, and Wormillian stuck with her through her ordeal with the severe burns, helping Antianna change Wormella's dressings and nursing her back to health. He worried her disabilities would hold her back, but she had the highest CAT score of the chi and scored higher than the ants that designed the test.

Roachard and Wobbert bumped into Wormillian after his cyborg selection.

"Mill, it's great that you and Mell got into the cyborg program," praised Roachard.

Wormillian untwisted himself from a pretzel-like stance he used to perform isometric exercises. "Yes, Mell had such high scores they couldn't refuse her, even with her disabilities." *She had the top CAT score among all insects.* He released a shiny smell. "Archiant hired her for his firm after she recovered from her burns, and he taught her some telekinesis. But her doctor says she also developed compensatory neuromotor controls to overcome her incapacities." *I cherish that worm, and I admire her strength of character in overcoming her injury.*

"I guess they wanted to take you as a leader in the business world, just like Roachard and me," added Wobbert, as a stuffy smell enveloped him. "It seems they had to start with the top of the heap."

"By the way, I saw they selected another roach named Roachelia. Do you know her?" asked Wormillian, who devoted himself to his close RoACh and WoBB friends.

Roachard locked himself into an impressive stilt. "I heard she had the highest CAT score among roaches. I only met her once before, but I'd like to know her better."

⁂

The ant scientists created a final seventh insectoid family as an afterthought when they realized they needed extra transportation aids. The missing step was the production of bins to carry large quantities of nectar back to the colony and honey to the vaults. Ant bioengineers completed this task by designing a new category of insectoid clones using genes from the DNA of extinct spiders. They genetically engineered these cyborgs, known as BUGs, for bipedal unibodied golems, to produce a gluey thread that they spun and hardened into bins to transport nectar or honey. Bipedal meant these insectoids walked upright on two legs, although they also had six upper limbs for spinning and weaving. They designed them to make BUGs as distinct from spiders as possible. Except for their hairy, bug-like appearance, they looked like pot-bellied men standing on two legs. Their stout unibodies contained the space needed to hold the spinning thread they used to make bins.

Pleased that the final innovation was complete, Antstrong exclaimed, "These BUGs with their bins and a RoACh as a bus, together will carry the load for all of us."

Cyborg creation was the insects' crowning achievement up

to this point. But they did not know yet whose head the crown would adorn.

⚬ ⚬ ⚬

Within a hexade, the number of insectoids grew exponentially, with each new model having more inventive characteristics, improving the honey production abilities of the cyborgs. Antianna and Anthiery played a prominent role in cyborg manufacture. Soon they reached design model VI for each insect family. Being bigger, stronger, brighter, and with the promise of longer lives, very few insects did not want to be cyborgs. Of the leaders, only some of the older higher-ranked soldiers resisted since they already had prestigious positions, and they mistrusted the educated types running the insectoid show. Likely, most would have converted, but the slots were far fewer than the demand. With the cream of the crop transformed into cyborgs, the remaining insects were older or uneducated ones who didn't know what to do independently. A more senior soldier, General Wiseant, saw the writing on the wall that they would not select him, as his CAT scores were low and his age too high. He met with a like-minded colleague, Lieutenant Spyfly, to discuss what to do about the situation.

Wiseant began, "Lieutenant, I know Antstrong and his crew are still planning to construct thousands of cyborgs, but they have made most of their selections. We are not among them, and there are millions more like us." *Once I was a military star, but now I'm close to retirement, and I don't want to be a cyborg.*

"Yes, I agree, and many rejected insects are distraught," said Spyfly.

"The big-brained cyborgs are taking over everything—civil governance, the UNIT, and their large burrows have taken over the colony. We need to do something." *I hoped that insects and insectoids could share the colony, but I see the writing on the wall.*

"We can't fight them, General. They're too big, and they'll crush us." Spyfly expelled a brisk bouquet.

Wiseant concluded insects must give way to cyborgs. "We must convince non-cyborgs to accept their fate and leave the colony. We can live off the land, in a more primitive style, like our Earth ancestors from Antuna's time." *Let the cyborgs squabble amongst themselves.*

"But will the masses follow us and leave peacefully?"

"We must convince them. We either leave or get decimated if we fight. There's no living with the cyborgs," declared Wiseant, radiating a baked bouquet. "All these young elite insectoids have nothing but power and greed in their future. They don't understand that their new idol, honey, imprisons them, and some hexay they'll beg to be freed." *They may be stronger, but we are the wise ones, making the right choices.*

"You're right. A revolt would be futile. We should move out to the countryside. We can survive, no, thrive in the wilds and live as we choose," responded Spyfly. "Should we be made and not laid, like our big cyborg cousins? Or take control of our destinies and lay eggs by the dozens?"

Discouraged by their failure to become cyborgs, many ordinary insects needed a leader and a stance to follow. That leader was General Wiseant, and their cause was a back-to-the-wild, anti-honey philosophy that stressed that honey was only for bees. General Wiseant convinced the remaining insect masses that honey was evil and they should leave behind any society built on its proceeds. When he heard that some of his fellow insects did not want to leave without exacting some revenge on the cyborgs, he told them they would, but only when the time was right.

As the hexs passed, the insects that left the colonies flourished in the wild. There were no restrictions on their reproduction, as they no longer lived in city-like burrows that restrained growth. They also had no predators, so the hundreds of eggs they laid all survived. Spyfly's argument that non-cyborgs could procreate as much as they wanted became a manifest destiny, and some believed they could take over the planet again if their numbers were significant enough. The forests and jungles had also spread throughout the globe, so natural food was plentiful.

Some distinguished non-cyborgs still lived in the colonies, including Innovant and Renaissant. Because of their advanced ages, neither of them became cyborgs. Given their distinction in society, the cyborgs asked them to join them, but both declined, stating that the new generation should take over as cyborgs. Some insectoids pushed to replace the old guard with cyborgs, but Federant and Legisant, now insectoids, blocked the ousting of Innovant as UNIT principal and Renaissant as President.

After turning down the cyborg offer, Renaissant asked to meet with Antstrong, Antianna, and Anthiery.

In Antstrong's office, Renaissant looked up at them and joked, "I expected you three would be giants in your fields. But I never expected you to be so gigantic." *I disagree with Wiseant. Cyborgs should take over. It's a natural progression.*

"Well, we may tower over you. But we'll never outgrow your stature," flattered Antstrong.

Renaissant crawled up the leg of Antstrong's desk and spoke from the surface so the others could better see him. "Thank you for that acknowledgment, Antstrong. I appreciate the praise from such an amazing visionary as yourself. And I am glad you finally got your bionics. Your colossal intellect deserved a large frame." *I'm so proud of all my students and what they accomplished.*

Antstrong offered Renaissant a drop of water and noted, "Thank you, President. But I know you didn't come here for pleasantries."

Renaissant wet his mandibles and responded, "Yes, I have some terrible news. My good friend Innovant passed away in his sleep last night." *How could I not accept the cyborg revolution when my esteemed friend Innovant started the program?*

"I hope he went peacefully," lamented Antianna.

Renaissant nodded. "Yes, and at a ripe old age."

"Please extend our condolences to his family," Anthiery offered on behalf of Antianna and himself.

"I will. Antstrong and I already spoke. And he agrees with what I am going to propose to you." He addressed Antianna and Anthiery. "I've asked Antstrong to take over as principal of the Unit, as it was Innovant's wish. I also suggest that the two of you take over from Antstrong as Dean of engineering and the team leader of the cyborg project. I leave that up to you three to decide among you," proposed Renaissant. *I leave our colony's future in good claws.*

Antstrong broke his gaze from Renaissant and turned to look at his colleagues. "I accept the position of UNIT principal, and I endorse the promotion of the two of you. Principal duties need my full attention, and I am confident that Anthiery will make a great cyborg team leader and Antianna will make a stellar new Dean."

"I don't know what to say …," muttered Anthiery, pleased with the opportunity but now weighing the responsibilities in his mind.

"Are you sure?" questioned Antianna uneasily. "A female has never been Dean of engineering."

"I decided that I'd like to shake things up a little with the new insectoid community," explained Antstrong. "I could have gone the other way, but this feels right, especially with you being a princess. Anthiery has an inventive mind, and I want him to lead the cyborg production team. He's already running the show."

"I am flattered," said Anthiery before looking at his mate. "I hope Antianna will still have time as Dean to work with us on the metallurgy side."

Antianna stepped away from Antstrong's desk and looked out the window. "I would die if I only sat behind a desk administrating."

"My thoughts exactly," agreed Antstrong. "Antianna's contribution to the team will continue to be instrumental."

Renaissant flexed his antennae and released some alert pheromones to get the others' attention. "I am pleased that you have sorted this all out. But there's something else I need to tell you." *I'll shock them with this.*

Antstrong raised his eyebrows. "There's more?"

Renaissant continued steadily, "Yes, I kept it secret, but I am quite ill. I'm afraid I have little time left." *My death may be imminent, but I want all my apprentices and students to achieve as much success as possible.*

"I am so sorry to hear this," declared Antianna.

"I will step down as President," Renaissant started strongly. "I have told your cyborg colleagues, Federant and Legisant, that one of them should take over as president. They both agreed that there should be an election to let the colonies decide. It will be like turning over a leaf to the insectoid generation. Insect cyborgs will take over as President and Principal of the UNIT. It's what you might call progress. Or better yet, evolution," he concluded. *I've had my time.*

"Well, if you think it's best," said Antstrong with a hint of sadness, pulling at his tone. "But insectoids and insects alike will miss you."

Renaissant reared up again, emanating a ripe reek. "It's the cycle of life—hatch unknowing, die transfixed, and grow as much as you can betwixt."

❧ ❧ ❧

Antilla reeled when he heard they selected Antianna as Dean of engineering at the UNIT and Anthiery as the head of the cyborg production team. He still hated Anthiery for stealing Antianna from him and telling Archiant about the fire prank that injured Wormella. Antilla was also against a female Dean of engineering or any other faculty at the UNIT, especially one that jilted him. He also hated the UNIT because his faculty had asked him to leave his business program when he failed too many courses. His father consoled him by saying that one could only learn about business in the real world and that Antilla should study with him. He had heard some good news, though. Antilla was ecstatic when his father learned the program selected him to be a cyborg.

Antilla closed the door to his office after he offered Antrich a chair. "Father, I am so glad you'll be a cyborg. I thought they took no one over sixty hexs." *It's the most fantastic news I've heard in hexs.*

"Well, no business ant contributed more to this project than I did. So, there was no question it would happen," bragged Antrich.

Although happy about Antrich's news, Antilla could not hide being upset about something else. "Father, I am furious about the direction the UNIT has taken. Can you believe they picked a female as a dean? What is this world coming to?" *Damn, females. I hate them all.*

"Females should stick to mothering and foraging," agreed Antrich. "They don't even belong in the UNIT, let alone as Dean."

Antilla slammed the morning news scroll down on his desk. "And that double-crossing squealer, Anthiery, is heading up the cyborg production team." *I could kill him.*

"You already put him in his place. Remember that, son. You're getting rich off him, and he's only a glorified civil servant."

"Yes, that is a satisfying thought." Antilla pressed his claws together. "But I'd love to crush him if I could."

Antrich crawled from his chair up onto Antilla's desk. "Some hexay you will."

Antilla picked up the news scroll again. "And there are rumors those two UNIT liberals, Federant and Legisant, will run against each other for President. Instead of stinking academics, we should try to get a business-ANT in there." *I hate the UNIT and all the academics running the cyborg show.*

Antrich, who had crawled onto the news scroll as Antilla picked it up again, scuttled up his forelimb to get close to his antennae, and spouted a steely stench, "Son, now that I'll be a cyborg, I can use my means for better things than Antstrong's program."

"What do you mean?" asked Antilla. *I love my dad, but he's always so elusive.*

"How'd *you* like to run for President?"

Antilla lowered his forelimb down over the desk and gently shook Antrich off.

"Who me? I'm not qualified." *Wow, I didn't expect that.*

Antrich reared up and excreted a screaming stench. "Qualifications, you don't need those! You just need great backing, and I can buy a lot of votes."

Antilla smiled, thinking about the possibilities if he won. "Father, you are the greatest—you've always had my back." *President Antilla! That sounds great to me.*

⁂

Anthiery, Antianna, and Beetrix decided it was time to get their friends together to make plans to best influence the outcome of the elections. Beetrix invited Anthiery and the girls into her burrow and offered them some honey before speaking. "Anthiery and Antianna, I want you to meet Shebee. She's the amazing journalist that mentored Flynette for her senior project. And the program recruited us together as the first cyborg BEEs."

Shebee lowered her head to bow a little. "Flynette and I are starting a news outlet we're calling PIN-point for Poo-ponic insect news. Insectoids will get to know me on their telescreens," crowed Shebee, "Considering your experience and insight, I'd love for the two of you to give us one of our first interviews."

"I'd be happy to," replied Anthiery.

"Yes, how could I refuse a friend of Beetrix and Flynette?" promised Antianna.

Flynette stepped forward from her position in the background. "I agree, these two will make great subjects, a dean and a princess, and cyborg team leader and an Antunite," beamed Flynette, proud of her friends.

"Let's not show bias, Flynette, since I am assigning you to do the background research," teased Shebee.

"Let me tell you why I brought us together," interjected Beetrix. "Anthiery has taught me about insectism, and I know Shebee and Flynette are keen on it."

"Renaissant mentioned it when I studied with him, and I assume it influenced his views and how he ruled. That's why he was so beloved," added Shebee.

"Anthiery, Antianna, and I met earlier, and we agreed that as cyborg leaders, we should inspire two things within our new insectoid society. First, there needs to be press freedom," Beetrix declared.

"Flynette and I are all for that," remarked Shebee.

Flynette urged her on. "And what's the second point?"

Anthiery moved into the light next to the burrow window to emphasize he was about to introduce the main point of the meeting. "There are new elections to replace Renaissant, and we want to start a movement to push for the candidates who support insectism."

Shebee's antenna straightened. "PIN-point needs to be neutral, but I realize our platform will have a significant influence. In my mind, insectism is at the heart and soul of our Constitution and Bill of Rights. Although we can't endorse specific candidates, we can hold them to the laws and the spirit of our government's founding principles," responded Shebee.

"That's what we want to hear, Shebee," approved Beetrix, offering more honey to her guests.

This diverse group of friends became the forerunners of a new political force based on insectism.

Flynette wiped honey off her mandibles. "Anthiery, have the views on insectism changed now that the rulers and elites are insectoids? And should we now call it insectoidism?"

"That's a brilliant question. Insectism is about treating all insects the same, no matter what family and how big or small," responded Anthiery, taking a delicate sip of honey. "Cyborgs are insects at the core, and our souls do not differ from our small cousins, so the term insectism still applies."

"And even if they left the colonies, we should still look out for the non-cyborgs' best interests," added Antianna.

"Hear, hear!" broadcasted Shebee.

As a former professor at the UNIT, Shebee was up on the latest technology and ensured PIN-point was up with it. The key innovation that allowed them to air their views in the first place was a pheromone-to-chemical structure interpreter. This invention allowed them to provide subtitles for the insects' communications on-screen during their interviews. Shebee and her assistant Flynette worked hard to get the network up and running to cover the presidential race. It delighted them to land Renaissant as their first interviewee. As expected, Renaissant stepped down as President and announced free and fair elections to determine the new leader.

After Shebee offered Renaissant some water, she carried him to a spot on a pedestal next to the pheromone interpreter and got right to the core. "President Renaissant, we are disappointed to hear you are stepping down, and can you tell our audience why?" *Landing such a critical interview should establish PIN-point as the dominant news program.*

Renaissant shook his antennae to clear his voice. "Thank

you, Shebee. I am not so young anymore. I haven't been well, and to be honest, I don't want to die in office."

Shebee gasped. "That is shocking news. I am so sorry, Mister President. Can I ask what the ailment is and how long you have to live?" *I thought it would make waves but never expected this interview to be such a tsunami.*

Renaissant looked downward. "Well, let's just say I can't finish the next session of Congress."

"What is it that would take such a powerful ant down?" questioned Shebee.

Renaissant paused and answered, "I don't want to say, other than old age."

Shebee didn't waste a moment before asking, "Can you talk about the plans for your succession?" *His stepping down begs so many questions.*

Renaissant answered, "We are to have free and fair elections. Two members of my cabinet will be running."

"That is a great scoop," exclaimed Shebee. "Can you say who?" *Will he tell me?*

Renaissant sipped some water. "I've already said too much. You'll have to wait until they announce it."

Shebee's journalist instincts took over. "Since there are only four members of your cabinet, and two of them wrote the Constitution, should we presume that Federant and Legisant will run?" *He has to say yes. My viewers need to know.*

Renaissant smiled. "I can't say, but that's as good a presumption as any."

Shebee chuckled. "Oh, Mister President, you are very diplomatic."

Renaissant's eyes twinkled a little. "Yes, it's part of the job. And by the way, I have another scoop for you."

"Mister President, do tell." *I have charmed him, I'm sure.*

"I will appoint Microant as interim leader since Macroant told me he wasn't interested," Renaissant offered.

Shebee cracked a wide grin. "This is quite the scoop and a back-clawed statement that further supports my presumption." *I got him now.*

Renaissant laughed. "Perhaps it does."

Shebee got more serious. "Will the election be for all insects—cyborgs and smaller?" *I support Anthiery's ideas about insectism and believe government officials need to safeguard all insects and insectoids.*

Renaissant stiffened. "As most non-cyborg insects have left the colony and no longer want anything to do with us, the cabinet decided that the election would be only for insectoids."

"Do the non-cyborgs agree?" probed Shebee with a fat fragrance. *I think they should choose.*

Renaissant squirmed a little. "I reached out to General Wiseant, but he never answered."

Shebee challenged the notion. "So, they're out. But it doesn't seem fair." *There's nothing you can do?*

Renaissant re-established his diplomatic demeanor. "Yes, it seems so, but remember, most of them are poor, uneducated insects that don't vote, anyway. Still, I have assurances from my cabinet that we oversee them well, even if we disenfranchised them in the wilds."

Shebee shrugged. "I am skeptical about that. Do all insectoids get to vote?" *Am I right? He's rejecting insectism.*

"Yes, much like our previous elections for the Congress, it will be one insectoid, one vote," Renaissant declared.

"And who is eligible to run?"

Renaissant fidgeted. "As described in the Constitution, all insectoids can vote for their favorite ANT."

Shebee barked back, "It's still an antocracy?" *As I thought. A typical ant leader!*

Renaissant responded, "I never liked that word, but we can't stray from our Constitution."

Shebee fought hard to keep her composure, glancing down and then back up. "Is that fair to other insectoids?" *It seems to me you could do more.*

Renaissant paused briefly. "You can take that up with the new leader. I am not about to change the Constitution at this point."

"That's reasonable," agreed Shebee. *The ant is dying, and I should give him a break.* "But how will you keep busy once you step down?"

Renaissant sighed, "I will read and rest. And write my memoirs, as long as I still can."

"Well, Mister President, I look forward to reading them. Thank you so much for this interview and your distinguished service to our colonies." *I'll take it up with his successor.*

"Thank you. And the best of luck with this new PIN-point venture," responded Renaissant, smiling.

🐜 🐜 🐜

Although Federant and Legisant announced their candidacies almost immediately, there was a one-hexth period to accept any more nominees that might declare. Federant and Legisant were both very well educated, founders of the central government, and esteemed. But neither was charismatic nor had they run a campaign before, as Renaissant claw-picked them for his cabinet. Their running created little enthusiasm in the general electorate, and their campaigns continued for a couple of hexeks without generating too much excitement.

Halfway through the campaign, Antilla submitted his nomination and announced his candidacy in a splashy event paid for by his father. Antilla became somewhat of a sensation in the business world after the production and rentals of his automated honey extractor. And since the proceeds of the invention paid him a generous salary, he didn't need to work hard to secure his business career. Antilla spent most of his time promoting himself and living the high life as a wealthy celebrity play-ant. He was a much more glamorous candidate to business types and insectoids that were not academics. He also proposed several policies like deregulation and reduced business taxes popular with the business community, the most likely voters. His father suggested another critical policy called dribble-down economics. He maintained that lowering taxes on the wealthiest ANTs would cause a boom in the economy, as their spending and hiring practices would cause honey to dribble down to feed hungry chi mouths. Antrich also had hundreds of high-profile insectoid business leaders under his claws because they owed him honey or favors or feared his powerful reach.

※ ※ ※

Back at PIN-point, Shebee and Flynette had a meeting to discuss election reporting. Shebee started, "Flynette, do you think we are covering the three candidates equally?"

"Yes, Shebee, but the public is lapping up our coverage of Antilla," replied Flynette.

Shebee sighed, "Yeah, I guess his splashy lifestyle captures everyone's attention." *Why do we allow unqualified candidates to run?*

"And I assume we have followed him a little more because we know the public finds it interesting," continued Flynette.

Shebee stiffened. "I'm sure more viewers are watching when we report on him." *Antilla's frivolous exploits excite the public.*

Flynette looked down at the polling charts she received. "I hope we're not boosting his chances."

"No, the public is smart enough to know he's too much of a joke to win," concluded Shebee. *At least, I hope so!*

Flynette shuffled the pages. "I'm not so sure about that. The public is easy to fool, and in high school, we all knew Antilla was both ignorant and a jerk, but he always got what he wanted."

≈ ≈ ≈

Although polling had Legisant leading until a few hexays before the election, a rumor spread that Legisant had a drinking problem, and the public shouldn't trust him as a leader. Antrich paid off some of his connections to fabricate a list of receipts for extensive strong sap purchases by Legisant over the hexs. The gossip spread far and wide and damaged Legisant's campaign, and the lies even affected Federant's polling because everyone knew the two were close. The feeling was that if one of them drank too much, they both did, as colleagues and good friends. Shebee warned the public that this was fake news, and she interviewed Wobbert, the primary seller of strong sap.

Shebee motioned Wobbert towards an interpreter and started. "Wobbert, have you heard these rumors that Legisant is a lush and drinks every hexour?" *Can the audience see from my body language how much I doubt these reports?*

Wobbert chuckled, "Yes, of course, the word is all over the planet."

I must remain serious, despite this frivolous story based on rumors. "Antilla's campaign says they have receipts showing Legisant is a regular customer and often buys strong sap from you."

Wobbert straightened up and effused a stocky scent. "Shebee, from what I've seen, these receipts are fraudulent. They even misspelled my name on the banner."

"Well, there you have it, folks. Straight from the beetle's pheromonal glands," Shebee concluded. *I'm happy Wobbert confirmed my suspicions.*

Despite these facts, the lies had their intended effect. As they say, the public cares more about rumors than the truth. The election was close, and Antilla finished with 38% of the vote. Legisant and Federant split the remaining ballots almost 50/50, with 30.5% for the former and 29.5% for the latter. One could have stepped down to avoid splitting the vote, but historians hypothesize that neither expected a political neophyte to win.

CHAPTER 4

Is war ever civil?

Deception is the master of corruption.

Not a surgeon but it doctors, not a baker, but it fudges.

And when it cuts or takes a slice, the
knave be sharper than the knife.

And the needless loss of life becomes a relative indignancy

when the doctor's orders have baked in malignancy.

ANTILLA TOOK THE reins of the government at a time of massive change. Since insectoids were enormous compared to their insect ancestors, they needed much larger accommodations and public halls. The tiny insects occasionally surveyed the colony and marveled at the construction. Spyfly had a discussion with Wiseant about the changes in their old settlement.

"Can you believe all the building going on in the capital?" Spyfly asked.

Wiseant spread his forelimb wide. "Insectoids are so big. They need to expand their structures accordingly."

"And the WoBBs can fell trees so quickly. They're constructing large buildings with wood." Spyfly continued, "Antilla built himself a massive palace he calls the Woodhive. He says it's the insectoid's house of government. But he built it so he can live like a king."

"So, they made it of wood?" asked Wiseant.

"Yes, they used the highest trees in the forest to build it. The structure is the tallest in the capital. It must be three insectoid stories high."

"Well, remember I promised our most rebellious friends that we would get back at the cyborgs for pushing us out." Wiseant cracked a broad smile and transmitted a seasoned scent. "Our guys love the taste of wood again, and I think it's time."

※ ※ ※

A few hexeks later, Antilla was in the upstairs bathroom of the Woodhive taking a bath. As usual, he had Decadant attending to him.

"Deca, I'm finished with my honey bath. Could you draw my royal jelly bath so I can unsticky myself?" *Honey does wonders for my shell, but it's so hard to get off.*

"Yes, I've already filled the jelly bath, and I'm heating some water for your final rinse."

"Be sure to fill them both up to the brim. I don't care if it spills over," complained Antilla, puffing a plump perfume. *I hate only getting half covered.*

Decadant sighed but complied. "OK, whatever you say. I'll bring up some extra jelly and hot water."

Shortly after Decadant carried up the extra jelly and water, creaking noises sounded from the floor below.

"Tilly, there's a funny noise downstairs. I'm going to check it out."

Antilla didn't respond because he had just moved into the royal jelly bath, where he typically hummed marching tunes at the top of his scent glands, and he fogged out any other fumes.

When Decadant reached the ground floor, he realized the sound came from outside the building, so he stepped outdoors. Just then, the front side of the Woodhive swayed and collapsed, and the three tubs crashed down to the ground. Antilla was still sitting in the royal jelly bath when the other tub flipped over and covered him with honey. As the Woodhive was on a hill, the jelly tub slid down the grade with Antilla hanging on for dear life. The tub careened down the slope and crashed into a totem pole with insect carvings that Antilla erected in the main square. A sticky jelly- and honey-covered Antilla stood up and watched as his bust at the top of the pole splashed into the marsh. A seething stink polluted the square. A small group of non-cyborg beetles and ants leaving the area had to stifle their urge to laugh out loud at their sweet, just deserts.

～ ～ ～

After Antilla had been in power for a couple of hexs, Antianna and Anthiery discussed the future of the insectoid society. Scarfing down some berries and honey, Anthiery boasted about the accomplishments of the cyborg program. "Model VIII cyborgs are nearly perfect, and I don't think we'll need any more major design changes." *We've done a great job.*

Antianna grabbed a berry and congratulated him, "That's great, Thiery, but I wonder whether we are building too many.

We started this to produce more honey, but now we need more honey to feed insectoids who eat much more."

Anthiery looked down at the large bowl of honey on the table. "Well, we've got many more insectoids to produce the honey, so that's not a problem," he surmised. *We need to focus on the positives.*

Antianna frowned, losing her appetite, "It also seems like most ANTs can never get enough honey. Other cyborgs only take what they need, but ANTs are greedy and are stockpiling it."

Anthiery put a claw to his temple. He was so proud of the cyborg program that he only just realized how ANTs used it to their advantage at the expense of others. "Yes, they're also trading for more, and Antilla's policies seem to help them amass the bulk of it." *How could I have been so blind to their greed?*

Antianna picked up her bowl and put the honey back in the cupboard with a look of worry. "I am afraid the ANTs are getting richer, and all the other insectoid families are getting poorer."

Antianna mainly worked on the metallurgy side, was less invested in the cyborg construction, and could distance herself from the program more than Anthiery. Anthiery focused on producing as many cyborgs as possible, and he had difficulty seeing the big picture. Yet, he realized that although Antianna may have been frivolous in her youth, through her mistakes, she had developed a pearl of wisdom that compelled him to listen to her.

"You're right. As an Antunite, I am ashamed that I was oblivious to what was going on. We should try to do something about it," declared Anthiery. *I'm glad you set me straight again.*

Indeed, Antilla's early policies were pro-business, and he

pushed through bills that reduced regulations on businesses and lowered taxes on their wealthy owners. As expected, the rich ANTs got more affluent, and a small group of ANTs at the top got even wealthier.

❦ ❦ ❦

Anthiery felt he needed to stand up to Antilla, but worried that getting politically involved might compromise his position at the UNIT. After agonizing for hexays, he sought the advice of his old employer, Queen Beeanna.

Anthiery bowed before the Queen BEE. "Queen, I am so happy you agreed to see me."

"You are always welcome here." Beeanna motioned for him to sit next to her. "I have followed your progress over the years. A student leader, a young engineering professor, and now the cyborg team leader. You are a star so bright I need to avert my eyes."

Anthiery blushed, "Oh, thank you, Queen. I strive to do my best."

"I am so happy you took my advice and kept learning." Beeanna cracked a wide smile. "And you snagged Antilla's girl."

Anthiery chortled. "Yes. Antianna wised up to that tyrant, Antilla." *Lucky for me.*

"But I guess Antilla is on your mind again. No?"

Anthiery sat up. "Yes, he represents the opposite of everything I've ever stood for. And he's pushing me to fight, but is it suitable for someone in my position?" *Help me decide.*

"Only you know the answer." Beeanna put a claw to her head. "You are a UNIT chief, in charge of many young minds who follow your leadership." She placed another claw over her heart. "But you are also an Antunite. So, you must inspire your charges to oppose injustice."

"Thank you, Queen. I knew you'd understand." *I'm happy to get an outside perspective.*

Beeanna stood tall and spread her wings wide. "Anthiery, you have a strength within you much more powerful than your bionic parts. You are a natural leader; I could tell that back when you were in high school."

Anthiery beamed and was full of conviction and energy. "My mother always said I was strong-willed, and I must have a lot of Antuna in me. If young Antuna could oppose Malevolant, I can stand up to Antilla."

Beeanna smiled. She was proud of her former attendant. "Yes, you have not only the means, but also the fire in your genes."

❧ ❧ ❧

After meeting Beeanna, Anthiery called together Antianna and their friends to organize further protests. Beetrix, Flynette, and Shebee shared Anthiery's views and, with Antianna, endorsed his insectism movement. Wobbert now mistrusted Antilla because he lied about Legisant's strong sap purchases to get elected and became president because of his father's power and influence. He grew to hate Antilla's policies, which favored ANTs, questioning his actions. Together, these insectoids formed the core of an expanding anti-antocracy protest movement that stood up to Antilla's moves with repeated marches that attracted many UNIT students.

❧ ❧ ❧

A short time later, after the cyborg leaders introduced model

VIII insectoids, Antilla invited Antrich to his office to ask his advice. "Father, I know that my tax reductions were popular with our rich friends. Now I want a policy that makes a statement that I'm a power to reckon with. " *I need to get approval ratings higher than Renaissant, and I'll do whatever I can to achieve that goal.*

"Yes, I agree," said Antrich. "The insectism group has been attracting attention with their marches. If their crowds grow, you'll look weak."

Antilla pounded his claw down on his desk, dwelling on the hatred he still felt for Anthiery and Antianna. He suspected they were the leaders of the protest movement. "I should crush them all, especially that infuriating Anthiery." *He's such a traitor to my rule.*

"No, I don't think you should mess with any insectoids yet," advised Antrich calmly. "It could backfire. It would be best if you concentrated on non-cyborgs."

Antilla puzzled, "What, those vermin that hate honey? What can they do? They're poor, uneducated, and harmless. They're only heathens and savages." *You've got to be kidding me.*

Antrich raised a single claw. "Exactly, they're easy targets."

Antilla paused briefly, then concluded, "I know they hate me because I made my fortune from honey. General Wiseant has also been a pain in the neck, asking us to stop expanding colonies into the forests. I also heard they had a population explosion and are eating all our essence-producing plants." He thought some more. "And one of my builders said he found small insect bore tracks in the wood framing that failed when the Woodhive collapsed." *Maybe non-cyborgs are not so innocuous as I thought.*

Antrich clapped his three forelimbs together. "Now you're talking. You created a justification for war."

Antilla puffed out his abdomen, oozing a smoldering stink, proud of himself and his ideas. "Yes, a war I can't lose will make me very popular." *Commander Antilla! I like the ring to that.*

Antrich walked over to the window, lingering on the thought. "Everyone loves a commander who's a winner."

Antilla smirked. *I can see my presidential ratings soaring.* "Decadant, are you listening to this?" Antilla called out towards his antechamber.

Decadant answered from his desk just outside the room, "Yes, sir, great idea."

"Get me General Prudant," ordered Antilla, grinning from antenna to antenna.

President Antilla gathered his cabinet and argued they needed to deal with the menace of the non-cyborg insect over-population. Then, after meeting with General Prudant to confirm the victory would be easy, Antilla convinced Congress.

⁂

When Wobbert heard the news about Antilla's call for war, he met Roachard and Wormillian from the New Honey Guild. He had an epiphany about his earlier excessive pride and the elitism of the group.

Wobbert appealed to his friends, "I propose we reconsider the purpose of our club. I met with our old buddies, Anthiery and Antianna, and I recognized the evil of entitlement and greed. By swanking our wealth, I realize that we're no better than that wicked Antilla who stole the election and is now pushing for war with small insects." *I hate that evil ant.*

Roachard stilted himself and spurted a stout scent. "Bert, you're right, I've known since I was a pupa that we must protect those who need it, and now many chi need physical protection and financial aid. We've been just flaunting our wealth—maybe we should use it to help the less fortunate."

Wormillian raised himself in his chair, "I agree. I was never too comfortable with our club's exclusiveness—I just wanted to join you guys. And I'm all for doing anything we can to counter that jerk, Antilla. I know he burned Wormella, despite him getting off. I expect he's just starting the war to make himself more popular with the electorate."

"Well, if we all agree, I'll start making plans to set up a charity to replace the guild. And if you both want to stand up to Antilla, come along to Anthiery's next protest group meeting," suggested Wobbert. "I'll bring Wobbin and invite my colleague Bugbert and his mate." *Together, we'll take him down.*

All agreed, and they raised a glass of strong sap to cheer on their new mission.

⁂

Despite calls for tolerance and leniency from Federant and Legisant, who both won by-elections to enter the Senate, Congress passed a decree of death to the tiny masses of non-cyborgs to combat the bane of insect infestation in the forests and jungles. Many insectoids and the government believed Antilla's arguments that the hordes of non-cyborgs living in the woods and jungles were consuming so many plants that the essence needed for honey production would run out.

In response to Antilla's war declaration, Anthiery called together his insectism enthusiasts. This group included the organizers of a much larger group of demonstrators that amounted to thousands and many splinter groups in other colonies. Anthiery's upbringing as an Antunite and interactions with Antilla as a teen helped him develop into a formidable leader who knew how to accomplish his goals.

Anthiery told the group, "Antuna once said, 'Insects did not weave the web of life; we are but its strands that fray with strife. We must mend the discord we sew and allow nature's lattice to grow.' All life on Poo-ponic is interconnected, and any harm we bring to others we bring upon ourselves."

His aspirations were further attainable given the support he received from Antianna. Included in the group was Flyhero, who, as the fastest fly around, was Antilla's private messenger. But now, as a fly spy, Flyhero could pull a fast one on Antilla. Firefly was another critical member since she had an entire network of FLYs at each of the other colonies eager to protest Antilla's policies. Finally, Wobbert recruited many of his friends and colleagues.

※ ※ ※

Despite the protests, Antilla announced the decision over the airways to insectoids in the colonies that they must rid the planet of the tiny insects. ANT chemists revived old chemical warfare techniques, and insectoids tolerated inferior honey vintages during the warring hexs. Under Beefarm's instruction, BEEs used tree sap for honey-making until they extinguished most insects. Then they avoided using tree sap while they targeted the wood-boring beetles.

The non-cyborg insects fought back using their chemical warfare, as they had done against termites and spiders. But their smaller bodies and brain sizes rendered their production techniques far inferior to their insectoid enemies. ANT cyborgs could kill several insects with a single caustic attack using their formic acid spray and much more with chemical warfare. Still, it was a test of wills between Generals Prudant and Wiseant. In one skirmish, known as the *Battle of Lily Valley*, the non-cyborg insects fought valiantly against their insectoid foe. Tiny insects were often at a significant disadvantage. However, because of their small size, insects made great spies and, on one occasion, literally had a fly on the wall during a strategic meeting of the insectoid brass. General Wiseant's lieutenant, Spyfly, accepted a dangerous spying assignment and overheard the plans for a secret raid to destroy the tiny insects' central command.

Spyfly flew overnight to the command cocoon to warn General Wiseant of the attack. "The cyborgs are coming! The cyborgs are coming! We'd better get our defenses a-humming," she warned. *I swear by the wings on my back.*

On General Wiseant's orders, the insects mobilized hundreds of millions of their troops to a narrow valley on the path the raiders needed to take. Wiseant invited Spyfly into the command cocoon. "Captain Spyfly, I want you to supervise the preparations for the ambush. You have proven yourself worthy of my trust."

"Sir, it's lieutenant," corrected Spyfly. *I'm a loyal soldier and never take more credit than I deserve.*

General Wiseant barked, "Please don't interrupt me, Captain, or I'll change my mind."

"Ah, thank ..." Spyfly stopped herself in a rush, releasing a scrawny scent.

The general interrupted, "Have the worms dig holes under the large boulders that line the valley's slopes south of here."

Spyfly questioned, "The one with the lilies?" *I bet he has a brilliant plan.*

"Yes, have them dig so that the rocks are ready to roll down the grade with the slightest push." Wiseant reared and made a shoving gesture with his forelimbs.

"Yes, I understand," responded Spyfly. *I'm happy to glean Wiseant's meaning.*

Wiseant continued, "And have our wood-boring beetles bore into the trees on the ridge."

"To where they're about to fall?" Spyfly responded. *I am a quick study.*

"Yes. And have the roaches and worms ready to molt throw their old skins onto the valley floor," instructed the general.

Spyfly shrugged and puzzled, "Sir?" *This trick is something I've never heard before.*

Wiseant explained, "When the cyborgs get close, order the soldier ants to hide in waiting under the slough of old exoskeletons with their jaws and sprays at the ready."

Spyfly raised a single claw. "Ah, I see." She smiled. *That's impressive, but Wiseant's military creativity never surprises me.*

The general spread his forelimbs wide. "And have the molted roaches line the dales on both sides, hiding amongst the lilies."

Spyfly flapped her wings. "And the bees and flies?" *We can bring it on too!*

"You guys do what you do, but make sure you have millions ready to swarm," advised Wiseant.

With Spyfly standing by his side, General Wiseant assembled the masses under his command and inspired his troops, "Our foe may be large, and our chances small, but we'll take down many before we fall."

Under General Wiseant's orders, the non-cyborg insects pounced upon the arriving insectoid platoon like a spider on its quarry.

Two unknown cyborg soldiers entered the valley, unaware of the impending doom. The first soldier spoke to his buddy, "I think it might rain. Look at that dark cloud."

His buddy answered, "That ain't no cloud. It's moving too fast."

"I think they're bees, but what are they doing?"

As they stared, bees in mid-flight formation, with a swarm the size of a mighty oak's canopy, began repeated shimmering waves. The bees in the middle first, then adjacent, and outward to the perimeter, flipped their bodies with hive mind-like precision. Their wings reflected, then deflected the light, causing hypnotically expanding concentric ripples that transfixed their cyborg enemy.

"I'm getting dizzy. We'd better look away," advised the first soldier.

"Watch out. It's bees, and they're getting closer."

Then, the air around the cyborgs became so thick with millions of flies and bees that the soldiers could not see those in line right in front of them.

"Where are you? I can barely hear you over all the buzzing," answered the second.

"I can't breathe. There are so many flies they've clogged my spiracles."

"Ouch! I just got stung." A freezing fragrance chilled the surrounding air.

They did not dare yell as their exoskeletons burned from

many stinger jabs. Else they tasted the bitter venom as the stinging bees flooded their mouths.

"Duck! The trees are falling."

"Jump! There's a boulder coming," cried the first soldier. "The whole place is booby-trapped."

As boulders toppled them and trees crushed them, survivors reported the lilies of the valley uprooted themselves and fell upon them with jaws snapping. Broken and staggering, the few still standing slipped on smooth roach shells and slimy worm skins as tens of millions of ants came from nowhere and swamped them, crawling all over them and gnawing their tender shells.

"Oh, my Queen! Those lilies have jaws, and there are ants everywhere. Get the heck out of the valley," exclaimed the second soldier.

In keeping with General Wiseant's plans and Spyfly's preparations, falling trees bashed in skulls and impaled thoraxes as rolling rocks crushed bodies and snapped exoskeletons. The venom of a thousand bee stings collapsed airways, and the bites of hundreds of thousands of ants and roaches stripped exoskeletons bare, evoking the stench of hemolymph and raw flesh everywhere. Finally, the two unknown soldiers broke ranks, fled the valley, and barely escaped with their lives.

This skirmish was one of the hundreds of battles fought, and most went the other way, with small insects massacred by the millions. With their incredible strength, the insectoids transported massive quantities of toxic chemicals throughout the planet. At first, they employed the same techniques used in the Spider-Termite wars, spreading chemicals that either killed on contact or contaminated the insects' food supply. They also devised ways to vaporize the neurotoxins, using fogs to gas the insects over extensive areas. But Antilla wanted the job done even faster.

Antilla called his general to his office for an update. "General Prudant, we need to speed up this war. Protests are mounting. And the *Battle of Lily Valley* humiliated us with those loser cyborg troops. Should I be thinking about relieving you of your command?" barked Antilla. *Incompetent fools surround me.*

"No sir, Mister President," defended Prudant. "You'll like my new plan that will rid the planet of our enemy once and for all." Prudant realized Antilla was displeased with the time required to defeat their enemy.

Antilla raised his eyebrows. "That sounds more like it. Tell me more."

Prudant moved in close to his commander, happy that he reacted positively. "Do you remember the fiasco with the attempts to make sugar-honey?"

"Yes, of course, those damn insects were getting into the hives and gumming up my extractors," complained Antilla. "They kept breaking down. And the lots were full of the pests." *Don't remind me.*

"Yes, insects can't resist sugar," Prudant continued. "That's why we stopped making it."

Antilla turned away from Prudant. *That damned Anthiery set me up with that sugar-making debacle. I'll never live it down.* "Get to the point, soldier."

"Yes, sir, we will poison sugar cane stalks and leave them out for them to eat," explained Prudant briskly, realizing Antilla's attention span was short.

Antilla smiled, exuding a shifty stink. "Sounds like a splendid plan, but will it take long?" *I want this done yester-hexay.*

"We'll start immediately, but we need some time to do it right," replied Prudant. "We don't want our enemy to get suspicious and avoid the sugar cane altogether."

"If you think it will work, go ahead." Antilla grabbed the scroll Prudant held and scribbled his signature on the battle plan. "But get on it fast!"

❧ ❧ ❧

General Prudant, a patient strategist, instructed the cyborg army to grow hectares of sugarcane and distribute stalks throughout the planet for many hexths. He knew the non-cyborg insects could not resist them, and he made sure insectoids knew about the plan. At first, the insects did not touch them, fearing poison. But as time passed, some undisciplined ones tried them and reported that they were safe to eat.

Spyfly requested a meeting with her general to inform him of the development. Wiseant was troubled about the course of their war effort and anxious about hearing more bad news, but he met with her anyway. "General Wiseant," she started, "some of our folks have been sampling the discarded sugar stalks. They haven't poisoned them. Much of our natural food perished in the war, and everyone's hungry."

Wiseant scratched his forehead, emitting a shaky scent. "The cyborg society has become so wasteful. I expect they extract the best parts of the sugar cane, fortify their armies, and discard the rest. If they seem to be clean, I don't see a problem. It may even give our remaining troops more energy." *Our troops are dejected and can use sweet nourishment to cheer them up.*

"There's some down the path. Would you like to try it yourself?" Spyfly offered.

Wiseant waved his fore limbs. "No, not right now. That stuff is addictive." *I've got other things to worry about.*

As time went on, the non-cyborg insects ravished the discarded sugar cane stalks, devouring as much pulp as possible. The non-cyborgs became hooked on sugar after many hexths passed. At that point, General Prudant implemented the devious part of his plan. The plot involved instilling minute quantities of toxins into the stalks that did not kill until the insects ingested a considerable amount. Some got sick, and a few died, but they did not attribute it to the pulp they had eaten for hexths. Prudant also arranged for a period when the sugar canes were scarce, knowing that the addicted insects would go into a frenzy trying to get more. Then he tripled the dose of poison within the stalks made available after hexths of dearth.

❧ ❧ ❧

When the stalks were ample again, the non-cyborgs gorged on as much pulp as possible. They gathered and ate all they could, worried there might be another sugar famine. With the triple measure of poison, many of them overdosed on the large amounts of laced sugar they consumed.

Spyfly reported to Wiseant on the recent events, "General, sugarcane is available again, and our troops are gorging on it like there's no tomorrow."

"Well, hopefully, it will give them some energy," said Wiseant. *Our losses have demoralized the troops.*

"There's a problem, though," explained Spyfly. "Many insects have been dying under mysterious circumstances."

"I heard. There must be some virus going around," surmised

Wiseant. *I can't imagine Prudant would be so patient and conniving with the cane stalks.*

"Is it possible they poisoned the sugar cane?" asked Spyfly.

"No, I had some myself just yester-hexay. It tasted great," replied Wiseant. "Oh, remember several hexths ago when some insects died, it was probably the beginning of a plague. Tell everyone to keep their distance and don't share food." *If Prudant were going to poison the stalks, he would have done it from the beginning. Anyway, the sugar cane is too good to be bad.*

Spyfly shrugged. "OK, if you think so."

"I've got some here. Let's have some and put these worries behind us." Wiseant offered his captain a large piece. *That'll take our troubles away.*

All the illness and death devastated the survivors. Scared and distraught, they turned to their happy drug, sugar, to overcome their grief. But, addicted to cane-pulp, they repeatedly fell prey to the same tactic. Several repetitions of sugar cane famine and glut led to the extermination of every tiny insect.

General Wiseant made this prophetic statement as he was dying of poisoned sugar cane and realized too late what had happened: "Nations, like each insect, are punished for their transgressions. In time, Antilla's crew will pay for these aggressions."

⚜ ⚜ ⚜

Insectoids had more vigor than ever, achieving near-perfect insectoid creation and solving the non-cyborg insect population explosion. Antilla believed nothing could stop them from producing as much nectar and honey as possible. Yet, things were not as rosy as the insectoids thought. Extracting large volumes of essence from plants instead of taking small quantities of nectar was deadly for many plants. This result likely explains where the term 'essence' came from since, when taken in large amounts, the plant lost its life essence and died precipitously after that.

In their efforts to amass as much honey as possible, the insectoids tapped the sap and burned trees in a clear-cut fashion. WoBBs targeted all trees in a line, bore in, and once the sawdust dropped, so fell the trees. The precision of the operation amazed Wobbert and Wobbin, who admired the instructions provided by their ANT supervisors. Yet, without non-cyborg insects feeding on them, the dying plants and unused branches from the trees became petrified. They turned to stone rather than rejuvenating the soil, so clear-cutting the forest killed it entirely. Although they had fungi that fed on excrement, no fungi broke down dead plants. Soil rejuvenation depended on small insects boring through the wood, breaking up old vegetation, and turning over the soil. The ground looked like either hardened lava or dusty ash, and no plants grew. Without tiny insects around, the insectoids saw 'spent land' expand at an alarming rate.

～ ～ ～

Antilla arranged a post-war meeting with his father to discuss his administration's new directions. Antrich returned the intelligence report Antilla had given him the night before.

"That group of insectism activists has shifted their focus," Antrich commented. "They're using their old anti-war network of rebels to protest environmental issues. And they've been pushing their philosophy of equal rights for all insectoids from the beginning."

Antilla steamed, "Father, I know those WoRM lovers have been working on the Congress to end the ANT-only rule and let betas and chi into government." *Don't they realize only ANTs are smart enough to rule? I can't imagine betas and chi in the government, watching over me and telling me what to do.*

"Yes, they convinced the Congress that since betas and chi gave their lives to fight in the Great Small Insect war, they can run for office too," cried Antrich.

Antilla threw the scroll across the room, squirting a fiery fragrance. "That's not right. Can you imagine RoAChs scurrying across the Hive of Representatives and WoRMs sliming up the Senate?" *It's too gross even to consider.*

"Well, Congress will pass it and change the Constitution," Antrich stated. "You'll lose too many voters if you veto it," he warned.

Antilla crossed the room and picked up the damaged scroll. "Damn it! I know you're right, but we can reverse it after the next election if we can get more members elected that share our view." *I'm angry, yet I must still consider my options.*

"Son, you're getting the hang of this political game," gushed Antrich. "I am so proud of you."

Antilla dropped the scroll into a filing cabinet and locked the drawer. "Well, you gotta play the game if you want to win." *I love it when I impress my father.*

Antrich stood up and headed towards the doorway. "Or you could make up *new rules* for the game."

Antilla followed Antrich as he entered the antechamber. "Yes, I'll have to remember that—especially after I get more supporters in Congress." *My dad is always so clever.*

Antrich saluted Decadant, who was at his desk, then turned towards Antilla. "Son, you know I don't have many hexs left, but I will make that happen before I go."

Antilla nodded at Decadant and waved at Antrich as he left. "Father, you get me that majority, and I'll make you proud.

Make *new rules!* I love that." *Imagine what I could do with all that power?*

Antilla was so vain that he used a pheromonal transcriber to record conversations in his presidential office. He chronicled all his pheromonal secretions for posterity, whether they smelled good or bad.

THE SLIPPERY SLOPE

Like toppled dominoes in a line, the
numbers fell to his dominance.

Like spinning power balls in a drum that dance,

the lots were drawn down the tubes by
the chance to know his power.

But all too soon, the jitterbug vibe
swung from glee to cower.

ANTIANNA BUMPED INTO Beetrix on her way out of the Senate building. "I am so proud of you and Beebuzz for getting elected to the Senate. I thought it could never happen that non-ANTs could hold office." *I am so thrilled that members of our group positively responded to my encouragement for them to run.*

Beetrix beamed like a young bee that found her first wildflower cluster. "Thanks, Flynette and Flyapper are also in the

Hive of Representatives. We couldn't have done it without the support of you and Anthiery."

Antianna extended her forelimbs to offer Beetrix a congratulatory hug. "No, you did it yourself. And Wormillian became Chief WoRM, Wobbert the Master WoBB, and Roachard the Topshell RoACh; also, fantastic achievements." She spread a sunny smell all around. *I'm so proud of you all.*

"It's so much better to fight from the inside. Finally, we don't have to carry those protest placards everywhere," Beetrix joked.

Despite a majority vote of ANTs to allow these concessions in that election cycle, Antrich came through with his promise to Antilla and ensured that a large majority of ANT-only supporting candidates entered the next Congress. This bloc of members comprised the newly formed PEE Party, which stood for Pooponic Electoral Exclusivity, understanding the word 'exclusive' referred to the ANTs. As a result, the voters elected Antrich, who led the PEE party, to the Senate.

After the PEE party swung the Congress back to a majority of members that supported ANT-only rule, Antilla was keen to pass a law that would institute the change. However, Antrich suggested Antilla wait until he had enacted a few bills that would demoralize the beta and chi Congress members.

Antrich leaned in close to Antilla, sporting a devious grin. "Now is not the time to kick them out. Let's first show them what we can do with a supermajority."

"But what policies would best irk them?" asked Antilla. *I don't know where to begin.*

Antrich got the waffling whiff of Antilla's air and held

his grin. "You're the President, do whatever you want. What annoys you most about them?"

"I'm irritated that the chi are starting up so many businesses," ranted Antilla. "We should make it more difficult for them to succeed." *Maybe there are some things I could do.*

"Anything else?" asked Antrich, glancing at Antilla with an 'atta boy, keep going' look.

Antilla giggled. *I feel like a debater on a roll.* "I hate it that females like Antianna and Beetrix are becoming leaders in society. They should take care of pupae in their nests, not become Deans at the UNIT and senators." *There's another. I like this.*

"Well, let's propose a bill to rectify the situation," suggested Antrich, feeding off Antilla's energy.

"And I still want to crush Anthiery," said Antilla. *I'll do it myself. Just give me some time to choose the most painful method.*

Antrich grinned. "I think we can arrange that, too."

Antilla introduced a bill that placed a hefty tax on non-ANT-led businesses. It was such a high tax that companies forced to pay it could not stay afloat. When the beta and chi business community heard about the tax, they saw it for what it was, which upset everyone.

🐜 🐜 🐜

A couple of hexths after Antilla implemented the new law, Wobbert called together his friends Roachard and Wormillian to his office next to his strong sap warehouse. He also invited Bugbert, the bin supplier he used for crating his bottles.

"Mil, I'm glad you could make it," greeted Wobbert. "It's great that we've stuck to our plan and refused to pay that ridiculous tax."

"I agree," said Wormillian. "We'll all go out of business if we pay it." *I can't wait to crush Antilla.*

"Roachard said he'd be a little late," continued Wobbert. "But here's Bugbert now. I'm trying to convince him to join our protest and refuse to pay the tax. It seems we were the only ones bold enough to resist."

After introductions, Wobbert stated his plea to Bugbert.

Then Roachard arrived, very rattled. "Hey guys, sorry I'm late, but I've been getting complaints from my customers." He panted like he'd been running from a menacing fly swatter. "Many of them are getting sick after eating my last batch of fungi."

Wormillian shook his head. "That's strange. You've had no problems before." *It must be Antilla's doing.*

"Do you think Antilla poisoned your fungi because you're not paying the tax?" questioned Wobbert.

"I know Antilla's a political tyrant, but I don't think he'd go that far," surmised Bugbert.

"I wouldn't put it past him," added Wormillian. *Wobbert has it right.*

Suddenly, they all heard a small blast from the far side of the adjacent warehouse. They ran from the office to see what had happened.

"What the heck!" yelled Wobbert, trembling like a beetle on a falling leaf. "My warehouse is on fire. Stay back! The entire building could blow." A shrill stink drenched the air.

Wormillian slithered over and panicked at the sight of the fire. "Wobbert, my crew is digging the foundation for your new warehouse. They're over there near the fire!" *I've got to save them!*

No sooner had he said it when there was a massive explosion, and it blew the entire south wing of the warehouse sky-high. The four friends were far enough from the blast to escape injury. But the explosion consumed the area where Wormillian's crew was working.

Wormillian stretched his longitudinal muscles to the max and prepared to dive. "Wobbert, I'll tunnel under the fire to get to my boys." *I'll save them! If they're not already dead!*

"I'll follow you to secure the tunnel," added Wobbert, staring at the flaming warehouse. "Roachard and Bugbert, you go get help."

As soon as Wormillian and Wobbert disappeared underground, a third more enormous explosion rocked the earth, and the ground around the excavation site collapsed. If flames did not overcome Mil's crew, falling rocks and soil likely crushed them. Wormillian and Wobbert's tunnel also caved in, and their two friends worried the sudden landslide might have squashed them.

Roachard and Bugbert sprang into action like lazy workers alerted to their supervisor's arrival. "Bugbert, use your six claws to dig as much soil as possible, and I'll bulldoze it away."

"Yes, we need to act fast," exclaimed Bugbert, surveying the magnitude of the soil compression. "Mil can probably dig the two of them out, but the collapse may have injured him."

"Hurry, let's get them outta there," fretted Roachard.

You never saw six limbs move so quickly when Bugbert got the knack of digging, and Roachard pushed the soil away like water flowing down a gorge. Before long, they reached Wormillian and Wobbert, who were dumbfounded by the blast. The explosion disoriented Wormillian, and he had tunneled deeper into the ground. Wobbert's shell was flattened, and he wasn't breathing.

"Mil's confused but OK," Roachard exclaimed breathlessly. "But Wobbert's in big trouble." He shot a screaming smell.

"I have CPR training," yelled Bugbert, shaking the soil off his limbs. He had his two claws opening and clearing Wobbert's mouth, another two claws squeezing his breathing spiracles, and the remaining two massaging his heart through his thorax.

Hexonds later, Wobbert coughed and spat out some dirt. "I, I thought we were goners." His frame bowed out as he gasped like a trapped miner taking his first breath of fresh air after rescue.

Bugbert threw his six arms around Wobbert and sighed. "It's good to see you breathing again."

Roachard chuckled at Bugbert's gangly hug and scooped the two of them up onto his back to carry them to safety. "But where's Mil?" asked Wobbert.

Wormillian then encircled the three, embracing his old friends and new friend and rescuer. "I may have lost my crew, but at least I still have you guys." *Antilla's going to pay for this.*

Wormillian's crew did indeed perish. It was an extensive project, and most of Mil's team worked on it. Everyone on the job was instantly incinerated or crushed by tumbling rocks. The next hexay, after recovering from the shock of the experience, the four of them returned to the site. As they approached the charred remains of the warehouse, Bugbert noticed a trail of silver powder littering the area leading towards the now obliterated south segment of the warehouse. He sniffed at the powder and licked a speck stuck to his claw.

"This is pure sodium," Bugbert exclaimed, wincing from the burning sensation on his tongue. "I know it from another factory I make bins for."

"And there's a funny smell in the air," noted Wobbert,

puckering at the vinegary aroma. "I'm pretty sure that's formic acid."

"Holy crap!" shouted Wormillian, glimmering as he remembered a childhood story. "My mother was obsessed with the old tales of Antuna and the early settlers on Poo-ponic. She read them to us as bedtime stories. I'm sure Antuna said that mixing sodium and formic acid would cause an explosion." He thought of the president and fumed. "The fire was Antilla's work. He's trying to sabotage all of us." *He burned Mella and now my whole crew.*

"You're right, Mil," added Wobbert with dismay. "I see ANT tracks in the mud. They must have doused the sodium with their formic acid sprayers. The initial blast ignited a fire that triggered further explosions when it set the strong sap ablaze."

Although Wobbert and his friends concluded Antilla was the culprit, they heard later that Antilla had Anthiery arrested for arson related to the disaster. In addition, there was some cooked-up story about a feud between Anthiery and Wobbert and a supporting history that Anthiery had purchased suspicious flammable substances, including white phosphorus. As a result, they apprehended Anthiery, holding him in prison without bail.

※ ※ ※

Not long after Anthiery's arrest, Antilla enacted a new law banning females from holding high office, including Deanships at the UNIT and membership in Congress. The law immediately eliminated the positions held by Antianna, Beetrix, and Flynette. After hearing the news, the three friends met to discuss their options, feeling defeated in more ways than one.

"Antianna, I can't believe Antilla framed Anthiery for blowing up Wobbert's warehouse," exclaimed Beetrix, reaching for a hug with tears filling her eyes. "What are you going to do?"

He's got Anthiery caged like a bottled firefly. Antianna gasped. "I don't know. Since the blast killed several WoRMs, they won't release him on bail." She pounded her claws on the desk. "I know Antilla caused the blast and blamed Anthiery for it. He has hated him since high school." Antianna trembled. *Stop shaking, girl. I must be strong.*

"Antilla detests chi and wants all their businesses to fail," interjected Flynette. "With the fungi poisoning, strong sap warehouse explosion, and WoRM crew deaths, our three friends lost their businesses."

"He targeted them because they refused to pay the unfair taxes, and now our positions are gone too," seethed Antianna, imagining what she would do if Antilla were standing in claws-reach of her. *I've never wanted to hurt someone so badly in my entire life.* "Antilla must have a vendetta against the leaders of our protest movement. But he's also targeted all females in power. Even Beefarm is now out, despite her contributions to increased honey production."

"Antilla is going after every group he despises," Beetrix cried. She swallowed her fear and continued, "But how can we help Anthiery?"

"Maybe Roachard and his friends can break Anthiery out? I'm sure they are itching to get back at Antilla," replied Antianna, now standing tall and rattling her antennae like sabers. "As for our sacking, we haven't lost our voices even though we've lost our positions." She polluted the atmosphere with inflamed incense. *We'll scream out for all to defeat Antilla.*

Next Antilla pushed for an ANT-only referendum, hoping to oust Congress's remaining BEEs and FLYs. But they did not count on an opposition party of non-ANTs encouraging the masses of betas and chi to vote against the proposition. A new coalition had emerged, calling themselves the POO Party for Poo-ponic Opposition Officers. Congress-FLYs, Flyapper, and Flynette started the group with encouragement from Anthiery. It was only natural that former Senator Beetrix took over as the party's leader. Although Flynette and Flyapper founded the party with FLYs swarming the POO, the movement gained more traction after Beetrix took up the cause. The ANT-only proposition failed once the opposition received widespread public support. The referendum's result so angered Antilla that he immediately called for a quick vote in both Hives of Congress. The poll was on a bill banning future referenda and elections and vetoing the current one. The move was typical of Antilla, who was often hot-tempered, vindictive, and over-the-top, as he could not control his impulsive recklessness. Despite the unconstitutional nature of the bill, President Antilla expected he had enough support from PEE Party members.

With Anthiery's protest group in disarray, most of the criticism of President Antilla's proposed bill came from the multi-insectoid free press, with PIN-point leading the charge. The top anchor-insectoid of PIN-point, Shebee, had a considerable following in the lay insect population, which buzzed. Shebee was a straight-up commentator who preferred hard news to fluff, and her viewers trusted her. As a reporter and anchor, she never let a politician get away with anything, and she would not start with Antilla.

Shebee met with Antianna and Flyhero during the mayhem after the referendum to discuss how far she should go in condemning Antilla, who started calling himself Antilla-the-One. She knew from Beetrix that since Anthiery's arrest, Antianna was the protest movement leader, and she could tell Flyhero was Antilla's disgruntled messenger.

Shebee flapped her wings hard to spread a blazing bouquet around the room. "Antianna, I can't believe all of Antilla's recent moves, especially this latest bill," started Shebee. "We insectoids cannot allow this decree to go on! It's unconstitutional! What comes next—more insectigone?" *We have to do something!*

Antianna nodded. "Shebee, you are right to go after Antilla and the PEE Party. We worked hard to get representation in the government. They shouldn't be able to take it away."

"Yes, and the things I'm overhearing from Antilla," added Flyhero. "I can't imagine what he'll do after he turfs all our guys out."

Shebee started, "I am glad you can keep us up to date, Flyhero. It's helpful that he's kept you on as his messenger. Has he ever suspected you as a FLY?" *I heard he is very suspicious of FLYs.*

"He hates FLYs and WoRMs too," answered Flyhero. "But he keeps me round because I'm the fastest messenger. He don't suspect nothing. He's sharp, but he also dull."

Shebee stared hard at Flyhero, thinking what a poor leader Antilla was. "I know he hates me, too." She then shifted her gaze towards her fellow female. "Antianna, you know Antilla hates females, and he has a disdain for the press." *How did we ever elect this guy president? He's dangerous.*

She feared Antilla would spread mistrust of the press among his supporters and someday shut her media outlet down. True to Shebee's worries, Antilla's repetitive reference to the media outlet as SIN-point rallied many lay ANTs and PEE Party members, who believed the outlet published false news.

⁂

Antilla smoldered after Shebee revealed cabinet transcripts from leaked i-mail messages, showing why he pushed for the ANT-only rule. He feared the beta and chi Congress members would discover that for hexades, ANTs had done nothing about the spent lands. One of the message lines read: '*We could deal with it if we choose, but if news of our inaction gets out, we're sure to lose!*' The transcripts also showed that the cabinet had considered transitioning power to an autocracy. The line read: '*We need to pare the leaders down until the boss can wear a crown.*'

"Antilla, we're going to have to be careful about this. It could take you down," reported Decadant, handing him the morning news scroll.

Antilla passed the scroll back to Decadant as his anger dissipated. "Don't worry so much, Deca. We only have to keep denying it, and the public and the press will tire of it." *The electorate's attention span is no better than mine.*

"But you should read the transcripts Shebee published. They're damning," exclaimed Decadant. "Someone on our team must have released it."

Antilla exuded an acrid aroma at the idea of disloyalty. "All leakers are traitors who use fame as a crutch. They are treasonous and must be treated as such." *I'll kill him myself.*

"I'll get our *Ant*orney General to look into it," assured

Decadant. "Leakers are like spies, and spying on the President is a big deal. And when we find the spy, we'll make him squeal."

"And what do we do about Shebee?" Antilla fumed. "She is a traitor who should go to the morgues. It's clear she's an enemy of us cyborgs." *I despise females with power.*

"We can't just kill her," responded Decadant with a seasoned smell. "We'll have to frame her and arrest her. Then we could take over the network."

"I like that idea!" said Antilla, patting Decadant on the shoulder. *Shebee behind bars would be perfect.*

⁂

Despite Antilla's bullying style, demonstrations continued for hexeks and only grew. Several young chi led the charge, including Firefly and her network of dissenting FLYs across the colonies. Antianna and her friends still did their best to aid Firefly. Crowds of angry protestors lined the streets chanting: "Hey hi, hey ho, Antilla's gotta go!" and "We won't end these noisy rants till we root out all crooked ANTs."

After hearing Antilla's denials about the leaked transcript, Shebee interviewed the ousted Senator Beetrix and Representative Flynette on PIN-point. It surprised her when Antilla's chief of staff accepted her invitation to provide a counterpoint.

"Decadant, I am glad you agreed to this interview," started Shebee. "Many say that Antilla's move to suspend elections is unconstitutional. What is your response?"

Decadant sat up tall. "Your President works hard to make everything right, as is usual. And he's got the final say on what's constitutional. When times take a toll, he can choose to stop the poll." He smiled. *I couldn't have said it better.*

Shebee looked at the opposing side. "Former Senator Beetrix, what do you think of our reports that Antilla is trying to remove non-ANTs from Congress and trim the government?"

"Well, it's atrocious, but not unexpected from a government that wants to return to an antocracy and a leader who won't stop until it's an autocracy," condemned Beetrix.

"Would you like to add a rhyme for our record?" asked Shebee.

Beetrix puffed herself up. "Death to the bill the President has introduced. Suspending an election is undemocratic, and he has no excuse!"

Shebee looked back towards Decadant. "What do you say about these released transcripts?"

"They're all lies. We never released such pheromones," deceived Decadant. *No one will believe those reports.* He gave a dismissive shake of his head.

"But I have sworn statements from my sources who attest to their accuracy," Shebee rebutted, rattling the report in her claws.

Decadant secreted a slimy scent, "Though my reply on this matter may give you woe, it relies on the alternative truths that I know."

Shebee shrugged and looked now at her old friend. "Representative Flynette, how do you feel about Antilla's new bill?" enquired Shebee.

Flynette flapped her wings vigorously. "Well, it's completely unconstitutional and wrong. It will set us back hexs, and it's a terrible message to non-ANTs everywhere."

"Would you like to add more to the record?" asked Shebee.

Flynette held her wings still and pronounced, "Yes, how can President Antilla, on one claw, introduce this corrupt bill, and on the other claw, claim we're disloyal to question his will? If these stories are true of the plot he deployed, he must relinquish his power back to insectoids."

Turning again towards Decadant, Shebee asked, "I assume Antilla has been following his new bill's protests. How does he feel about it?"

"They're attempting a coup," exclaimed Decadant with a stifling stench. "Antilla says we should jail or exterminate the leaders of the protests. These betas and chi are treasonous traitors, you see, and Antilla knows what to do to such treacherous scree!" he threatened. *I agree protestors should be exterminated.*

Decadant had instructed one of his staff to slip into the back room during the interview and place large canisters of honey into Shebee and her producer's lockers. He also planted a doctored ledger of PIN-point's advertising revenues with their forged signatures, omitting the missing honey pots. Two hexays later, after a raid on PIN-point's offices, Decadant announced trumped-up fraud charges that caused the firing of Shebee, her producer, and her top reporters at the media outlet.

Decadant took over at PIN-point and announced the charges on air. "Shebee and her team had their claws caught in the till. Now imagine her face locked up behind a grill." He flashed a devious grin. "Shebee is not only a traitor, but a fraud. We must bring her to justice and have her ceremonially declawed." *I'm going to love this job.*

With Decadant at the helm, PIN-point published only flattering stories about Antilla. Most of the public believed the smear campaign and supported the revamping of PIN-point. However, others saw through the plot and called the media outlet KING-point—recognizing it for what it was—a propaganda machine for the emperor.

Hearing that Antilla's BUGs arrested Shebee, Beetrix became enraged, and on Antianna's advice, she urged members of the POO party to step up their opposition. She convinced all BEEs to refuse to pay the rental for Antilla's automated honey extractors and had queen BEEs limit the amount of honey that ANTs could gain. Antilla met with both Antrich and Decadant after hearing about the tactics.

"Deca, I'm happy with how things turned out with Shebee, but now that bitch Beetrix has become intolerable," ranted Antilla. "We must do something about her immediately."

"I agree," concurred Antrich. "That daughter of a bee has become a thorn in our hindguts."

"I suggest we poison her with the same toxins we placed in Roachard's fungi, but we'll give her a triple dose to finish her off," advised Decadant with a smarmy stink. "Then we can say she died from overeating Roachard's fungi. She's getting so large; everyone will believe she overindulged."

"Another great idea Deca, and father said I pay you too much," joked Antilla.

"Hilarious," retorted Antrich. "But we should also ban that damned POO party and imprison any queen bee or hive mistress that doesn't drop Beetrix's schemes."

Antilla scoffed. "Everyone will cooperate after they find Beetrix dead." A scalding stench warmed the room. *Or they'll meet the same fate.*

The next hexay, Antianna and Beebuzz visited Beetrix's hive

to discuss additional actions the POO party should take to counter Antilla.

"Beetrix is not answering her door," said Antianna. "She knew we were coming." *I don't understand. She is usually so welcoming.*

"Maybe it's open," said Beebuzz. "She doesn't always lock the door. Try it."

"You're right. It's open. I'll look in Beetrix's back chamber. Maybe she slept in." *I hope everything is alright.*

"Yes, she's a heavy sleeper," Beebuzz added, slightly blushing.

But when she arrived at the back chamber, horror filled her. "Beebuzz, come quick! Beetrix is on the floor. She's ill!" She could die! Antianna worried. *I don't know what happened.*

Beebuzz picked up a glass that Beetrix had dropped on the floor and rubbed it with his antennae. "Oh no, I think they poisoned her. The glass smells like licorice. They must have used jimsonweed." He passed the glass to Antianna. "Wobbert said his customers tasted licorice in his last batch of fungi. I bet they used the same poison on Beetrix."

Hearing the word jimsonweed, Antianna thought back to when she helped her mother collect natural healing medicines, and her instincts kicked in. "Sometimes young insects would eat jimsonweed by mistake, and my mother had a remedy that helped them." She emitted a flickering fragrance. "Wait, I remember—it was beach apple. Quickly, go find the small apples on manchineel trees." *I hope we're not too late!*

"Those trees are everywhere. But aren't the little apples poisonous too?" fretted Beebuzz.

"Yes, by themselves, but their poison is an antidote for jimsonweed. Go get some, promptly." *We need to act! She could die any hexond.*

Beebuzz rushed outside and found some beach apples not far away, flying back as fast as possible. Antianna crushed the apples into a sauce and forced it down Beetrix's mouth.

"Is it going to work?" worried Beebuzz.

"It depends how much poison she ingested." Antianna pushed more sauce into Beetrix's mouth. *We can only hope.*

"How long before it takes effect?" asked Beebuzz.

"Not long. Luckily, you BEEs have fast metabolisms." *If only we were on time!*

Sure enough, in hexutes, Beetrix came to and sat up, looking at her two friends. "What's the buzz, guys? I wondered when you two would show up."

Antianna's eyes popped out. "Trix, we almost lost you! Antilla poisoned you. I don't know what I would have done without you," she cried. *The poor girl doesn't even know what happened.*

Beebuzz reached down and lifted Beetrix to her pods and declared his deep affection for her. "Nor I, my sweet princess. My life would be stingerless without you." He squeezed her tight.

Antianna beamed a wide smile towards Beetrix, who looked back and winked while she swooned in Beebuzz's strong limbs.

❋ ❋ ❋

Decadant broke the news to Antilla that the poisoning of Beetrix had failed. Antilla blamed her illness on Roachard's fungi. Then he arrested her for sedition, throwing her in jail with Anthiery and Shebee. Word got out that Antilla poisoned Beetrix. Still, Decadant used PIN-point to convince the public that she overdosed on jimsonweed that got accidentally mixed into Roachard's last batch of fungi.

The following hexek, Decadant announced that Antilla's bill had passed both Hives of Congress, causing riots to break out. Chi set fire to government buildings, and the betas were buzzing the ruling ANTs as they shuffled between their offices and the Congress. Antilla commanded a platoon of RoAChs to encircle the Woodhive and Hives of Congress, where the members voted to implement martial law. For the next hexek, Antilla ordered insectoids to stay in their nests each hexay after the setting of the solar star.

It was a perfect time for Antilla to release his secret weapon. He unveiled a new group of model IX BUGs, which he had secretly commissioned and trained. It thrilled the chi at first, as they thought the latest release was a peace offering by Antilla. But the early excitement promptly soured as they realized these BUGs were spider-like warriors. They spun webs, spit thread, and stung with deadly spider toxin. Antilla had arranged for secret genetic engineering programs to alter their DNA. The model IX BUGs could now kill like their spider ancestors.

"Deca, aren't these creatures fantastic?" exclaimed Antilla. "I had my genetic engineers make them look as menacing as possible." *I'm as giddy as a nanitic schoolboy on the first day of classes.*

"Yeah, they don't look like the old BUGs," said Decadant. "Their legs are longer, and they seem leaner. I'm guessing they don't need the large round bellies to store bin-making fibers."

"Look at the skull-shaped, red pattern in the middle of their hairy backs," Antilla smiled and scattered a stuffy scent. "Their fronts are hairless and transparent, so they allow a view of their guts and the last meal they ate." *These guys are frightening. I made sure of that.*

"What's that acrid stink?" asked Decadant.

Antilla rubbed his claws together. "That's the venom in their saliva. It drips from their fangs and lubricates their toxic spitting thread. Watch, I'll have them do target practice on one of those traitorous protest leaders." *You're going to love this!*

Antilla released a FLY into the chamber where two of his new BUGs were waiting. One of them spat out his thread, ensnaring the FLY like a net cast over a wild animal.

"That bitter aroma is a sticky mace that coats the thread. It'll stun and burn the FLY," Antilla explained. *I'm so excited.*

The FLY writhed briefly but then froze—paralyzed by the toxins. The second BUG approached the unwitting victim slowly. This slightly larger BUG was Bugthug, Antilla's BUG secret police captain. Selected as the best reflection of Antilla's most brutal tendencies, one cannot imagine a more vicious or sadistic commander than Bugthug. Rumors circulated he sucked the poison from his lieutenants' venom sacks so that he would have the most lethal sting. He insisted that whenever they captured a rebel, they summon him to the scene so he could take the first seizure-inducing bite.

Antilla cracked a wide grin. "As the spit paralyzed the FLY, he won't react when bitten. But each fang will enter his flesh like a dagger and feel like the stings of a thousand bees focused on a single point. So, it has just two purposes—intense pain and agonizing death." *I designed it myself.*

"Gosh, I'm tingling," said Decadant in a falsetto tone. "And what was that awful, shrill sound? Is the FLY screaming?"

"No, these BUGs let out a glass-shattering squeal when excited by their kill," Antilla snickered. "It's designed to raise the hairs on the backs of all insectoids." *They're so devious that I'm delighted.*

Antilla trained the BUGs to be extra ruthless and fiercely

devoted to him; they were his goon squad. Finally, by some freak accident, the manipulation of their DNA also extended their lifespans even longer than other insectoids, and these vile creatures lived for hexuries.

"So, Bugthug, I assume you enjoyed tasting your latest victim." Antilla laughed. "Tell Decadant your plans for the other protestors." *Or should I say our plans?*

Bugthug menaced, "We will hunt down the leaders of this coup." *Drool, slurp.* "And on your orders, sting the whole crew."

～ ～ ～

Antianna organized a meeting of the insectism activists in response to Antilla's crackdown, determined to fight back.

"Wobbert, I hope you and your friends might help break Anthiery, Beetrix, and Shebee out of prison." Antianna started. *I'm furious with Antilla but fearful for my friends.*

Wobbert nodded to Roachard and Wormillian, who reciprocated, and then he turned to Antianna. "Say no more. We'll do it," he promised.

Antianna sighed and oozed a fizzing fragrance. "I want to introduce you to two new members of our group. Wobbert convinced his new friend Bugbert to join us, and he brought along his mate, Bugabelle. They are both members of the POO Party, and you may remember that Bugabelle was once Grand Spinner of the BUGs," announced Antianna. "Welcome, you two. We're honored to have you join." *We must all fight the evil Antilla.*

"The honor is ours," responded Bugabelle. "We'll do anything to counter that scoundrel, Antilla."

"I agree," added Bugbert. "We heard about your group

from Wobbert, whom I know through our business dealings. He had great things to say about what you are doing here."

Antianna walked over to greet the newcomers. "I hope you can teach us something about Antilla's new BUG police. We need to know everything we can about them. You should stand by your friends, but you need to understand your enemies before they stand over you." *And these guys stand tall.*

Bugabelle shook Antianna's claw and responded, "These thugs are a whole new breed of BUG, but we'll do what we can to learn about them."

"Now Flyhero has something to say," continued Antianna.

Flyhero stretched out his long wings and flapped them once. "I am sorry, but I can no more work for Antilla. He is killing FLY protest leaders everywhere. I still fly for you."

"We will be sorry to lose a great spy, but it's getting too dangerous," responded Flynette, standing next to Antianna.

Antianna looked at Flynette and Flyhero, then cautioned all in the room. "Although I feel like I want to crush Antilla, we must curtail our demonstrations until we know it's safe." *We need Anthiery safely back before we irritate Antilla anymore.*

"Yes, and we can use your speed right now, Flyhero. You and Firefly should split up and fly around the planet to warn our network of resistance leaders," recommended Flynette.

Antianna snapped her pinchers once and concluded, "You know what to do. Begin and be careful." *We must save my dear Anthiery.*

CHAPTER 6

Aim for the moon!

What is bravery but to stand up to
slavery and characters unsavory?

To buck the fearful throngs and call
out your leaders' wrongs.

And comport not as the fowl when your
name risks food for gravery.

THE NEXT EVENING, after the solar star set, Wobbert, Roachard, and Wormillian headed over to the prison where their friends were incarcerated. Wobbert learned which cells to target from Flyhero's contact at the Woodhive, and discussed the breakout plan while hiding next to the jailhouse in the shadows.

"Mil, you dig under the building and break through the floor into the prisoners' chambers," explained Wobbert. "Each one is about two WoRM-lengths from the exterior wall and a WoRM-length long and wide. Beetrix and Shebee are being held together in the middle of the building." *Anthiery's a great friend. I want to organize his break-out.*

"I'll start here. I can tunnel to the girls in hexutes," said Wormillian. "But where's Anthiery?"

Wobbert pointed towards the front of the building and explained where Anthiery was.

"No problem," responded Wormillian. "I should get there in fifteen hexutes."

Wobbert touched Mil on the back. "I'll follow you in case there are any problems." Then he looked over at Roachard. "You wait here as a lookout. You can transport us back to safety. The BEEs can escape on their own. Okay, let's go!" *I need to break my friends out of jail and contribute to the rebellion. This plan will work.*

Wormillian dug under the jailhouse. Wobbert followed him and shored up the ceiling and walls of the shaft. Roachard moved forward to cover the hole. It didn't take long for Wormillian to tunnel under the chamber with his BEE friends, but his progress slowed as he dug up towards the floor.

"What's the problem, Mill?" queried Wobbert. "Can't you get through?" *We've got to get them out!*

"Looks like they lined the floor of each cell with a rock barrier," explained Wormillian, panting heavily. "It's going to be harder than I thought. I can wriggle my way through, but you'll have to push the rocks out of the tunnel."

Just then, one rock dropped onto Wobbert.

"Ouch, you just had to ask me. You didn't need to hit me over the head," joked Wobbert. *I need to relieve the tension.*

Wormillian wriggled a few more rocks free, and Wobbert pushed them out of the tunnel. When Wormillian removed enough rocks so the BEEs could escape, he listened carefully through the remaining dirt floor to ensure he had the correct cell. Then, when he heard the BEEs buzzing, he broke through the remaining earth.

"Mill, is that you?" Beetrix released a pale perfume. "I knew you'd come!"

"Quick, slip down through the tunnel," he hissed. "Wobbert's there. He'll help you out."

"We can't move, Mill," gasped Shebee. "We're pegged to the wall."

"I wouldn't dare break the wall," exclaimed Wormillian. "We don't know who might be on the other side."

"We need to do something fast," cried Beetrix, feeling herself panic. "The guards will check the cells before lights out."

Wobbert then popped out of the hole in the floor and piped in, "No problem, girls, I can drill through those pegs in no time."

Before Wobbert started on the pegs, Beetrix overheard something and pushed him back toward the hole. "The guards are coming!"

Wobbert jumped into the tunnel. "Quick Mil, plug the hole from underneath," he urged, "and girls sit on Wormillian's back to hide him." *I just hope they don't come in.*

Beetrix and Shebee had just enough chain to move over and block the hole, then sat there waiting for the guards to arrive.

One guard peeked through a slot in the door, then scoffed. "You two should be in your bunks, but sleep on the cold hard floor if you want to."

"Okay, they're gone," cried Shebee. "Send Wobbert back in to work on these pegs. Don't worry. They won't come back until morning."

While Wobbert drilled through the pegs, Wormillian

submerged himself into the tunnel and headed towards Anthiery's cell. When the pegs broke, Beetrix and Shebee crawled out of the tunnel, then Roachard urged them to fly back to the burrow where the others were waiting. Wobbert then crawled through the new tunnel and pushed more rocks out of the way. Wormillian listened again before he broke through the floor of Anthiery's chamber. He heard footsteps and one guard saying: "I'll throw him into the interrogation chamber and let him stew a bit. Then I'll get Bugthug so he can torture him some more."

Wormillian turned to Wobbert, who caught up to him. "They're taking him to the interrogation room. Do you know where that is?"

Wobbert thought for a moment. "No, but it may be like a dungeon underground. Maybe it's at the back of the building." *We can't leave Anthiery behind. It's our only chance.*

"I'll tunnel straight towards the back," exclaimed Wormillian, liberating an itchy incense. "Maybe we'll get lucky. Let's hurry. Bugthug is coming."

Wormillian dug toward the rear of the building and soon hit a wall of rocks. "You were right. This area must be a dungeon below the other cells, and they've reinforced the walls."

Wobbert pointed at the obstruction. "Let's get working on those rocks. We don't want to meet up with Bugthug." *I'm glad I guessed right, but we still need to spring Anthiery.*

It was easier to break through a rock wall than a ceiling, and they soon found Anthiery unpegged and got him out.

"Thanks for doing this," exclaimed Anthiery. "Let's get out of here!"

"This way," whispered Wobbert, gesturing toward the exit. "Quick! I hear footsteps." *We can't fail now!*

"It's Bugthug," said Anthiery. "I can smell him."

Wobbert and Anthiery raced through the tunnel, and Wormillian pushed enough rocks back to plug the hole. Bugthug entered the room as Wormillian drove another layer of stones up against the first. Luckily, the dungeon was dark, and the inner walls were rock-lined. Bugthug suspected nothing. However, he found one rock on the floor and thought: "My claw-smashing rock, I wondered where that went." He waited a while, assuming the ANT guards had not yet brought Anthiery to the room. Meanwhile, Anthiery, Wobbert, and Wormillian squeezed into Roachard's storage compartment, and the RoACh whisked them back to their hiding place.

Flyhero and Firefly planned and executed their flights to warn the planet-wide FLY protest leaders. The two FLYs split their assigned message targets to reduce flight distances. They warned all but one, who was clinging to life, entangled in a web nearby the main burrows of his colony. When news of his subsequent death spread, riots erupted throughout the land and became violent. Yet when Flyhero and Firefly returned home, they got worse news that stunned the whole rebel community.

Free at last, Anthiery arranged another meeting with his group. They met in a meeting nest they used before, which they thought was safe.

Anthiery spoke softly, barely able to say the words, "Despite my delight that you broke us out of prison, I have terrible news." He moved closer to the group. "Flyhero received a memo from his FLY friends at the Woodhive about something

Decadant will soon announce on PIN-point. It said: 'Protest leaders around the planet are found dead! Everyone in the movement has gone into hiding.'" *Antilla's on a rampage. We must be on our guard.*

Antianna, fearful for the fugitives, looked at Anthiery. "I am sure Antilla has discovered that Beetrix, Shebee, and you have escaped. You're not safe here."

"Yes, we must hide," added Anthiery. *He'll find us in no time.*

Antianna continued, "I found an abandoned nest just west of here. No one will suspect you're there."

"Firefly and Flyhero, come into hiding with us too," advised Anthiery. "You can't stay at home. Antilla is targeting FLYs right now, and his spies may have seen you alerting the others." *He seems to hate FLYs most.*

Just as Anthiery finished his point, there was a loud noise, like the slamming of a door. He checked one of the two entrances to the meeting nest while Flyhero checked where the bang came.

Flyhero rushed back to the group. "I got to the door, looked out the window, and saw his BUGs running away," he cried. "I tried to chase 'em, but the door stuck. They blocked it."

Anthiery arrived back as Flyhero spoke. "They jammed the other exit, too, and there is a strange package in the hallway leading to the door. I'm pretty sure it's a bomb! It's ticking with less than 50 hexonds remaining." Anthiery sprayed a pealing perfume. *We need to act fast.*

"Let me check it out," cried Bugbert. "I can weave a super-strength bin over it to contain the blast." Bugbert was calm under pressure. You could count on his bravery without fuss. "Bugabelle might have been the Grand Spinner of the BUGs, but she learned everything from me," exclaimed Bugbert as he started working.

Bugbert generated some thread and spun up a bin in no time. He then reinforced the container to create a sturdy box, using quick-dry saliva resin to ensure that the fibers gelled rapidly. With his six arms flying all over the place, Bugbert finished the bin in about 40 hexonds. Then, he and Anthiery ran as fast as they could to the site of the suspicious package, which was several hexonds away.

Bugbert commanded, "Stand back, Anthiery. No sense, two of us risking our lives." He conveyed his message with a perfect mix of bravery, urgency, and pragmatism.

"There's no time left," screamed Anthiery. "Cover it now!" *We'll be blown to smithereens.*

Bugbert stumbled over a wire that Antilla's goons had set around the device. It's not sure whether the wire tripped the detonator or time had just run out, but the bomb went off as Bugbert fell with the bin extended in front of him. Since Bugbert was long-limbed, he stretched far enough to drape the container over the bomb just as it exploded. The bin took most of the explosive force, but there was a small space under the bin's rim where the volatile gases spewed outward, tearing off one of Bugbert's hind limbs. The spark from the detonator on the far side also caused flames to flash out and ignite a fire that set ablaze several wooden chairs stacked in the hallway near the exit.

"Bugbert, you squelched most of the blast," shouted Anthiery. "But are you okay? Oh, no! Where's your leg?" *I must remain calm and help my friend.*

"I'm okay, but we better get out of here," screeched Bugbert painfully. "This smoke will asphyxiate us in no time."

"Hold your breath," Anthiery shrieked, dragging Bugbert away from the growing flames. "I'll use my sash to tie a tourniquet. It'll stop you from losing hemolymph. I can replace your limb later."

Anthiery helped Bugbert back to the main hall and alerted the others about the fumes. "We have to get out of here," he said. "The fire is spreading. It may be in the far hall, but the smoke will take us all down." *We need to be creative, or Antilla will snuff us out.*

"But they blocked both exits," screamed Beetrix. "We're doomed!"

Then Wormella, who attended the meeting, stepped forward. "Wormillian and I have got this," she exclaimed. "Anthiery and Flyhero use the large display scrolls to block the smoke from entering the room. Mill and I can dig a tunnel out of here. No way Antilla's gonna burn me twice."

🐜 🐜 🐜

The narrow escape and news of the dead resistance leaders convinced everyone that Antilla had become 'the One' all on Poo-ponic dreaded. Anthiery's group was keen to join him and Antianna at their new hiding place. When Antilla introduced his new cabinet, everyone realized the thing they feared most was happening. His cabinet members were his lay-mate relatives: insectoids that the cyborg-building team created from eggs laid by the same mother. The antocracy was now a full-fledged autocracy.

After the bomb incident, Antilla and Decadant discussed recent events.

Decadant updated him on the news he had. "The BUGs

returned to the scene and found the meeting nest burned to the ground."

"That's great. I finally crushed Anthiery and got those bitches Beetrix and Antianna," Antilla gloated. *First, I got his invention, and now his worthless life.*

"But they also found a tunnel under one exit," continued Decadant. "Some might have escaped."

"Confounded WoRMs, they dug the prisoners out, and now this. I hate those slimy creatures." He released a scorching scent. *I should kill them all.*

Decadant tried to reduce Antilla's anger by changing the subject. "I see you put your new cabinet together."

"Yes, most of them are my twins and agree with me on everything," said Antilla. *We're all of the same mind.*

"I'm surprised you have so many twins," said Decadant. "Didn't Antstrong try to prevent that?"

Antilla pondered the question for a moment. "I believe he said: 'It's important for the health of the insectoid community that we scramble up the eggs to ensure our immunity.'" *It was a worthy idea, but not one my family agreed with.*

"I guess they made some mistakes and let a few twins slip through," surmised Decadant.

"You could call them mistakes," conveyed Antilla with a sticky stink. "I call it serendipity by duplicity."

By chance or devious circumstance, most of Antilla's cabinet members were his twins and had not only exoskeletons that looked alike but also similar temperaments and ideas. They were the greediest of the ANT world and the most power-hungry. Foremost, they were devoted to Antilla, who now called himself Emperor Antilla-the-One. With the government now run by Antilla, and his twins, he ruled the planet as a dict*ant*orship.

He revealed his supreme power when one of his twins who disagreed with him was found webbed and beheaded—another victim of his BUG secret police.

"One twin wasn't that loyal," said Decadant. "Good thing you nipped that in the bud."

Antilla bragged about the matter and laughed deviously, "Yeah, you cross me, and there will be no judge. I say the word, and you'll face my new BUGs."

❦ ❦ ❦

Antilla's twins were already rich, but they became even more affluent once they became cabinet members. Despite their poor qualifications, Antilla also appointed his twins as Cabinet Secretaries of the honey production and civil government departments. None of the cabinet members were good at their jobs, but they efficiently used their positions to amass more honey for themselves and Antilla. Although the cabinet members swore allegiance to the Constitution and promised they would work to improve the lives of all insectoids, they did the opposite. As a result, Antilla's cabinet slashed programs assisting the poor, with more honey diverted to and fewer taxes on the wealthiest ANTs. They also cut the SOT program designed to "Save our Trees."

Although inept, the cabinet was excellent at deceiving the public. Antilla and his cabinet repeatedly used PIN-point to drive home their messages. Eventually, most of the populace believed Antilla worked hard and reduced the spent land. Antilla convinced them he was capable of unparalleled greatness. Many said he was the most intelligent ANT that ever lived, even though Antilla had not even graduated from the UNIT. Others said he was not an insectoid, but a demi-ant-god that grew to cyborg size because of his incredible brilliance, and only such a steady genius could reverse the significant forest degradation as he had. With PIN-point now a propaganda machine for Antilla, they had a huge budget. They even had a polling division that tracked the opinions of lay insects. Historians have used many of these surveys to document public sentiment contemporaneous to Antilla's time in office.

Anthiery's group moved to the abandoned burrow to hide and huddle together, planning their next move. Firefly had left their last meeting to get her things, but was late getting back to the new hiding nest. When she never arrived, Antianna disguised herself and took a stroll to see what was up.

Antianna returned to the small, dank nest where the dissident insectoids hid. She trembled, and her antennae twitched uncontrollably. "I saw her as they cut her down from the sticky mesh. They ripped off her wings and legs. There were holes in her flesh." *I've never seen anything so horrific.*

Antianna recounted Firefly's vacant stare, stuttering out, "She was not yet dead, but her body was rigid, and her eyes fixed open. She had a gaze I can't forget. It was brain-drain." *Poor girl. I wish I could have saved her.*

Anthiery reached out to hold Antianna because he saw her trembling.

"I almost fainted when I saw her," Antianna continued, issuing an icy incense. "I had to look away to avoid the horror." *But I couldn't show my emotions.*

Antianna wept as they had never seen an ANT weep before, and she shook her head from side to side. "They tangled poor Firefly up in the web, so she had no chance. She had so many fang wounds. I hope she went fast into a trance." *Even with my eyes closed, I cannot shake the vision in my mind.* She sat down and wailed. *Everything inside me feels broken.*

Anthiery tried to console her but did not know what to say because he felt the same despair. "I am so sorry for Firefly. I should have gone with her."

"No, you'd be dead, too," cried Antianna, crumpling into her chair. *What am I doing? With Anthiery, I am a leader here, and I must beckon all my courage. But everything keeps getting worse, and these losses are hitting me harder than ever. How do I summon the strength of mind and body when I feel so helpless?*

"I'm sorry you had to find her like that," agonized Anthiery.

Antianna composed herself, stood up, and addressed all present. "It is clear that Antilla accepts no dissent. I fear there will be many others to lament. With his spider-like BUGs at his side, the best we can do is run or hide." *We don't have the numbers to fight, so we need a plan.*

Anthiery stood tall next to Antianna. "Yes, until now, most of us were lucky to escape all his plots to thwart us," he added. "But if we don't get away soon, we'll all end up like Firefly."

❦ ❦ ❦

Indeed, as his cult-like support grew, Antilla took advantage, locking up or exterminating his remaining opponents. His BUG secret police rounded up dissidents by the hundreds and made them disappear. The remaining opposition members conformed to Antilla's views or went into hiding. Anthiery's small group of rebels decided they could not live under Antilla's rule and needed to find somewhere to disappear permanently. They knew he'd locate them soon in their new hide-out.

"We need to escape, but where can we go?" pondered

Antianna, considering their options. "Antilla has his spies all over the planet."

Anthiery inspired the group, releasing a bulky bouquet. "Our history has shown us there is nothing we can't do. If we put all our heads and thoraxes into the stew."

"Flynette, you're a top-notch researcher," chimed in Antianna. "See whether you can find a hidden cave or sinkhole where we can create a secret base."

"Before getting into journalism, I studied geography," said Flynette. "I'll get on it."

"No offense, although Antilla hates me, he doesn't even know who you are," added Shebee. "Your time in Congress was so short. I expect you'll be able to get to the UNIT library safely."

Flynette nodded at her former boss, comforted by her accurate reporting of the circumstances.

Antianna surmised, "That's true. He doesn't even acknowledge females exist unless they adore him or cross him." She considered it, then suggested, "Flyhero, go with Flynette and fly back for help if they try to arrest her."

Flyhero walked over to Flynette and offered her his claw. "I honored to help. I told Antilla my father was sick and dying, so I quit, and he no suspicious of me. His spies no see me on my warning flights."

Anthiery patted Flyhero on the back. "Good, we have a plan."

Flynette and Flyhero returned after long hexays of research in the Geography and Geology sections at the UNIT's main library. Flynette buzzed with excitement, and her wings flapped uncontrollably. "I read about many caves and craters across Poo-ponic to find a potential rebel base site. And I discovered something amazing," bubbled Flynette. *None of you will believe me.*

"It so amazing, I no imagine it possible," exclaimed Flyhero.

Flynette stilled her wings and gushed a buoyant bouquet. "Listen to this!" she explained. "I found these old stories about how the forests of Bilaluna had grown after a large meteorite strike on Poo-ponic." She panted. *I must calm myself.*

Antianna jumped forward. "I remember my grandmother's old folk song about Bilaluna. 'A moon so gray and lifeless became an orb so green. If only we could get there, we'd find wonders yet unseen.' Are you saying the song is not a may-fly-tale?" probed Antianna.

"Exactly," said Flynette. "The geological and astronomical records show that Bilaluna changed color after a giant mete-orite hit Poo-ponic many hexennia ago." She pointed out the window towards the moon. "Most researchers think the meteor impact opened a wormhole to Bilaluna, transporting our veg-etation there." She sputtered, unable to contain her delight. *How else would it be so green?*

"It's like the one that brought our ancestors to Poo-ponic from the tales of Antuna," exclaimed Antianna. "And if there's vegetation, there should be oxygen."

Anthiery pulled out his pocket map of Poo-ponic. "Where did the meteorite strike?"

"It's not too far from here," answered Flynette. She pointed to a spot on the map close to Poo-ponic's capital. "Right here. You could walk it in a few hexours or less."

"I fly it in hexutes," piped in Flyhero.

"Are you saying if the wormhole is still there, we could escape to the moon?" cried Shebee.

"Yes, it was the largest meteorite strike on Poo-ponic. After a powerful impact, I read that a wormhole can remain intact forever," beamed Flynette. *I did it. We'll all be safe.*

Shebee eyed her former mentee like a mother bird watching her fledgling take flight. "Flynette, your impeccable research skills always saved my butt at PIN-point, but you may have saved us all from a tyrant." She paused for dramatic effect. "The early bird might get the worm, but the late working FLY found the wormhole."

Flynette grabbed onto Flyhero and pulled him close. "Please don't forget my pal here. He was not only a bodyguard. He sped around the library, fetching all the scrolls I needed. I couldn't have done it without him." Like her former journalism boss, she finished strong. "Both discrete and fleet. He kept my probing replete." *He's the best.*

Beetrix grabbed the map from Anthiery. "Did you find any other possibilities on Poo-ponic?"

"No, Antilla has troops in all the caves I found," replied Flynette. "They used the best ones when storing sugar cane for the war with the non-cyborgs. And they still occupy them." *There's only one choice, and we need to jump on it!*

Anthiery pointed upward. "So, we aim for the moon. Nice work, Flynette and Flyhero—this is more than we ever expected. Bilaluna it is!"

The group prepared a plan to escape to Bilaluna. When everything was ready, Anthiery called them together again. Antianna polled everyone to confirm they would risk transit through the portal and the dangerous trip to the meteorite crater. Anthiery ensured everyone understood they would leave behind their nests, families, and friends and that there would be hardships having to start a brand-new colony on Bilaluna. Luckily, they had within their group at least two members of each insectoid family, one male and one female, to create a new colony of cyborgs on Bilaluna. As they waited for Flynette to complete her research, they determined who would come to the new base. The escape party would include four mating pairs, with WoRMs (Wormillian and his mate Wormella), BUGs (Bugbert and Bugabelle), and WoBBs (Wobbert and Wobbin), along with the rebel ANTs (Anthiery and Antianna). The other eight included three not yet mated pairs of RoAChs (Roachard and Roachelia), BEEs (Beebuzz and Princess Beetrix), and FLYs (Flyapper and Flynette). Two older unmated insectoids, Flyhero and Shebee, completed the cluster.

Anthiery pulled out his map again. "As the last step, we better send out some scouts to check out the portal site at the crater." *Planning is my forte, so let me take charge.*

Just then, Flyhero arrived, returning from flying some errands and checking in with some trusted friends from the Woodhive. Flyhero took a moment to catch his breath and informed the others, "My guys tell me Antilla knows we holed up here and plannin' escape. His BUGs are checking all over the burrows, and they come here when it dark."

"Well, that settles it," declared Anthiery. "There's no time for exploration. We have to leave tonight." *No matter how stellar my plans are, we need to be flexible.*

Anthiery suggested that two flying cyborgs go first and explore the route to the wormhole site, checking for any traps or ambushes. When he sought volunteers, the two older unmated insectoids knew it had to be them and stepped up.

Flyhero buffed his wings and chimed in, "I may be old, but

I still the fastest flyer among us. I won't let you down. No need to fuss."

Shebee added, "I'm not so fast as my friend here, you might say. But more than a thing I've seen in my hexay."

"Thanks, friends. You spoke not only with courage but also dignity. When we get to Bilaluna, our new colony will never forget your bravery," declared Antianna.

Anthiery worked out a plan, and he and Antianna explained it to the group as a vigorous vapor circulated through the burrow.

"Roachard and Roachelia will carry Wormillian and Wormella in their storage areas since they cannot escape fast enough without legs," started Anthiery. "The four of you will leave as soon as possible, as you'll take much longer than the rest of us who will be flying." *You guys can do it.*

Indeed, RoAChs were not as swift as the flying cyborgs but were fast runners. And their size and armor allowed them to break through webs and ward off stings, projectiles, or other attacks.

"Flying insectoids will leave just before dark, carrying smaller wingless ones," said Antianna. "Beebuz, you carry Bugbert, and Beetrix, you carry Bugabelle."

"Flynette and Flyapper will take Antianna and me," Anthiery added. *I've always wanted to fly.*

Wobbert apprehensively inquired, "Have you forgotten about Wobbin and me?"

"No, as you two are much smaller, we figured that Beetrix, as a large BEE, would have no problem taking you as well," explained Anthiery. *Don't worry. I rarely miss even the slightest detail.*

Beetrix flapped her wings and crooned, "As a princess, it is rare that I take to the air. But I'll carry as many as my wide wings will bear."

Anthiery pointed out the path on the map. "And Flyhero and Shebee will go first to check over the route." *May luck be with us.*

❧ ❧ ❧

The two WoRM-loaded RoAChs left with Shebee and Flyhero. The flyers left early to ensure Antilla's spies were not surveilling the route. Roachard covered his and Roachelia's shells with leafy branches to camouflage them for their journey, and Wormillian and Wormella slid inside for the ride.

Wormella was enthusiastic about beginning the adventure. She chanted, "Not exactly a luxury ride. But a RoACh is my coach, and who am I to deride?"

Not far into the journey, Flyhero returned to warn the RoAChs and WoRMs.

Flyhero breathed heavily and spoke, "Those sons of bees … er bugs, I say, they block path that is your best way. Ain't no enemies, just enormous boulder on the road."

When they arrived at the obstruction, Roachelia exclaimed, "Oh dear! We can't climb that boulder. It's way too big and steep."

"They placed that barrier such that there's nowhere to crawl," panted Roachard, pointing at the drops on either side of the road. "If we try to go around, we will fall!"

The WoRMs wriggled out of their compartments and pushed the large rock to a broader part of the path, with Wormella saying, "No problem, crew. It's what we do." Though excited, she was sensible. An earthy essence enveloped them.

Flyhero caught up to Shebee in no time. A fast flyer, Flyhero set the insectoid air-speed record at almost 200 mph as a fast flyer in his prime. He was slower at his advanced age but still

defeated most model VIII FLYs in short races. He and Shebee
flew on together, with the taste for freedom pushing them on.

~ ~ ~

As the second group left their hiding place, they spotted a squad
of four BUGs headed towards their concealed nest.

Alarmed, Antianna shot a squealing scent, "We must
promptly leave our snugs. The place is crawling with BUGs!"

The BUGs noticed the party leaving, and two of them ran
after the group, while the other two ran back to the Woodhive
to alert Antilla.

BUGs did not run fast, so they had no chance to catch the
laden BEEs and FLYs. And since the two BUGs headed for
the Woodhive would take some time to get there, the party
was confident they could get a good head start before Antilla's
loyalists chased them.

~ ~ ~

Back on the trail, the fugitive RoAChs quick-marched their way
onward. As they progressed, they came across another roadblock.
Antilla's BUGs built a wall across a causeway that crossed a
large marsh.

"Here we go again. Antilla's goons blocked the path,"
cried Roachard.

Roachelia paced left then right, spewing a shrill smell.
"Yeah, the path is wider, but they built a wall right across."

Roachard surveyed the landscape and exclaimed, "We can't
climb that. There are marshes on both sides. And we can't swim
fully loaded."

Again, the WoRMs wriggled out of their RoACh coaches.
They dug a tunnel under the wall to the other side this time.

Again, the WoRMs were more innovative than credited by other insects.

When they finished, Wormillian slithered back towards his coach and declared, "Don't tax the clerk. It's all in a hexour's work!" Wormillian calmly expressed the level-headedness he shared with Wormella.

Flyhero arrived first at the meteorite impact zone and flew so fast in the dark that he did not notice the thick web spread across the wormhole. Antilla's BUGs guessed the rebels were planning to use the portal, and they blocked and guarded it. Flyhero flew into their trap and entangled himself in the sticky, stringy mesh.

As Flyhero struggled to free himself, he noticed the web was quite thick and likely impenetrable for the RoAChs. Instead of working his way out of the web, he forged forward. He bit as many strands as possible to weaken the web for the convoy. Although most of the BUGs stationed near the wormhole were sleeping, the commotion in the web alerted two sentry BUGs guarding the entrance. They were on the far side of the obstruction, allowing Flyhero to gnaw away at several strands, weakening the web. As he progressed forward, Flyhero became more and more entangled.

Noticing his wings were completely enmeshed, he gasped with his last remaining vigor, "If I can't beat 'em, I'll bite 'em!"

Then Flyhero nipped off his wings, allowing him to reach and chew through many more strands, but ensuring that he would never escape. Although he continued to gnaw away at the web to the end, he was like a beetle stuck on its back, unable to flip over when the BUGs got to him. He was hardworking and proud his whole life, and his sense of duty did not abandon him even when faced with certain death.

Shebee arrived as the BUGs descended on Flyhero, and although she struggled to rescue him, she was too late. She surprised and stung one of the BUGs to death as it prepared to devour Flyhero. She kept her stinger somehow and fought the other BUG, but her large wings became entangled in the sticky strands of web that lined the opening Flyhero had gnawed. The remaining BUG descended towards her head-on, expecting Shebee had lost her stinger in killing the first BUG.

The smug BUG advanced and snidely remarked, "You can't sting, and you can't fly. So, taste my venom and prepare to die!"

The BUG pierced the immobilized Shebee with her sharp fangs, but a moment later, Shebee freed her stinger and stung the withdrawing sentry, preventing it from warning the other sleeping BUGs.

Shebee broadcasted quietly to the flying rebels and their passengers as they arrived together at the meteorite crater: "It's all clear, it's true if you can only break throu...." She foamed at the mouth, and with that last gasp, Shebee was no more.

Beetrix gaped at Shebee's limp body and then Flyhero's hanging on the web, and she stood frozen in disbelief. She imagined nothing could take down her cherished friend or the speedy, ageless Flyhero. She looked toward Flynette, trembling as she reached for her, and they both sobbed uncontrollably. They exchanged no words, as neither knew what to say. After a long hard cry, they marched in lockstep up to the web and cut both Shebee and Flyhero down. They needed to detach Shebee's wings to free her from the sticky strands. They lay their lifeless and wingless bodies down on the cold ground. As they looked sorrowfully at the group, Antianna stepped forward and gave them both a tender hug while the others watched in reverent silence. Later, Anthiery and Wobbert carefully climbed up the web and worked free the wings of their compatriots, bringing them down and laying them beside their lifeless bodies.

When the remaining crawling insectoids arrived at the wormhole, Roachard and Roachelia broke through the weakened web, clearing the way for the others to enter the portal.

The ordinarily shy Roachelia burst her way through the mesh and seeped a pale perfume. "Thanks to Shebee and Flyhero, the web is weak. So, follow us through this mess to find the wormhole we seek."

Before leaving Poo-ponic, Wormillian and Wormella moved a pile of rocks in front of it to conceal the entrance. They also considered burying Shebee and Flyhero, so the savage spider-like BUG secret police would not eat them. They rejected the idea in favor of bringing the two heroes through the gateway and burying them on Bilaluna.

Anthiery announced mournfully, looking down at his two lost friends. "These heroes need a place of honor on our new moon. Not in the bellies of brutal BUGs, who may find them soon."

Tears dropped from Antianna's eyes while she held Beetrix and Flynette. "Yes, 'twas bravery we shan't forget. Lest forever we shall regret."

Thus, the oldest graves on Bilaluna became a monument to the Great Escape of those who were later called the *Fabled Fourteen* and their two fallen heroes. Since then, young insectoids on Bilaluna have recited these simple refrains about Flyhero and Shebee as they passed the monument.

A more valiant BEE or selfless friend simply could not be found than the double stinging Shebee that lies beneath this ground. And ne'er was there a FLY so fast, nor a soul so very brave, as the heroic Flyhero who fills our moon's first grave.

They still teach young insectoids this elegy in low school, and historians discovered the first print of the scrolls issued to memorize the lines.

EPOCH II: DEATH OF A PLANET

CHAPTER 7

THE DRONE ON THE THRONE CLONES AND HONES!

Some civilized see others as brutal and savage.

Yet 'civilization' needs but slight
changes to beget 'evil nation.'

Remove the third 'i' and flip the first one on the cee,
and again, ninety degrees, counterclockwise, turn the zee.

Ɛ vil ᴎation

AFTER THE REBELS escaped, the BUG secret police wanted to chase them through the wormhole to Bilaluna to bring them back to justice for treason.

Chief Bugthug sharpened his fangs and shouted out his desired plan, "We'll march through the portal and hunt 'em down. We'll catch 'em, try 'em and eat 'em clowns." *My boys will track 'em down.*

Antilla assumed the traitors had perished in the wormhole and did not want to lose any of his precious BUG secret police to such a death trap. He also did not want others to discover the portal.

Bugthug tried to further his case with Antilla, "Emperor, my troops are hungry for more victims. If we can't go after the defectors, some will starve." *Give us a break.*

Antilla smiled, "Don't worry, Bugthug, I'm sure you'll find more rebels hiding under rocks or underground. Before long, there will be many to sate your hunger."

Bugthug did a double-take. "Emperor, you are making me drool. What are you planning?" *Don't keep me in suspense!*

Antilla turned to walk away but secreted a spiky scent. "Now's not the time, but there are too many chi cluttering up the planet. And I don't trust any of them."

"We'll be ready when you are," Bugthug promised. *I'll do whatever you ask, especially if it means killing insects and making them suffer first.*

Antilla looked back at Bugthug. "As for Antianna and her gang, I want everyone to forget them. Having disappeared off the face of Poo-ponic, everyone will assume we massacred them. So, they'll fear us even more."

"If we bring them back and put their heads on stakes, wouldn't that scare them more?" asked the drooling Bugthug. *I'm craving the taste of hemolymph.*

Antilla stamped one of his tripods. "No, I don't want them remembered as heroes. Dead or alive, they're all just zeroes."

"Okay, Emperor, you know what's best," responded Bugthug, squelching his urges.

🐜 🐜 🐜

Although Anthiery's band of rebels had escaped, and other vocal dissenters either hid or reluctantly supported Antilla, there was still displeasure among society. Yet with PIN-point's propaganda, most of their viewers believed Antilla could do anything—walk on water, fly with the BEEs, grow trees with the wave of his forelimbs.

Meanwhile, the rich got more prosperous, and the poor got poorer. Less honey was available, and it became more valuable. Destitute chi families died of malnutrition and related illnesses. The public still accepted Antilla's argument that further reductions of taxes on the rich would have honey dribble down and improve the lot of the poor. After all, Emperor Antilla had said it—so it must be true.

🐜 🐜 🐜

At the end of the second hexury of Antilla's rule, the emperor considered his mortality. He had always intended for one of his offspring to succeed him as the supreme ruler. Yet, the more Antilla thought about it, the more he concluded this plan was not good enough. So, he called Principal Antstrong, who recruited the top genetics and molecular biology professors at the UNIT.

Antilla explained his sinister wish to them. "I have a request. Please don't take it as dire. I want my clone to rule when I expire. And don't take me for a fool. You do this, or I'll have you satiate Bugthug's drool." *Do it, and I'll spare you.*

It only took a few hexths for the UNIT professors to develop the technology. The team determined how to use traditional genetics, cloning, and advanced epigenetic manipulations to ensure the clone had the same DNA with a similar epigenetic environment.

"Antstrong, I thought one's genes and that DNA stuff were fixed at conception," puzzled Antilla.

Antstrong shrugged and shifted his gaze away from Antilla, hiding his disdain for the ruler. "Yes, Emperor, one cannot alter DNA. But epigenes are the wrapping around the DNA. Unlike DNA, which is immutable, epigenes react to prehatching and early-life environmental factors that affect one's personality."

Antilla offered Antstrong some honey. "So, you make sure the epigenes don't change?"

Antstrong waved off the honey tray but was favorable to Antilla's question, "Exactly, sir. We used cloning and strict environmental controls taken from your hatching and early-life records."

Antilla giggled and spewed a spiny smell. "So, my clone will be a replica of my greatness." *I can rule forever!*

Antstrong frowned and showed Antilla a chart explaining the process, highlighting 97-99%. "Your clone will be not only an identical twin on a physical level but also a near-perfect match on mental and emotional characteristics. These are traits usually not shared between monozygotic twins or clones." Antstrong inspired his team to develop the innovation out of duty, yet he recoiled, thinking of Antilla living on through his clones.

Antilla clapped his claws together and laughed. "So, you did it. Quite a scientific achievement and Bugthug will have to remain hungry." *Now get out of here. I still hate the UNIT and you academic types.*

Antstrong reluctantly handed Antilla another note. "Here is my statement for PIN-point: 'A scientific discovery ne'er before so clever. Ensures Emperor Antilla will rule forever.'"

The result was as close as possible for Antilla to replace himself with himself. By this means, Antilla-the-One could rule forever, with successive Antilla-the-One-II, Antilla-the-One-III, etc., running the planet for eternity. The plan was popular with his cabinet and the wealthy ANTs since they knew continuing Antilla's policies would reward them. It was necessary to ensure that the rich got richer because honey output steadily declined. Despite further advances in honey acquisition techniques, increasing forest degradation cut productivity and profits.

With the declining honey available, the ruling class suspected a growing black market in the honey trade hampered the economy. It seems charitable BEEs scraped some honey off the top of the hives to provide needed sustenance for the poorest of the chi, which would otherwise starve. Antilla installed BUG secret police in the hives to monitor all activities and clamped down on the fleecing when he discovered the honey skimming scheme. Instead of revealing the discovery, Antilla sent out a press release to PIN-point: 'Rings of black market FLYs are off their blocks. And are to blame for reduced honey stocks!'

Decadant reported on PIN-point, with a spiky smell: "Captain Bugthug has arrested a ring of FLYs, which were stealing honey and selling it on the black market before our eyes. Over six hundred kilos of honey were seized after a FLY accomplice was forcibly squeezed."

Antilla had a justified feeling FLYs were becoming too bright and were on to his corrupt policies. Most of the underground dissenters of his policies were FLYs. Antilla's fake stories about the staunching of spent lands did not fool FLYs and BEEs, who flew through the forests daily. They could see the devastation had increased to 65% of the planet. It was false that FLYs had created a honey black market; they were too honest and law-abiding to steal. Antilla instructed PIN-point to stage and record fake sting operations where the BUG secret police caught black-market FLYs, who became known as black-FLYs, in the act of illicit honey deals.

The public was at first offered honey rewards for turning in suspected black-FLYs. At one point, Antilla and Decadant imprisoned half the FLY population, and the insectoid courts could not handle the backlog. The authorities ordered special burrows built as jails since they apprehended many FLYs. The WoRMs dug the tunnels so fast that the largest one of them collapsed, killing the FLYs inside before they saw justice. Later, Antilla told the FLYs they could avoid prosecution if they turned in two other FLYs they suspected were black-FLYs. The public supported these moves because of the sacred status of honey and their desire to end its illegal trading. Eventually, Antilla introduced emergency laws to institute the death penalty for black market crimes, and he created make-shift courts to try cases quickly so the jails did not overfill. In time, he accused and exterminated all FLYs. Antilla hated how dissenting flies like Firefly had rebelled against his policies. He also had a memory from early childhood of a swarm of flies carrying off his dead mother. She was sick and dying, but Antilla could not remember whether she died before or after they came. Whether they hastened her death, he just remembered that flies took her from him.

❀ ❀ ❀

Two hexuries later, under Antilla II's reign, poverty and deaths by starvation were mounting. Antilla II instructed PIN-point to publish a story reporting that with no FLYs around to run the black market, WoRMs took over the dark web. Antilla II knew his predecessor hated worms. His father had always told him they were lazy and had no real purpose. Antrich spent hexs complaining to his son how he wished the slimy creatures had never come to Poo-ponic. Antilla adopted his father's anti-worm sentiment that WoRMs did not deserve any respect, as they were not insects. His clone kept an eerie collective memory of his predecessor's motivations and prejudices, and as more impulsive, he acted on them without delay.

Antilla II then spoke to Antifact about Decadant. "I read in Antilla's diary how your father served him well both as a chief of staff and the anchor at PIN-point."

"Thank you for saying so, Emperor," Antifact blushed. "I know my father was loyal and worked hard." *I hope I can be just as dedicated.*

Antilla II handed Antifact a golden honey spoon. "Antilla meant to give this to him when he retired, but he died so suddenly. So now I am pleased you filled his claws here and at PIN-point. It's like we're the new generation taking over together."

Antifact's eyes watered up. "Thanks for this, I agree. I only hope I can do half of what he did." *I haven't known Antilla II long, but I'm already in awe of him.*

Antilla II smiled. "Stick with me, boy, and you'll achieve double or more."

"I'll do my best." Antifact wiped his eyes and grinned. *Anything for my Emperor.*

Antilla II returned to his desk and looked at his calendar. "Okay, I want you to start by reporting that with the FLYs gone, WoRMs have taken over the black market. Antilla hated WoRMs, and I agree they should not exist. We should have slaughtered them like the non-cyborg insects," barked Antilla II.

"They are distasteful creatures, aren't they? They're slimy and don't even have legs." Antifact agreed.

"I can see we are going to get along famously." Antilla II grinned so hard his mandibles made a crack sound. "It is unclear why we created cyborg WoRMs. Poo-ponic would be better off without that slimy brown skin race."

Antifact nodded his approval. "Indeed, there's already much discrimination out there in public. They'll be easy to convince. Many insectoids hate WoRMs already." *And rightly so.*

"So, you understand my plan?" questioned Antilla II, as he exuded a sneaky stink.

"They'll go the way of the FLYs?" replied Antifact, dribbling a flat fragrance.

Antilla II convinced his cabinet that since there were already enough burrows, WoRMs were expendable. PIN-point pushed stories about how WoRMs were not only running the black market but were also tunneling into insectoids' nests and stealing their honey. Rogue WoRMs reportedly dug their way into the honey hives and stole honey from the source, and they attempted to auger their way into the honey vaults at the Supreme Bank.

Before long, the public began rallies shouting, 'Poo-ponic for the insects, all WoRMs are dirty suspects,' exhibiting their growing hatred for their non-insect neighbors. No one cared when Antilla II destroyed all WoRM eggs and stopped creating new WoRM cyborgs, and Antilla ordered Bugthug and his secret police to kill WoRMs on sight.

Bugthug yelled to his lieutenant, "There's one there. Get it!"

The lieutenant grabbed the WoRM's tail as she attempted to slither underground.

"Pull her out and bring her to me," ordered Bugthug.

The lieutenant yanked the WoRM out of the hole and plopped her in front of his captain. Before the worm could even wriggle more than a few inches, Bugthug sliced both her head and tail off with his two dominant claws. He then used another claw to eviscerate and skin the WoRM. He laughed and threw the skin over his shoulder and took it home.

Bugthug and his crew massacred hundreds of fleeing WoRMs on the spot. Even chi lay-insectoids created swarms to lynch WoRMs, which they called non-insect scum. Antilla II placed a price on the heads and tails of all WoRMs, and many insect families formed hunting parties to *get some WoRM skin*. The expression had some meaning because their hides were warm and waterproof, and the skins made for coveted blankets in the damp underground burrows. Soon after the demise of the last FLY, WoRMs too became extinct. With the help of PIN-point and ever-growing discriminatory sentiment in the insectoid world, they exterminated all WoRMs. Antilla II had implemented what his predecessor started, with the 'familic cleansing' of two families of Poo-ponic insectoids. Most ANTs were happy, as there was more honey for them.

Hexuries later, when Antilla III took over as emperor, many working BEEs reported that the spent lands had grown out of control and complained that the problem needed a solution. Some chi held protests. The public had a feeling that although Antilla III was as ruthless as his two predecessors, he was a little more tolerant of peaceful protest. If you didn't cross him hard, you could get away with some opposing debate. He preferred to use deception and coercion rather than fear to control the masses unless they angered him. He still had his BUG secret police force, but used them less. He insisted, however, that he did not want to be called Antilla III, stating, "Am I not the drone's clone? So Antilla is how I'll be known. You'd better drop the three, or from your life, I'll set you free."

Recognizing the public's growing concern about the spent lands, the new emperor urged the Dean of Forestry at the UNIT to go on PIN-point and appease the community. Dean Beetree was the head of a research team that used sophisticated tree counting techniques to track the declining forest over several hexades. His group used destructive tree sampling to estimate the mean biomass density for the average tree and multiplied that by the area of each forest sector. They compared this to advanced remote sensing techniques to determine the total forest biomass. Complicated formulae for the average lay insectoid, but his findings showed forests decreased every hex no matter how you counted it. He found the forests declined about 0.35 to 0.7% per hex.

Antilla arranged a meeting with Beetree to discuss the spent lands.

After shaking Beetree's claw, he immediately got to the point. "Professor Beetree, I want you to go on PIN-point and tell the public that the spent lands are rapidly declining."

Beetree scowled at Antilla's fishy fragrance, "Respectfully, Emperor, you realize that I have studied forest decline for hexs, and the trend is the opposite. Why would I want to say otherwise?" *He must know I'm a hardworking scientist. I take much pride in my meticulous research methods.*

"Do you realize I could shut your faculty down and have you arrested?" bullied Antilla with a spiny scent.

Beetree shook his head from side to side. *I must express my views. I will not cower before the emperor.* "Yes, but to deny my life's work and deceive the public is not right."

Antilla sneered, "You can be right and detained, or a little wrong, and have your research team's funding enhanced. I hear research can be expensive."

Beetree grasped his options. "So, my choice is riches or imprisonment?" *That's how this guy works.*

Antilla cackled. "You academic types are clever, aren't you?"

"Yes, and our first government, when run by academics, could run circles around yours." Beetree snapped. *I must show him who's the boss.*

Antilla fumed at the Dean's insolence. "And you'll fly in circles if I cut off your left wing."

Beetree reluctantly agreed to state that with Antilla's great wisdom and support, the UNIT had come up with ways to stem the forest degradation problem. However, he only agreed with Antilla's request because of the threat and the large grants Antilla promised for his faculty's research projects, as biomass estimation was not cheap. But when he appeared on PIN-point, Beetree's conscience got the better of him, and he reported the bald facts.

He ended with a bold statement, "Our research shows spent lands are now at seventy-five percent. The forests could disappear in one to two hexuries to the greatest extent."

The report caused an uproar in the beta and chi communities and panic in the burrows. Dean Beetree was immediately arrested and thrown in jail without charges or a trial. Many BEEs flying daily into the forests confirmed the Dean's reports and concerns. The spent lands were not only expanding, but the planet was also becoming a wasteland. The petrified branches and stumps left behind after logging turned to stone. With no tiny ants, termites, beetles, or plant-eating fungi to break them down, they sat as granite-like monuments to the majestic trees to which they once belonged. Antilla refused to take any action to reverse the growth of spent lands. Small trees, shrubs, and flowering plants, which had the essence sucked out of them, withered and dropped to the ground where they turned to ash, littering the cement-like dirt which hardened with no small worms or insects to turn over the soil. The landscape was like the Earth's moon, barren and desolate, a forsaken land that the insectoids preferred to avoid rather than rehabilitate.

～ ～ ～

Around this time, a group of young students took a class trip to explore the forests and jungles near the edge of the spent lands. As part of their environmental science class, their teachers divided them into teams of two and had them perform a scavenger hunt to look for various flowers, leaves, ferns, and fungi. Two young insectoids that were teamed up did not know each other well, but both students loved everything about nature. The two were a female ANT, Gretant, who was very shy, and a male BUG, Thunbug, who was quite outgoing.

When teamed up, Thunbug approached Gretant. "I think we can win this thing. You are always picking flowers and plants at the playground. I bet you know which ones are which."

Gretant stared back at Thunbug. "You've been watching me?"

Thunbug swallowed hard. "No, not watching you. I just noticed you like nature. So do I." *And I do think you're cute. But you are an ANT, and I'm a BUG.*

Gretant turned and looked away. "Cause I like to stay to myself. I'm not so good with others."

Thunbug stepped around to get in front of Gretant. "That's

okay. Nature's more interesting than most kids, anyway." *Except perhaps you. I like your style.*

Gretant smiled but lowered her head. "I know all the flowers on the list and where to find them."

Thunbug grinned. "I knew it. And all the ferns too?" *This girl is sharp. I hope she'll be my friend.*

Gretant nodded. "Yep. Here's one."

"I guess you're shy," surmised Thunbug. "I'm friendly with almost everybody, but I also like nature. And I got a big fungi collection. Now, if only we knew which leaves are what."

Gretant muttered, "My Dad's a dendrologist."

Thunbug raised his eyebrows. "A what? I thought I knew all the professions, and you came up with that." *I'm impressed.*

Gretant chortled. "He studies trees. He taught me to recognize just about every leaf."

Thunbug reached for Gretant's forelimb. "What are we waiting for? We'll win this, claws down."

Gretant pulled back her limbs. "I'm not comfortable being touched."

Thunbug swiftly swung all six of his limbs behind him. "No problem, I may be all claws, but I can keep them out of your way. They are good for picking flowers, ferns, and leaves, though. You point and keep a list, and I'll grab them." *You can trust me.*

Gretant smiled. "Another advantage for our team." She pointed to a leaf. "Poke-me-boy."

Thunbug did a double-take. "What? I thought you said claws-off."

Gretant giggled. "No, that's the name of the shrub. It's on the list."

"Wow, I never heard of that." Thunbug clapped his claws together. "You're brilliant."

"It's a *Vachellia anegadensis* leaf." Gretant raised her nose. "It's part of the *Fabaceae* family."

"Odd, you don't seem so shy when you're talking leaf names." Thunbug grinned. *I kind of like shy girls. They let me do most of the talking.*

"True, but I think you're funny." She sported a crooked smile. "And somehow, you make me less nervous."

Thunbug picked up the leaf and threw it into his sack. "That's great. Now find us another leaf. One that doesn't make me want to poke you." He snickered at his joke. "Wait, is there a veiled lady on the list?"

Gretant shrugged. "Why, I'm not that shy."

Thunbug laughed. "No, it's a type of fungi. A cool mushroom. See it over there?" He pointed to a mushroom with a white lattice over it. "It's called *phallus indusiatus,* one of the stinkhorn mushrooms. Pretty to look at, but it's also pretty smelly." *That should impress her.*

Gretant laughed out loud. "Good thing it's not on the list, then." She looked fondly at Thunbug. "Seems you know your fungi, and I think we will get along."

"But can win this hunt?" Thunbug ran toward a patch of jungle. "C'mon!"

It didn't take long for Gretant and Thunbug to find all but one item on the list, and Gretant was adamant that they find them all. She motioned to Thunbug. "Let's go that way; it looks like the terrain where we could find a chaste tree flower."

Thunbug's eyes bugged out. "We were told not to go that way." *Wow, she's shy, but I detect a boldness in her.*

Gretant raised her forelimbs. "What? Now forests are off-limits."

"I don't know," Thunbug wondered. "There must be some

reason they don't want us to go there." He wiggled his claws. "Maybe there are some deadly spiders there." *I may be outgoing, but I follow orders.*

Gretant sighed. "Poo-ponic doesn't have spiders anymore."

Thunbug shook his head. "I see you're not shy about breaking the rules."

Gretant laughed. "I may be shy, but you're gutless."

"That's just wrong. Unlike spiders that dissolve food outside their bodies, BUGs have two guts and can eat more than liquid diets." Thunbug marched in the prohibited direction. "And you're also wrong if you are talking about my bravery." *I'll show her!*

"Wow, I didn't even have to dare you."

Thunbug looked back at Gretant. "Just know I'll blame it on you if we get caught." *This girl is going to be the end of me!*

The two walked for several hexutes in the barred zone until they popped out of the jungle and found themselves in the spent lands.

Gretant turned herself around in the hot sand. "Thunbug, what is this place?"

"I've heard my parents say that it's difficult to grow trees after logging." Thunbug looked in all directions. "It creates patches of unfertile land. But I didn't know it was so big. This place is a wasteland." *How did we not know this?*

"Let's go a little further," Gretant insisted. "I want to see how far it goes."

"I don't know," Thunbug flapped his spiracles. "I'm having trouble breathing." *We shouldn't be here.*

"Just close your spiracles," Gretant suggested. "We can hold our breath for a long time."

"I suppose," said Thunbug. "But what if the teachers notice we're missing?" *She's so persistent. I don't know.*

"Come on," Gretant urged. "Where's your sense of adventure?"

"Okay," Thunbug relented. "But we turn back in ten hexutes." *I'm going to have to watch out for her.*

The two walked on for ten hexutes, and Gretant talked Thunbug into ten more. They went into a twisty cave and were a little disoriented when they came out.

"We shouldn't have gone in there. It messed up my sense of direction," Thunbug said. "I'm not sure which way we came from." *We may get lost.*

"We can follow our pod tracks." Gretant pointed to the east. "They should be right there." Then she motioned to the west. "Oh no, it's windy, and there are no tracks!"

"Wait, I'm sure the solar star was shining in our faces when we got to the cave. We just have to go away from it." Thunbug pointed to the northeast. *Sometimes we just need to think and not panic.*

"I hope you're right, Thun, or we're toast." Gretant wiped her brow. "We have to breathe sometime, and the air here smells bad."

Thunbug marched off confidently. "Let's go. I know this way's right." *I think!*

The two walked for about fifteen hexutes and finally saw the tree line in the distance. Gretant jumped into Thunbug's forelimbs. "Oh, Thun, you found it. You saved us."

Thunbug pointed to a tree with long cone-like purple flowers as they got to the jungle's edge. "Is that a chaste tree?" *No way, it can't be. She'll know.*

Gretant jumped up and down. "It is! You found that too. We got everything on the list."

Antilla stayed the course, and the spent lands expanded as time passed. As a result, he had difficulty countering the public's concerns. So there was general civil unrest. Over the next few hexs, disastrous events occurred around the planet on a grander and more frequent scale. Large windstorms generated at the edge of the spent lands were piling up mounds of infertile dirt in adjacent unspent lands, smothering small plants. The outer forests looked like large sand pits, with stands of trees sticking up like rows of matchsticks jammed into a giant ashtray. Massive versions of these dust storms started further in the spent territories and sent enormous debris into the upper atmosphere. The dust rose in a smokestack-like column and spread out into a flattened sphere, so it looked like a rising mushroom cloud, reminiscent of nuclear fallout. The thick clouds blocked out the light from Pooponic's solar star, causing colder weather and a further reduction in vegetation.

As the climate catastrophes increased, the new principal of the UNIT, Truant, arranged for an audience with Antilla. He expected it would be a hard sell, but he could no longer ignore the crisis.

Antifact knocked on his boss's door. "Antilla, Principal Truant, is here to see you."

Antilla yelled, "I'd rather not have this meeting, Antifact."

Antifact got up and stepped into the doorway. "You've already skipped meeting him three times."

"Well, I expect he's used to it with a name like his," laughed Antilla.

Antifact pushed, "Shall I send him in?"

Antilla nodded in agreement, and he stood up to greet his visitor. "What brings our esteemed principal to my office, Truant?"

Truant extended his claw, shook Antilla's, and pleaded his case passionately. "Emperor, we have two top-notch environmental scientists at the UNIT, Professors Antland and Antrain, who tell me we have a serious climate crisis that needs immediate action." *I'm sweating. This guy makes me nervous.*

Antilla wiped his claw off with his handkerchief. "Oh, don't tell me they have dire predictions like that traitor of yours, Dean Beetree."

"They say the planet's atmosphere will thin since there is less vegetation to produce oxygen," Truant beseeched. *I must make my case hurriedly.*

Antilla sighed, "Again, predictions. I have no trouble breathing. Next, you will tell me our atmosphere will implode, hah."

"There's reduced water evaporation from tree leaves, which will reduce the size and number of rain clouds, so there will be less rain," Truant continued. *I must convince him it's urgent.*

Antilla glanced out the window. "It rained just last hexek. They're only making scary scenarios to justify their positions, and I don't believe it."

Truant spoke speedily, "But the reduced rain will cause droughts in the unspent lands, further speeding up the spent lands." *I'm getting nowhere.*

Antilla turned away from Truant and sat hard in his chair. "Spent lands, spent lands. That's all you scientists say. Just go plant more trees."

What a jerk, Truant thought. "But ...."

Antilla pointed his claw at the door and interrupted him,

"No, I mean it. Get out of my office and go plant trees, or I'll have you all fired."

A burly bouquet lingered as Truant stormed out of the office. But his concerns were quite valid. There were fewer trees, and many of the older, large trees were withering. They dried out as their branches and limbs became parched and brittle, as the roots could not absorb enough moisture. Lightning bolts that became more extreme in the remaining clouds triggered forest fires. Loud cracks of thunder shook the ground beneath them. Blinding inverted branch-like flashes illuminated the night sky. Sometimes, the tips of these bright explosions ignited the tinder-dry trees. The outer forests were ablaze, like an ashtray with fiery matchsticks and the flame jumping from stick to stick.

Forest fires sometimes came close to the nests at the edge of the insect colony, where the forests were healthier, and the wealthiest of the ANTs lived. Sometimes the insectoids could not tell when they surfaced from their underground burrows as the smoke was thick as a locust swarm.

🐜 🐜 🐜

Gretant and Thunbug met one morning on their way to school, as they did each hexay since becoming close friends.

"Thunbug, where are you? It's so smoky, I can't see you," cried Gretant.

"I'm over here. We'd better clear out," cautioned Thunbug, openly concerned about their safety. "The flames are approaching fast." *Come on, girl!*

Gretant repeatedly blinked to clear her eyes. "Don't worry. The fire's still far away."

Thunbug grabbed Gretant by the claw and led her away

from the burning trees. "There are so many ashes raining down, and I'm afraid the wind is blowing this way." *She must know we're in danger and shouldn't waste time.*

Gretant dragged her pods. "I can hardly hear you with the crackling and snapping. But, gosh, did you see the branch crash down?"

"Yes, keep moving, Gretant," cried Thunbug in a panic. "I can taste the charcoal." *We're going to burn!*

"Don't panic, Thun. It's not that bad."

Thunbug emanated a shabby smell. "It's getting hot too! We'd better run." *Now!*

After they got a safe distance, they watched the flames drawing closer to the outer burrows. Then they spotted a group of model VIII BUGs, part of the Fire-BUG brigade, rushing toward the fire.

"What are they doing?" questioned Gretant in shock.

Thunbug watched intently. "Looks like they're digging a moat and filling it with water from their bins. They're trying to save the insect nests." *I don't give them much hope.*

"Oh, no!" cried Gretant. "The wind changed direction. The flames are overtaking them. Can't we do something?"

"It's too late," warned Thunbug. "The fire's too hot. There's nothing we can do. The other fire-BUGs will have to save them or bring their bodies back." *Look away, quick! We shouldn't see that.*

"I've had it with this," cried Gretant. "I'm going to do my hex-end project on climate change. I want to make a difference."

Thunbug looked back at the blazing forest and quickened his pace. "Ever since we got lost in that desert, I've been reading about forest degradation. It's the issue of the hexury." *I'm relieved we're out of the fire's reach. Yet, I'm just as disturbed as Gretant about the state of the environment.*

Gretant turned back as well. "I hope those Fire-BUGs survived."

When the fire destroyed a large section of the outer nests, the wealthy ANTs living there expropriated the neighboring burrow, rendering many of the chi homeless. Having nowhere to go until the WoBBs finished new nesting districts, the chi slept out under the stars or the few seen through the smoke. Some mornings when the solar star rose, the authorities discovered that many of the chi could not arise with it, succumbing to some shadowy unknown plague in the night. Shortly after that, hundreds of homeless chi died under these harsh conditions. The coroner performed dissections but could not determine the cause of death. Toxic gases blowing in from the spent lands made breathing more difficult for cyborgs and likely caused the deaths. The thinning atmosphere had less oxygen, and there were air pockets throughout the unspent land with more poisonous gas than oxygen, so insectoids were dying. This scenario was conjecture from more recent times since they had not yet developed instruments to measure the levels of lethal gases, which were likely carbon, sulfur, and nitrogen dioxides.

CHAPTER 8

THE CLIMATE GETS UGLY

Plans made sans rhyme or reason.

A forest is lost for want of trees each season.

Arboreal breath, now birthed and died.

Things do come in threes. Or so it seems amid crises.

Like Peter and the crows,
'tis science, truth and reality denied,
ere climate is crucified.

GRETANT AND THUNBUG walked home together after spending time in the school library researching their projects.

"Gretant, the more I read about forest degradation, the more depressed I get," fretted Thunbug. "Our government has been ignoring it for hexuries. They call the desert spent lands, and it's far worse than Antilla lets on."

Gretant looked over at the burned-down forest next to the schoolyard. "I agree. I'm reading articles by UNIT scientists saying that burning trees affect the climate. And it's worse with fewer trees around. Did you know that trees produce the oxygen we need to breathe?" *I may not be as emotional as Thunbug, but I'm passionate about this issue.*

Thunbug sighed. "Yes, that's why it's so scary. Did you hear about the homeless chi dying? It might be because of the foul air. I know it's hard to breathe lately."

"Antilla has been trying to convince everyone it's a nasty flu going around," Gretant started. "But I expect you are right, Thun." *I blame Antilla and his cabinet for this mess, and I'm not afraid to show my anger about the government's inaction.*

Thunbug stamped out a glowing ember that somehow outlasted all the others. "I'm afraid that we may be too late. The situation is out of control."

Although still young, Gretant and Thunbug were dedicated students with a climate catastrophe wreaking havoc on their daily lives and seriously threatening their futures.

Gretant picked up a piece of charcoal and drew a tree on the walkway. "After we work on our projects, we should start some protest marches. It could be our joint mission," suggested Gretant. *I want to support this cause, and we need to fight Antilla!*

Thunbug took another charred branch and wrote SOT under the tree. "I'm with you all the way, Gret. Antilla may not like it, but this is too important."

Gretant stared with confusion. "SOT, what's that?"

"Just something I read in the history books about earlier protesters who pushed to 'Save Our Trees,'" replied Thunbug. "But won't Antilla come and get us if we march?"

Gretant took her piece of charcoal and wrote SOT across Thunbug's forehead. "Don't worry about Antilla. He will not care about some school kids' protests. *We've got to stand up to him.* You help organize, and next hexek, we'll march." She propagated a bold bouquet. *I've learned from Thunbug's style. He's helped me overcome my shyness.*

Thunbug spat on his handkerchief and wiped his brow. "Spoken like a true Antunite."

Gretant drew SOT across her forehead, although the 'S' was backward. "With Antuna and Anthiery's bloodline, my path to protest was already forged." *I may be shy, but I'm tough as RoACh shells.*

"By the way, I've read all about Antuna, but whatever happened to Anthiery?" queried Thunbug.

"No one knows. Some say Antilla murdered his entire gang," Gretant speculated. "Others say they escaped to another planet." *Anthiery was a tough dude I need to channel.*

Thunbug rolled his eyes. "That sounds far-fetched. I know some ants used to fly, but space travel?"

≈≈ ≈≈ ≈≈

The growing climate change and the many mysterious deaths alarmed the Departments of Atmospheric and Environmental Sciences chairs at the UNIT, professors Antrain and Antland. Although they could not prove toxic fumes caused the fatalities, they knew that the current state of the forests and the atmosphere approached a critical, life-threatening point. Unlike Earth, where gravity holds the atmosphere in place, Poo-ponic's lower gravity alone was not enough to maintain the atmosphere. Instead, the professors knew that Poo-ponic needed gravity and the ozone layer to hold the atmosphere in place, and the ozonosphere dwindled.

Professor Antrain from the UNIT's Atmospheric Sciences

department made an appointment to meet Professor Antland in Environmental Sciences.

Antland opened his office door after he heard a knock. "Professor Antrain, I am so glad to meet you. I read some of your articles, and they impressed me."

Antrain entered and grabbed a chair. "I have studied your work as well, Professor. When I read your latest article, I dropped everything else and came to meet you." *We need to act!*

"Are you as frightened as I am?" exclaimed Antland.

Antrain looked out the window towards the nearby lower school. "Yes, last hexek, these two young students, Gretant and Thunbug, came to talk to me about my research. They were so earnest and fearful about the future, and I realized I couldn't ease their worries." *Their futures are at stake, and we must help them.*

"Funny, they came to see me too, and I had the same feeling," responded Antland.

Antrain turned and looked Antland straight in the eyes. "I heard they organized a protest at their school, and all the kids joined in because they were worried about the planet's future. I can't say I blame them." *Antilla is letting our planet die.*

Antland gave Antrain a signed copy of his article. "I saw them on my way home. Gretant got the kids riled up. For a young insectoid, she's a very good spokes-ant on the issue. She even got the teachers to join in the protest by the end."

Antrain looked down at the manuscript and smiled. "The young are more open to new ideas and listen to reason. While adults can be so unmoved and downright resistant," he surmised. *We must stop this.*

"Yes, many adults ignore science and the facts," agreed Antland. "But the young know that their future is at stake."

Antrain paced across his colleague's office. "Gretant and her friend Thunbug made me realize that researching this topic is not enough. It's time for action. We must warn the public and be part of the solution," he stressed. *I'm ready to take it to the streets.*

"I agree," responded Antland. "If students are figuring this out, everyone else should understand. Insectoids are dying!"

Antrain stopped in his tracks and looked at Antland. "My concern is how Antilla will react if we protest. It might be short-lived if he imprisons or executes us." *I have some reservations about acting too rashly.*

"He didn't execute Dean Beetree, so our arrest is the only worry," reassured Antland.

"That scares me too, but not more than this looming climate crisis," concluded Antrain with a sigh. *Our planet will die.*

Inspired by the students, the professors descended their ivory towers and got down in the trenches to fight against the climate crisis.

Antland stretched out his claw towards Antrain, strewing a strapping scent. "Are we in agreement?"

Antrain grabbed and shook Antland's claw. "Yes, but our efforts might soon get short-circuited, so we should do something with a big impact." *We must be bold, or no one will notice or care.*

"Spot on!" Antland began with a thoughtful look. "Let's trick PIN-point into letting us make a joint statement."

Antrain scratched his head. "You mean we pretend Antilla asked us to talk about the problem and say it's not so bad?" *I think it could work.*

"Yes, exactly, but do you think PIN-point will believe us?" responded Antland.

Antrain thought for a moment or two, then revealed an idea. "My mate worked for Antilla before she discovered what a hindgut hole he was. She has some of his letterhead papyrus, and we can use it to prepare an official-looking letter, with Antilla insisting we make a statement." *I must shed my earlier misgiving. We need to act fast.*

Antland frowned. "Don't we need a signature or a seal on the letter?"

Antrain smiled. "The letterhead was pre-signed and sealed to save time."

Although the protest led by Gretant and Thunbug was successful and made waves at their school, Gretant wanted to have a more significant impact on the entire society.

She met with Thunbug on their way home from school. "I want to go back to the spent lands and take some pictures so we can show everyone on the planet how bad things are."

"No way," exclaimed Thunbug. "Don't you remember we got lost and almost died?"

"Don't be so dramatic. We weren't even gone a hexour." *I thought it was fun.* "And this time, we'll be prepared and bring water and a navigator."

"I don't know." Thunbug shuttered.

"Do I have to call you gutless again?" Gretant asked. "Because I will, and I'll go by myself." *And nobody can stop me!*

"No way!" Thunbug insisted. "I'll go with you. I don't want you to get lost. Do you even have a navigator?"

Gretant blushed. "I was hoping you did." *You always have my back.*

They planned their excursion for the next hexay, a school

holi-hexay. They followed the trail they had taken on their school trip and once again took the forbidden way out to the spent lands.

Gretant looked across the barren land and then over at Thunbug. "Since we've packed a lunch and are better prepared, I'd like to walk as far as we can in two hexours." *I hope he finds that reasonable.*

Thunbug nodded. "Okay, we'll stop then, have lunch, and head back. We will be back well before dinner."

Gretant and Thunbug walked in the same direction they had before. When they passed the small cave, Thunbug checked the navigator.

He pointed to the south. "We've been heading south, and we should keep going in the same direction. Then we'll know we're on track if we turn right around and find this cave again."

"Sounds good," agreed Gretant. "We can go for another hexour and a half and stop for lunch." *We can take lots of pictures to show the crowd.*

They continued on the same track, stopping to take pictures at several points. They captured images of dried swamps and dunes, lava-like rocks, and petrified tree stumps. At first, they had no trouble breathing, but the further they got, the worse the air seemed. They agreed to close their spiracles in the valleys and attempt breathing on the crests of hills or dunes. The plan worked as the air was better at higher ground. They stopped for lunch on top of a high hill where they could see for miles. After eating, they looked around in all directions.

Gretant pointed up in the sky over the eastern horizon. "What are those?"

Thunbug strained his eyes. "It looks like FLYs flying toward us."

Gretant shaded her eyes. "But what's dangling down?" *I think they're carrying something.*

Thunbug gaped as the FLYs approached. "They're transporting trees."

"Whatever for?" Gretant shrugged. "And where are they going?" *How come we don't know this?*

"I don't know, but get out your pictographer and take some pictures."

Gretant fumbled through her bag and found the pictographer. She took several pictures as the FLYs flew over them. "I think they're headed over there." She pointed to the west. *Maybe we'll see what they're doing with the trees.*

"Do you see smoke?" Thunbug asked. "Over there, where the flies are headed."

"I think so," Gretant replied. "It's clearer now, and I can see the tree line."

"Wow, did you see that?" Thunbug exclaimed. "The smoke got thicker and higher just after the FLYs got there."

"Yeah," Gretant answered as she took pictures of the large plume. "They must burn trees." *I can't believe it!*

Thunbug watched the smoke get thicker and thicker. "I guess that explains all this." He spread his forelimbs wide.

Gretant shook her head and put away her pictographer. "We better head back. It's getting late." *I think we got enough.*

Thunbug pulled out the navigator, set the course due north, and headed out. Then as they traveled about three-quarters of the way, Gretant noticed something peculiar.

She pointed to the north. "Is that another swarm of FLYs heading this way?" *This looks scary. We better shelter ourselves.*

Thunbug squinted. "No, it looks like a dirty cloud."

Gretant shuddered. "It's coming this way, really fast." *What can we do?*

"Quick, the cave is just ahead." Thunbug pointed at the opening. "Run!"

They sprinted and jumped into the cave. The winds hit like a sandblaster, and although the two were not hurt, the gusts tore Thunbug's bag from his back as they frantically tumbled into the cave. The storm left almost as quickly as it came and deposited several feet of dirt at the cave's opening.

Gretant trembled. "Has it buried us alive? Are we going to die in this lousy cave?" *Just our luck.*

"Don't dis the cave. It saved us. The wind could have torn us to shreds." Thunbug began digging. "Remember, I got six arms. I'll get us out of here in no time."

Thunbug dug for several hexutes but didn't seem to get anywhere. The more dirt he moved, the more it flowed back in.

He looked back at Gretant. "The wind was heading straight for the opening, and it piled sand high out there."

"What can we do?" Gretant sobbed. *We are going to die here!*

Thunbug tapped his temples. "I saw some light at the other end of the tunnel last time." He pointed further into the cave. "Maybe the other end didn't get buried so bad."

Gretant held back her tears. "You think the opening is big enough?" *Can we squeeze through?*

Thunbug shrugged. "We'll find out."

The two turned and ventured further into the cave. The cave was much darker than the last time, and it wasn't easy going. Thunbug went first, released a little thread, and weaved it three times over, so it was strong enough for Gretant to hold on to as she followed. He groped the cave walls with all six forelimbs, trying to find the opening at each turn. Finally, Thunbug got to where there were no more turns.

He called back to Gretant. "I think we're there. This area is softer, so it must be new dirt." He dug for a hexute. "I see hexay-light, and let's hope it is big enough to get through."

Thunbug had cleared all the sand a few moments later, and the two squeezed through. It was a tight fit, but they made it.

Gretant stretched and let the solar light flood over her. "Okay, take out the navigator, and let's get home."

Thunbug reached for his bag. "I forgot. The wind and sand ripped my pack off me, and the navigator was in it."

Gretant shook. "How do we know which way is home, then? Wasn't it just straight out from the opening?" *Don't tell me we're lost again.*

Thunbug pointed to a massive mountain of sand. "We left from the other end last time. And I can't tell which way the opening was facing."

"So, what do we do?" Gretant quivered. *We won't suffocate. We'll die of exposure!*

"Let me think." Thunbug scratched his chin. "It was about one hexour later the last time we were here." He pointed east of the solar star, which was due south. "And the solar star arcs about 60 degrees every hexour. So, we just need to aim that way." He pointed due north. "About 60 degrees towards the west compared to last time."

Not long after, the two reached the jungle near the colony.

Gretant leaned over and kissed Thunbug on the cheek. "Thunbug, you are a genius."

❦ ❦ ❦

Meanwhile, Antrain and Antland tricked PIN-point into letting them give an on-air public statement to warn the public. With the signed ruler's letter, Antland and Antrain assured the PINpoint producers that Antilla had instructed them to provide evidence that the changes in the climate were a sign that things were improving, that the forests were returning to full vigor. Once on-air, they broadcast their joint thesis with a dire prediction that a climate crisis would speed up the spread of spent lands. Riots erupted throughout the colony when they explained that this could lead to the planet's destruction within a hexury.

While on air, Professor Antland explained how trees and plants were necessary to produce oxygen and absorb toxic carbon dioxide. "Trees not only fuel our furnaces, but help cleanse the air we breathe. They are like giant air filters that nature unsheathes."

Professor Antrain described how trees absorbed water from the soil, and water evaporating from the trees created rain clouds. "Without trees, there'd be no oxygen or rain and far too much carbon dioxide to strain," he warned. He also described how burning too many trees increased the levels of carbon monoxide, which reacts with oxygen in the upper atmosphere, destroying the ozone layer. "The ozone layer protects us from solar radiation. And it keeps our atmosphere from leaving the station."

Professor Antrain had determined that the thickness of the ozone layer had shriveled and was close to collapse. This situation was a severe climate crisis—without rain, oxygen, or an ozone layer, life on the planet would end within their lifetimes.

Antilla denied these crazy climate crisis scenarios were imminent and immediately had his BUG secret police arrest the professors on treason charges. Antilla rationalized his actions to his cabinet. "These two rogue scientists fraudulently wormed their way onto PIN-point without cheer. They reported fake news about a climate crisis hoax, and we should poison them with the dioxides they fear."

～ ～ ～

Antilla immediately contacted his allies at PIN-point to plot his revenge. "Antifact, I want you to report that the deaths of the homeless chi cyborgs were because of a virus released by accident, which started a deadly insect plague."

Antifact looked down. "Who should I say released the virus?"

Antilla, wanting revenge and demanding prompt action, barked, "Careless UNIT scientists." *I'll get them back for this.*

Antifact put a claw to his forehead. "Yes, they'll believe it because most of the public mistrusts scientists."

"Then, after a few hexays, say you got more reports that suggest it wasn't an accident." *It's the more devious part of my ploy. I'll get the public to string 'em up.*

Antifact raised his eyebrows. "Are you sure, Antilla? The public will turn on the scientists."

Antilla pressed his claws together and wafted a vile vapor. "Exactly, that's what I want. And be sure to implicate those two traitors, Antland and Antrain." *Like my predecessors, I don't tolerate dissent.*

"They'll want to lynch them," warned Antifact.

"Yes, and most other scientists too," deduced Antilla. *I'll be happy to be rid of the lot.*

Antifact frowned, "You want that?"

Antilla smiled and liberated a vexing vapor. "Yes, the UNIT has outlived its usefulness and is full of treasonous know-it-alls. Do what I hired you for, deceive the public."

Antifact reported two or three times about the plague on

PIN-point. His last report ended with, "The docs at the UNIT have been up to no good. They released a deadly plague upon our neighborhood."

The public was supportive when Antilla mused about shuttering the UNIT.

The crowds shouted, "They did that! They did this! Jail for evil scientists."

They demanded the arrest of all scientists they believed had created the plague. They thought they did it to reduce the population, to get more honey for themselves.

🐜 🐜 🐜

Gretant met Thunbug the following day. "I can't believe they arrested Professors Antland and Antrain... right after we met them. Antilla must have hated the report they did on PIN-point." *I want to tear Antilla to pieces.*

"It must have angered Antilla that they told the public the truth," surmised Thunbug.

"Now PIN-point says scientists released a virus," cried Gretant woefully. "And the public is buying it." *They're so gullible. We must open their eyes.*

Thunbug rolled his eyes. "It's a lie, but the masses are easy to fool."

Gretant yearned to speak on the subject to her classmates and anyone else who would listen. She was introverted and shy about public speaking when she was younger. After befriending Thunbug, she became more confident around others and worked hard at overcoming her shyness. And the more she read about the looming climate crisis, she realized someone had to speak out, and if no one else volunteered, she would. Thunbug wanted to do what he could to save the planet, but he realized

Gretant was a much more captivating speaker, despite her earlier shyness. He also assumed the crowd was more likely to listen to an ANT. Thunbug was more extroverted and could motivate people behind the scenes. They made a great team. Gretant was the figurehead and Thunbug the rudder, and a growing crisis was the wind in their sails.

Thunbug grinned and continued the conversation. "I got some BEEs at school to tell their friends at other schools and spread the word to join our next protest."

"That's great, so schools around the colony will join the movement," rejoiced Gretant, scattering a bubbly bouquet. "We can show them all the pictures we took." *It'll be great! Again, you got my back.*

Thunbug beamed. "It's better than that. Remember our last protest? A large group of BEEs from several colonies were here for a school exchange."

"Yes, but didn't they leave right before our strike?" questioned Gretant. *What are you getting at? Tell me.*

"No, most of them stayed for a big party that night. A lot of them were at our protest and saw you speak. I worked the crowd and got the word out about our next protest. Schools all around the planet will join us," explained Thunbug.

"Oh, Thun, I can't believe it. With me speaking and you organizing, we'll take this planet by storm." Gretant raised all three arms above her head, and Thunbug leaned in to give her a big high-six. *My friend is a genius.*

～ ～ ～

Although PIN-point viewers were anti-science, others mistrusted Antilla and the media and became distressed about the climate crisis. Gretant and Thunbug did several more planet-wide school strikes and inspired young model VIII insectoids of all families. At first, only school kids and teachers recognized their efforts, but as the climate-related disasters intensified, they appealed to a broader audience. Although young, Gretant and Thunbug were political, not because they aspired to enter Congress, but because they worried about the potential demise of the planet.

Gretant stirred up the public with her fiery speeches, imploring the multitudes. "I want you to act as if your nest is on fire—because it is! And believe me, our prospects are dire." *Antilla has poisoned our planet!*

She wanted all insectoids to realize the ominous circumstances of their climate crisis. Gretant was vocal and chastised Antilla and his cabinet for their mistakes in managing the growing climate crisis.

She ranted, "Antilla and his thugs have robbed young cyborgs of our dreams. We must act before Poo-ponic comes apart at the seams." *The time to act is now! We have no choice.*

She wanted Antilla and his government to act to do something, anything, about the spent lands. During her speeches, she showed pictures of the spent land and the FLYs taking trees to the furnaces. Many insectoids did not realize the scale of the deforestation, and the images of the barren wasteland and plumes of smoke caused by blazing trees shocked them.

Thunbug never took the podium but was the behind-the-scenes organizer and moral support for Gretant, which she needed to take on Antilla. Antilla would have arrested Gretant for subversion if she were not young and popular, and he despised her after she received the All-Insect Noble Tremendous (ANT) prize for her work. Retired and emeritus UNIT professors selected Gretant for the award.

The former Dean of Arts and Chair of the History

department, Professor Antoria, presented the honor with a long-winded statement. "Gretant, and her friend Thunbug, with all they've tried, led us like aphids to sap as all-knowing guides." She sprinkled an effervescent essence. "They inspire us to respire our planet. Working so hard ever since they began it."

Antoria was so impressed with the young pair's exploits that she supported Gretant's nomination for the prize and befriended the young activists in the hexths following the award ceremony. Although the first Antilla fired all female politicians and Deans, his immediate successor relaxed the rule, and a few enterprising female professors progressed up the ranks. This group included Antoria, a meticulous researcher, and a perceptive historical analyst. Gretant admired her because of her feminist ideals. She loved her inspiring quote to budding female history students: "No tale is complete without history. But we can't believe his-story without her story."

❦ ❦ ❦

Not long after Gretant's award ceremony, Antilla leaked that his BUG secret police would shutter the UNIT. Gretant insisted to Thunbug that they go to the campus and check it out.

"Gretant, do you think we should be here?" fretted Thunbug. "Things could get ugly." *She's so persistent yet careless. I'm frightened.*

"I want to witness this!" insisted Gretant. "Anyway, they'll probably just padlock all the doors."

"It's sad," lamented Thunbug. "The UNIT's research and teaching have done so much for the insect and insectoid societies. And we'll never get to study here." *I really wanted to.*

"Maybe they'll only shut it down for a few hexths," Gretant supposed.

"What's that noise?" questioned Thunbug, responding to a blaring bouquet. He turned around and saw thousands of insectoids. "It looks like an angry mob, and they've got spears and torches!" *This situation could swiftly get dangerous for us.*

Indeed, an angry crowd overtook the UNIT. The multitude believed Antilla's lies and bound and gagged the professors and scientists. They prepared to burn the UNIT to the ground.

"Oh no, they've set fire to those labs," cried Thunbug, then warned, "We better get out of here!" *Listen to me, girl, I'm not kidding.*

"We have to stop them!" Gretant yelled, ignoring the instinct to run. "They can't round everyone up and burn the place down."

Thunbug grabbed Gretant by the forelimb, fearing for their safety. "There are thousands of them, and Antilla's BUG police are with them. There's nothing we can do." *Come on, let's go!*

Just then, there was a loud boom, and the building one over from where the young pair were standing exploded into a tower of flames.

"Run!" Thunbug shot a sharp stink. "These are the chemistry labs; the whole place will blow." *Believe me. It's time to scram!*

Antilla's BUG secret police led the hordes and set laboratories and offices afire, scorching the alpha campus to the ground. The flames reached high towards the heavens and required observers to stand back hundreds of feet to avoid hair-singeing heat. The beta campus remained intact, but the mob smashed laboratory equipment and looted the rooms of any honey or food supplies they found. Finally, the BUGs rounded up all scientists and academics in the arts, shackling them and throwing them into the jails previously used for black-FLYs.

Being retired and not considered an evil scientist, Antoria avoided the academic round-up and arrest. She met Gretant one afternoon on her way home from school. "Gretant, you and Thunbug need to go into hiding. They arrested so many of my friends, and I know he will come for you next," she implored. *I've studied history for a living, and I know what malevolent leaders can do.*

Gretant looked over both her shoulders. "But where will we go?"

Antoria wiped a tear from her eye, puffing a poignant perfume. "I found a hiding place for you. I asked Thunbug's folks to meet us at your home, and I'll explain the situation to both your parents." *Antilla is worse than you can even imagine.*

Gretant gave Antoria a hug. "I expected this might happen. What about our fight to save the planet?"

Antoria thought for a moment. "It is as if an illness has infected our colonies and compels us to destroy what we have contrived. This evil malady knows if we cannot stop our careless actions, insectoids will perish, and Poo-ponic will revert to the state it was before we arrived." *You've fought hard, but it's too late now.*

Gretant sighed. "We will only hide if you hide with us. You, too, are in danger."

Antoria explained she didn't think they would need to hide long since insectoids would soon turn on Antilla. But she warned, "For now, Antilla does not tolerate any dissension, and he will snuff us out like the plague would end my pension."

While in hiding, word reached Gretant that the defense team wished to call her as a witness in the treason trials slated for Chairs Antrain and Antland and the other UNIT scientists. Despite Antoria's appeals for her not to go, Gretant insisted she help. The prosecutor presented fabricated evidence that the two professors released the virus causing the plague. The prosecution also made its case that their motivation was to amass more honey for UNIT scientists and instigate a coup against Antilla. Gretant made several critical points about the desperate nature of the climate crisis and provided witness to the professors' strength of character.

After the testimony, the judge ordered both the prosecution and defense to summarize their arguments. The prosecutor closed his arguments, spewing a sticky stink. "These ivory-tower docs have planned this for hexades, conspiring to release this plague as their murderous blades. Their motivation was to fill their pockets to the brim. And to humiliate Antilla so we would oust him."

Gretant agreed to summarize the defense arguments and stated, "The plague was not unleashed by these honorable professors, but by the greedy actions of environmental transgressors." She continued, releasing a staunch scent, "It started with early cyborgs in the times of old, when they began raping our lands for liquid gold." She finally explained that Antilla's lies about how scientists released the plague led to the UNIT's destruction. "An ANT who can make insectoids believe in absurdities can make us all commit gross atrocities."

Convicted, despite Gretant's powerful testimony, Antilla had Antland and Antrain exterminated three hexays later by lethal inhalation in the public square. The other scientists and academics were tried in absentia and left in their cells, where their life sentences commanded they stay to rot. Luckily, in the commotion following the guilty verdicts, Gretant slipped away from the courthouse and back into hiding with Antoria and Thunbug.

From a historical perspective, it was fortunate that the insectoids were meticulous about keeping official documents, including court files, political papers, and presidential recordings. They stored most of these records in underground archives, recently discovered by a team of explorers from Bilaluna. Evidence suggests these records supported and expanded upon many of the accounts of the planet's survivors.

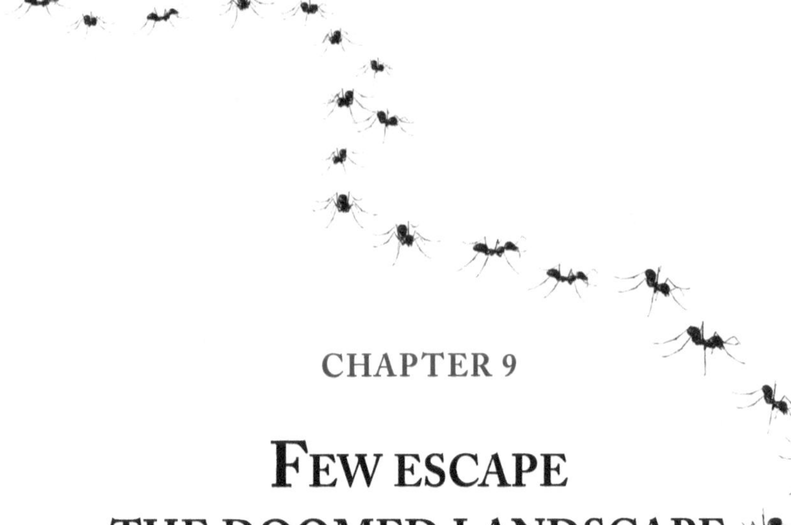

CHAPTER 9

FEW ESCAPE THE DOOMED LANDSCAPE

Death comes in five stages for planets like beings,
though two differ and three the same.

The first is denial. Next comes panic and
anger, and acceptance follows blame.

Ignoring signs until it is too late, the
crowd's terror fuels hate.

Amidst retaliation, there's no redemption, so
all must bear their deserved shame.

THE UNREST PRECEDING the treason trials dissipated for a short period. Yet, when another wave of the plague hit, civil society completely broke down, with thousands dying. Most insectoids concluded that if Antilla jailed the guilty scientists, they could not release any more of the deadly virus, which they knew did not pass from insectoid to insectoid. The calm period after the trial confirmed that the scientists were responsible since no one else died. But hexeks later, toxic gases again wafted in from the spent territories. It was a rude awakening that a virus did not cause the plague but poisonous fumes, although the word plague stuck. Gretant and Thunbug, who slipped out from their hiding from time to time, heard the cry from panicking cyborgs everywhere—*Must fly or run as fast as you can. Lest the plague rashly ends your lifespan.* This time, the cyborgs saw thick yellow clouds approach before they dropped in their tracks or escaped in the nick of time. The plague thrust the whole insectoid world into sheer panic, with the remaining hordes running for cover, though not knowing where to flee.

While the yellow clouds cleared and insectoids were safe for the time being, civility, law, and order never returned. After a violent outburst by protesters, Thunbug spoke to his friend. "Gretant, Antoria's friend, came over and described what's going on." *She was here while you were sleeping.*

Gretant perked up. "Yes, I heard from my cell—a swarm of angry chi blew up the furnaces and smashed the steam turbines and essence presses last night."

"Everyone's on strike, and those rich ANT cowards are hiding at the honey vaults," Thunbug scoffed. "They're staying close to their precious honey stores." He tilted his head towards the door. *I think it's safe to go out.*

They slipped outside and looked all around. "Yeah, and there was no one to stop the chaos because Antilla's BUGs are at the Woodhive or the Supreme Bank guarding his friends and his beloved honey."

"The UNIT professors' predictions are coming true," rued Thunbug, emanating a sapphire scent. He looked around. *I hope there are no yellow clouds.*

Gretant threw her forelimbs in the air. "Everyone is panicking that they're going to starve to death or get poisoned by the plague."

"It's not a plague. It's environmental toxins," corrected Thunbug. *They're such idiots, and we can't convince them.*

Gretant looked down. "I know, but everyone else thinks it's a plague."

Thunbug paused and said, "Antilla never cared about the environment, but now it looks like he cares nothing about insectoids." *He's the number one bozo in my book.*

Indeed, Antilla did not appease the public anymore and did not hide his intentions to save his rich twins and friends. When he learned the chi were protesting because they had no honey to eat, Antilla laughed and said: "Enough with their ranting poems. Let them eat honeycombs!" Honeycombs were a delicacy that only the wealthiest ANTs ever ate since eating the comb decreased the amount of honey produced. The idea of anyone eating honeycombs during such a despairing time was repulsive to the betas and chi. The public turned on Antilla, and there were calls for his head.

⁂

As the two tweens and Antoria prepared to go to bed, Gretant noticed something unusual in their hiding nest. She looked at Thunbug and Antoria. "Do you guys smell something funny?"

Antoria straightened her antennae. "No, but my sniffers have been going over the last few hexs."

Thunbug walked about the nest. "I'm getting a whiff, like the air in the spent lands, and it's getting stronger." *I better check this out!*

Gretant stumbled as she headed toward the source of the smell. "It reeks like rotting fly eggs."

Antoria felt a little dizzy and opened the window wide. "I think we're being poisoned."

Thunbug went outside and searched the area near where the smell was coming. He noticed a canister with a hose attached leading through a small hole in the burrow wall. Thunbug yanked the hose out of the hole and pushed the canister away.

He came back into the nest. "You were right! They were pumping gases through the wall, and I removed the hose." *Antilla's trying to kill us!*

Antoria helped Gretant to her feet. "Good thing for your sensitive antennae." She then thanked Thunbug for checking outside. "And good thing we stayed up late tonight."

Gretant stared at Antoria. "Do you think it was Antilla?"

"Who else?" Antoria replied. "We better find another place to hide. And no more going outside to look around."

⁂

Heroach, the great-grandnephew of Roachard of the Fabled Fourteen, was the chief of the Imperial Guard and worked closely with the deputy chief, Roachman. They were guarding the Woodhive one night when the protests got loud.

"Hero, I think we'll be here all night again," said Roachman. "This crowd is getting bigger and more aggressive." An explosive essence hung in the night air.

"We'll do what we normally do, stand tall and keep them from advancing," said Heroach. "Though with the policies this guy has been enacting, I feel like joining them." *I am loyal as leader of the guard, but I don't respect my ruler. I often think of Roachard and what drove him to rebel against the first Antilla.*

"Yeah, sometimes I wonder whether we're on the wrong side," agreed Roachman.

For hexours, the two sentries got pushed and shoved back, dancing the waltz they had countless times before. But this night, the crowd pushed harder than before and got closer to the Woodhive. An angry ANT threw a rock, breaking Antilla's chamber window, and the mob became frenzied, releasing a raging reek.

"Is that Antilla on his balcony?" asked Roachman. "What's he doing?"

"He's got the rock," replied Heroach. "Looks like he is going to throw it back." *I'm not surprised. What a jerk!*

Antilla then threw the rock out into the crowd, and it struck a small WoBB right in the head. Hemolymph spewed out everywhere, and the WoBB keeled over. The entire crowd hushed.

Heroach picked up the young WoBB, looked into his lifeless eyes, and declared, "He's dead." He glared back at Antilla. *He's so reckless. There's more hemolymph on his hands—the pointless loss of a young life. That's the last straw. I can't follow this brute anymore.*

The crowd stirred, and after one protesting BEE screamed a rhyme, everyone joined in yelling: "He's a killa, kill Antilla. He's a killa. Kill Antilla!"

Antilla cried back with a booming bouquet, "I'll kill you all one by one if I have to." He threw a candlestick at the mob and then barked an order to his imperial guard, "Crush them all!"

Heroach yelled with a raucous reek, "It's every Guard-RoACh for yourself. Choose your side. I'm with the crowd." *I'm proud to follow in my great grand-uncle's footsteps.*

"I stand with Heroach," cried Roachman. "Antilla's a tyrant!"

Most of the RoACh Imperial Guard then turned and

marched with the crowd up the steps of the Woodhive. A small group of RoAChs still loyal to Antilla tried to hold their ground while the emperor and a large group of his BUG secret police escaped through a tunnel leading to the Supreme Bank's vaults. Finally, the crowd with most of the RoAChs ransacked the Woodhive and burned it to the ground.

～ ～ ～

The following hexay, Heroach amassed a large group of now rebel RoAChs and met with Roachman in the main square.

"We're all doomed," bemoaned Heroach. "Antilla's inaction on the spent lands has killed the planet. Insectoids are starving, and he says eat honeycombs. He tried to turn us against our own. I want to rip his head off." *I have nothing but hatred in my heart for Antilla now.* A scorching smell flooded the square.

Roachman pointed to a poor homeless WoBB on the street. "There are so many insectoids starving. Heroach, we must do something. The RoAChs are up in arms. Everyone hates Antilla now, and they'll follow whoever wants to lead against him."

Heroach paced. "You should lead some of the RoAChs over to the hives. Tell the BEEs they must distribute what's left of the honey to the starving chi. I'll take another team over to the honey vaults and get that damn Antilla." *My hatred is at the boiling point. I must kill the scoundrel Antilla and as many of his cronies as possible. Let me at him.*

Roachman scanned the square. "There must be a thousand crazed RoAChs out there. It would be best to take the bulk of them with you and leave me a couple hundred."

Heroach and Roachman were long-time friends and maze-running teammates in their youth. They both had hard shells and were the strongest among the roaches. But beyond their physical might was the strength of their character. Both were magnetic leaders who embodied the typical roach characteristic of loyalty, but each had a solid moral compass that guided their path towards social justice and righteousness. When these two RoAChs spoke, other bugs listened, and other RoAChs followed in step when they scurried.

After Roachman left with a couple of platoons, Heroach approached the angry crowd and led the charge. "Get the wealthy ANTs and their wives. Let's bring them to 1% of their lives!" He continued, excreting a brawny bouquet. "Together, we'll march on the Supreme Bank and massacre the rich ANTs. Crush whichever ones you like, but leave Antilla for me." Although it didn't happen often, all insectoids knew there was nothing more dangerous than an angry RoACh. *I'm like a bull staring at a red cape after being jabbed by a matador's spear, but this matador is old and fat and has lost his sword*

Many RoAChs died—caught and stung in the extra thick webs the BUG secret police spun. Yet, Heroach and his RoAChs broke through the webs and crushed many of the BUGs. Bugthug and the surviving BUGs retreated to the halls of the Supreme Bank. When they got there, they found the rich ANTs in the large gallery outside the vaults having a sumptuous banquet and gorging themselves on the honey of the best vintage. There were even honeycombs on the table sliced for easy eating. The rich ANTs decided that if they were going to die anyway, they should go out in style. Despite their typical fierce loyalty, Antilla's BUGs, which had observed the mass starvation of chi, became incensed when they saw such gluttony.

One of Bugthug's lieutenants approached him, drooling. "I

don't care who trained us. This greed is not right. Insectoids are starving, and look what Antilla does."

"Insectoids say I'm cruel," added Bugthug. "Antilla is no longer worthy as ruler, and he deserves to be lunch." *I may be sympathetic to Antilla, but I've never seen my squad so angry and hungry. As they say, 'for every BUG that drools, there'll be a clawful of ghouls.' All this vitriol is sparking me to follow along.*

Bugthug turned to address his police BUGs. "BUGs under my command, you're free to do as you wish. If you choose to kill ANTs, do so—but leave Antilla to me!" *I am the captain of the BUGs, and I must right the ship. And, with the aroma of BUG saliva in the air, it's easy to change my tack.*

The BUGs swarmed and attacked the ANTs in the hall. Bugthug sought Antilla and approached him.

"Bugthug, I order you to stop your BUGs immediately," commanded Antilla.

Bugthug replied firmly, convincing himself he needed to do the deed. "You trained them to be ruthless with criminals, and they only now discovered who the real villains are." *I'm sure you can guess.*

"And you, do you think I'm a crook?" asked Antilla.

Bugthug hissed, "I knew you were from hexay one, and your predecessors too."

"But you supported our cause," pleaded Antilla, shaking from the betrayal.

Bugthug stepped forward again, his killer instincts over-taking him. "I followed you because it was my job. You had authority, but you've lost it now." *And you've gained me as your hunter!*

Antilla bumped into the wall as he backed up further. "Are you going to kill me?"

Bugthug grinned, drool welling up and triggering the inevitable. "Well, I *am* hungry, and you are the fattest hindgut in the room." *Slurp!*

Antilla got down on three knees and begged Bugthug to spare his life, oozing a smarmy smell. "Please don't do this, Thug. Remember the good times we had."

A foul-smelling drool dripped from Bugthug's fangs. "I am, and it's making me hungry. Right now, to me, you're only meat. Now, prepare to meet your maker." His jaws quivered and sprung open wide. Bugthug didn't even sting Antilla—he swallowed him whole. Then he proudly displayed his catch to the other BUGs through his transparent belly. No one even heard Antilla's futile screams while he suffocated and slowly disintegrated in Bugthug's fore-gut.

Having slaughtered and eaten all the ANTs, the BUGs stampeded and fought each other, scrounging and consuming the remaining honey on the banquet tables for dessert.

❧ ❧ ❧

Back at the central square, the smaller group of RoAChs, led by Roachman, stormed the honey hives to distribute whatever honey was available there to the starving multitudes.

Roachman shot a solid scent. "Let's blow the hives so the hungry can eat, with honey falling from the sky to the street." He reared and ordered his troops to double-stilt-march to the hives. *We must distribute all the honey.*

When they got into the hives, they found piles of dead BEEs throughout the tunnels. They learned from one of the dying bees that there had been a massive battle. The melee was between BEEs who wanted to dispense the remaining honey and those who tried to keep it for themselves. The combat was a bitter fight to the death, and most BEEs in the hives met their end.

As BEEs were generous to those in need, the dying bee said about the confrontation with his last breath: "To be a BEE or not a BEE, that was the question. I tried to stop them, and they ignored my suggestion."

A few smaller WoBBs snuck into the hives before the battle began and hid in the shadows while the mayhem ensued. Once the dust settled, they rushed out to tell other WoBBs what had happened, and hundreds of them in the area swarmed in and robbed the leftover honey in the hives. A young WoBB named Wobbella was among those hiding in the hive but was so horrified she froze in her hiding place until the RoAChs arrived. The RoAChs came after the other WoBBs had scattered. Besides finding the hundreds of slaughtered BEEs, they discovered the empty hives broken and in disarray.

Roachman approached the small WoBB veiled in a shadow. "Is that you, Wobbella? What happened here?" he asked.

Wobbella stepped out into the light. "We snuck into the hives, hoping to take a bit of the sweet honey out to the starving chi." She trembled. *Am I in trouble?*

"And the BEEs started fighting?" questioned Roachman.

Wobbella shuttered and spoke with an echoing essence. "Yes, the head honey comber watched the hive, and she had a large group of soldier BEEs with her to protect the honey. Then another group of BEEs demanded that they distribute the honey in the hive to the hungry masses." *It was such an ordeal. I'm so frightened.*

Roachman put a forelimb on Wobbella's shoulder, then questioned, "They wanted it all?"

Wobbella held two claws close together. "Yes, we had the

same idea, but we were going to steal only a little. And we were waiting until the BEEs fell asleep." *Honest! I don't lie.*

"How did the skirmish begin?" Roachman delved further.

"The head honey comber said: 'If you come to the combs with false blab, you'll leave this place on a slab!' She sharpened her stinger. They argued, then another BEE flashed his stinger," explained Wobbella. *I can't imagine what might have happened if they had discovered me.*

"And they fought to the death?" asked Roachman.

Wobbella shook. "It was a massacre; BEEs were killed everywhere. There is nothing sweet about it, I swear." *What a hemolymph bath! I've never seen such carnage.*

🐜 🐜 🐜

The remaining RoAChs at the Supreme Bank regrouped. Then, under Heroach's leadership, they stormed through the gates into the hall outside the honey vaults. They arrived to see dismembered ANT parts everywhere, and BUGs were wrestling over the last of the honey. The BUGs stopped gorging and squabbling and prepared to attack the RoAChs. But they surrendered when they saw the RoAChs outnumbered them.

Heroach cornered Antilla's chief BUG. "Bugthug, you are sensible to surrender." *I'm relieved there will be no more loss of life.*

Bugthug grinned, "Well, we don't want you to crush us after we have eaten an enormous meal."

Heroach looked down at Bugthug's belly. "You killed Antilla, I see." *He should have been mine.*

Bugthug widened his grin so much that his fangs popped out. "Yes, he's dead now, but his body will slowly dissolve as he goes through my system. I will show off my trophy to who-ever asks."

Heroach raised the spear he carried. "If he were still alive, I'd spear through your belly to say it was I that killed him." *Perhaps I should anyway.*

Bugthug frowned, "But I am your prisoner. You'd slay me too."

Heroach lowered the spear but still pointed the tip towards his foe. "You were his right-claw man, his assassin." *I hate you just as much!*

"So, you want to execute me?" Bugthug stood his ground.

Heroach opened his storage compartment and motioned for Bugthug to get in. "Yes, but I won't. I'll take you to the jailhouse like the others. Get in!" ordered Heroach. *Justice will suffice for me.*

At Heroach's command, the RoAChs locked the BUGs within their storage bins and marched their prisoners to the jails next to the courthouse. As they left the Supreme Bank, a large yellow cloud of toxic fumes descended on them and poisoned the RoAChs and the BUGs inside them. Directly exposed to the gases, most RoAChs died quickly, but the BUGs locked within the RoAChs died a slow death. They gasped for air, trying to escape from their coffin-like confinement inside their dead hosts.

Bugthug yelled from his cell, "Heroach, unlock the doors, let me out. I am going to die in here!" For the first time, Bugthug felt fear.

Heroach cried, "There's no use. The fog is too thick, and we're all doomed." *Why should I let you escape?*

Bugthug pounded on the doors and pleaded, "Let me

run and try to save myself." He desperately appealed for Heroach's compassion.

Heroach ignored Bugthug's cries and calmly professed, "It's a more fitting end. You swallowed Antilla, and now his inaction consumes you." Despite the dread, he spoke with a fluid fragrance. "Complicit in life with his ignorance. In death, you taste his virulence." His statement was his last, and Bugthug died soon after, claws worn down to his exoskeleton.

After the slaughterhouse of clashes at the honey hive and the Supreme Bank ended and the toxic clouds cleared, there was an eerie calm across the colony. The winds were kind to the remaining insectoids by blowing towards the spent lands—no forest fires or toxic clouds appeared for a few hexays. Wobbella and other WoBBs distributed the honey they had looted from the hives. The remaining RoAChs broke down the doors of the honey vaults and doled out honey to all who needed it in the main square outside the burrows.

Roachman crawled up to the small WoBB and hugged her. "Wobbella, I am so glad that you finally got your wish to feed the starving chi." *The poor girl has gone through so much.*

Wobbella looked up at the large RoACh and responded, "That was your desire too, no? And with Heroach dead, you are the leader now."

"Yes, and I'd better get back to it." Roachman turned and headed back to a group of RoAChs under his command. "We have other colonies to feed, too." *Our work is never done.*

"All we can do now is our best. Good luck," Wobbella waved goodbye.

Roachman addressed the RoAChs under his command

with a buffed bouquet, "Okay, crew, pack your compartments to the rafters before our friends meet their hereafters."

Sensing the calm after the storm, Antoria, Gretant, and Thunbug came out of hiding and volunteered at honey lines for the hungry.

Gretant urged the young cyborgs to aid the starving masses, "I know our future looks bleak. But we must fortify the hungry and weak." She fought long for environmental justice and was hopeful now that Antilla was gone.

When they finished, the three went back to Antoria's regular nest rather than their hiding place. While there, Antoria spent hexours looking through her old records from her time at the UNIT.

After quite some time, Gretant queried, "Antoria, you've been looking for almost a hexour. What is so important?" She worried about Antoria's well-being.

Antoria shuffled through some scrolls. "Our lives may depend on it." *We must leave this planet!*

"What are you looking for?" asked Thunbug.

"An article I read earlier tells of a large meteorite strike long ago," explained Antoria. "Some believed it opened up a wormhole to Bilaluna." *It's our only chance.*

Thunbug picked up a scroll and scanned it. "Do you think we could use it to escape?"

"Yes, if it's there. Everyone on Poo-ponic could transit to Bilaluna," promised Antoria. *I hope beyond belief!*

"So, it's true! Anthiery and his friends left this planet," speculated Gretant, buoyed to think her relative might have survived.

Antoria looked up at Gretant. "I don't know about that,

but I hope *we* can. We must find where the wormhole does stand and rescue all that we can." *This disaster is as urgent as it gets, and we need to escape.*

"Does the article say where the wormhole is?" probed Thunbug.

Antoria dug through another bin. "Yes, but I read it so long ago. And it was only a theory." *Please let me search!*

Gretant grabbed a scroll from the bin. "Let us help you look," she insisted, urging Antoria.

Antoria tapped her temples with her claws. "Where is it? I know it's here somewhere! Wish my memory would answer my prayer," she yearned, sifting through the many stacks of papyrus scrolls she packed up when she retired. *I put it in these files.*

During her time at the UNIT, Antoria had studied pre-insectoid history and wanted to make a final detailed account of the lives of the non-cyborg insects before the Great Small Insect War. If she had still been working, she would have lost her files as angry anti-scientist mobs burned down the offices and labs at the now-closed UNIT. She planned to write a historical treatise during her retirement.

Having regretted the war, she moaned, "They were our mothers, our fathers, but small. They didn't deserve such a fate, after all."

Antoria had sought the article earlier, but her desire became pressing. She had gone back to the UNIT before it closed to find other information sources, only to discover all records on the subject were missing.

After three hexays of searching, Antoria announced to Gretant and Thunbug that she had found the old essay she sought. She sprinkled a vibrant scent. "Eureka, I knew it was here. If only we had more time to cheer." *Now, we just need to find the wormhole!*

Gretant leaned in to look at the scroll. "What does it say?"

"Slow down and let me read it," requested Antoria.

After pacing back and forth, Thunbug implored, "Tell us already. Where's the wormhole?"

Antoria looked up briefly. "The author narrowed the wormhole location down to two potential craters." *Why is it always so hard? I can't do the far one.*

"Where are they?" Gretant blurted out, enthusiastic about a potential escape.

Antoria pointed out the window. "One is very far away on the other side of the planet, and the other is not too far from here." *Maybe we'll get lucky.*

As an early model VIII cyborg, Antoria was old and had little time to live. She hoped to find the portal to save as many remaining insectoids as possible, especially young cyborgs like Gretant and Thunbug. Antoria did not want to tell others in the colony about the wormhole right away, and to stir up false hopes since they might not find the portal.

"You two should check out the crater sites to see if we can escape," instructed Antoria. *I'm too old for this.*

Thunbug shrugged. "How can we tell?"

"The article says there should be an area when you get close, where you feel funny, like your hair stands up for no reason," Antoria explained. *I hope that's right.*

Gretant leaned in again to read the scroll. "Is there some way to know for sure?"

"Throw stones in every direction and see if they disappear," proposed Antoria. *But what do I know? I'm a historian, not an astronomer.*

Thunbug rolled his eyes. "That seems too easy and unlikely. You better come with us to make sure."

"No, I'm too old to do the scouting," moaned Antoria.

"We'll go to the closest one first," pushed Thunbug. "You said it would only take a few hexours."

Gretant grabbed her forelimb and pleaded to Antoria, "We can't leave you behind in the smog. It's not too far, and we won't make you jog."

Since it was unknown when the winds might change directions and bring death and destruction, Antoria agreed at last. The three friends, young and old, planned to leave the following hexay to find the lifesaving wormhole.

≈ ≈ ≈

When Antoria, Gretant, and Thunbug left on their trip, the breezes switched direction, blowing from the spent lands towards them. They were lucky that there were no yellow clouds or fires despite the wind's change. The wormhole was the one used by the Fabled Fourteen hexuries earlier. The path was overgrown as the first Antilla had closed off its access. In recent hexs, the old track was easier to find with the dying-off of vegetation. Yet, no insectoids had used it for hexades.

After hexours of walking, Thunbug got annoyed, as he carried most of Antoria's heavy stuff.

"Gretant, we've been plodding for hexours," panted Thunbug, leaching an onerous odor. "Antoria is so slow." *We should be there already!*

"I know, and she insisted we bring all these files," muttered Gretant.

Thunbug stumbled over a tree root. As he stood up and dusted himself off, he noticed a hollow in the land ahead.

"Hey, I think this is the place," announced Thunbug. "See the crater over there?" *I can barely take another step.*

"Yes, at last," cried Gretant. "See, Antoria, it wasn't that far."

"Perhaps for you youngsters, but I'm bushed," she gasped. "Look for the wormhole."

It annoyed Thunbug when he caught Antoria's whining whiff. "I see nothing, and I feel nothing." *What a waste of time!*

"It must be here somewhere," buoyed Gretant.

Thunbug paused and noticed a gentle breeze blowing from the west.

"The wind's blowing from the spent lands; we better watch out for toxic clouds," Thunbug warned. *What now! Does everything always have to be against us?*

"Keep looking around," insisted Antoria. She plunked herself down.

Tired and frustrated, Thunbug started throwing rocks in every direction as he walked on.

"Watch that, Thun," cried Gretant. "You almost hit me!"

"It's no use," said Thunbug. "We might as well go home." *I'm one step from giving up entirely.*

Thunbug looked back towards Antoria, still sitting and now a few hundred feet behind. She looked faint and coughed repeatedly.

"Oh, no!" Thunbug yelled. "There's a yellow cloud coming, and it's almost got Antoria." *I better run!*

"Get her, Thun," screeched Gretant. "She'll be dead in hexonds!"

Thunbug dropped Antoria's heavy gear and ran over to Antoria as fast as his two legs could take him. He threw her over his shoulder and ran faster away from the encroaching yellow cloud.

Thunbug slumped as he reached Gretant. She helped him and Antoria, whose breathing improved. Gretant pointed in the opposite direction of the mist. "Let's go behind that pile of rocks. Fast!"

Thunbug grabbed Antoria's pack, and as they rounded the mound, they blindly stumbled into the gateway. Sucked through the wormhole before the three realized they had found it, they began their rapid transit to Bilaluna.

Antoria wanted to let the other insectoids know the wormhole's location. But she, Gretant, and Thunbug staggered into the portal, escaping the toxic yellow cloud. There was no turning back, even if they could stop themselves from spiraling down the wormhole.

Travel through the portal was quick and painless, and they arrived on Bilaluna as expected. Yet, they landed in a depression through which a rushing river flowed. They plummeted into a calm pool on the river's edge, narrowly missing the raging waters just a few feet away. Large rapids crashed on the other side of a boulder, which diverted the powerful flow. Soaked but safe, Antoria began crying about the millions they left behind. "We have to go back. I wanted to bring the others," she insisted.

"I am not sure, but I think the wormhole collapsed," Gretant cried. "There was a loud boom right when we left."

Thunbug spread his forelimbs to block the others from re-entering the wormhole. "It's worse than that. Did you not feel it? There was a catastrophe decimating all life on Pooponic. I instantly felt the screams of millions of insectoids in my heart. It's too late! We can never go back," he wailed. *Pooponic is dead! I'm certain.*

"I sensed it too," groaned Antoria with a broken bouquet.

"I'm afraid you're right. There's nothing left. We would die too if we returned."

Thunbug reached out to console the distraught Antoria. "I know you must feel so sorry. But we must go on to tell the full story." *At least we survived.*

Indeed, the group heard a loud booming din marking the instant Poo-ponic's atmosphere imploded. They just escaped the disastrous events scientists believe unfolded right after, killing the remaining residents of the doomed planet.

Thunbug bemoaned, "Poo-ponic is now no more. I do fear it! I hope more young cyborgs come here, at least in spirit." *They are all gone. I can't believe it!*

❦ ❦ ❦

Hexuries later, Bilaluna scientists speculated that as the ozone layer finally erupted, the air in Poo-ponic's atmosphere shot away like the hiss from a popped balloon.

One scientist prepared a graphic description of how she thought it might have happened:

The sky would have blackened, and the few remaining BEEs flying to the last bits of forest would have dropped from the sky, as there was no air mass to hold them up. Without the ozone layer, solar radiation would have roasted the planet. Streams and rivers would have boiled, and all life under direct solar light would have incinerated instantly. Cyborgs inside would have heard the sizzle of burning flesh, with an aroma like burning hair and smoldering embers assaulting their antennae and fumes flooding their breathing spiracles. I expect that being below ground or under any cover would have only prolonged the agony. The sheltered insectoids would have suffocated because of the lack of oxygen and nitrogen essential for life. If their tracheae did not collapse under pressure within less than a hexond, they would have died with their next few breaths as they inhaled the poisonous levels of carbon, sulfur, and nitrogen dioxides. Their spiracles, starved of oxygen, would have burned. And their cerebral neurons would have burst all at once, like the crescendo of a fireworks display.

There was no escaping the plague that had started many hexuries earlier and finished in a dramatic climax. Evidence suggests that millions lost their lives instantly, and Poo-ponic became a dark, uninhabited wasteland!

EPOCH III:
PARADISE GAINED

CHAPTER 10

HOW ROBUST IS YOUR CONSTITUTION?

*Wisdom is the water that douses the
fire of reckless intelligence,*

*and enlightenment is the air that raises
the phoenix from its earthly ashes.*

*This ethereal mix fills voids and spawns
altruistic give from egotistic want.*

Bilaluna, Poo-ponic's only moon, five hexuries before Poo-ponic's demise

THE STORY RETURNS now to the fourteen refugees that left earlier for Bilaluna. They knew Bilaluna had vegetation, but they did not know what they would find when traversing the wormhole. The wormhole opened on Bilaluna in an area that had a depression. This hollow formed the bottom of a waterfall, swollen during the rainy season. A large river cascaded over the crater's lip down to its floor below, thrusting the fourteen insectoids into a gorge at the bottom of a waterfall that flowed into Bilaluna's largest river. The rapids were so strong that most of them could not escape the whirlpools that pulled the new arrivals into the depths.

"Antianna, are you okay?" screamed Anthiery before a large underwater eddy pulled him in.

Antianna spurted out of another vortex and grabbed onto an overhanging tree limb. Shaken but still breathing, she yelled back, "I'm okay. Where are you?"

Just then, Anthiery burst out of the water, clinging onto Roachelia, and the two crashed into Antianna's bough, which snapped under the weight of the three insectoids. The three then washed down through the gorge, clutching the broken branch.

"Hold on tight!" yelled Anthiery as they bobbled through the torrent.

The two WoBBs, Wobbert and Wobbella, were smaller and more buoyant. After an initial dousing, they popped out of the water like inflatable toys, riding the rapids like whitewater rafts bouncing over number five rapids. Rushing currents often washed over them but rarely pulled them under the surface. Wormillian and Wormella also had no trouble. Instead, they slithered through the river like water snakes, coming up for air at will. Flynette and Flyapper were both propelled towards a pile of shallow rocks and used the boulders as a launching pad, pushing off the solid ground and rapidly flapping their wings to take flight. Beetrix and Beebuzz did not fare so well. Their wings and fuzzy coats were heavy when doused with water. They could not breach the surface while swimming and could only breathe when the turbulent waters bounced them into the air at irregular intervals. Roachard also sank deep when he first entered the water and got stuck while being squeezed between two obstructions well below the surface.

"Wormella, was that Roachard we passed back there?" cried Wormillian when the two WoRMs met at the surface.

"I think so, but he wasn't moving," replied Wormella. "I think he got stuck between two rocks."

"I'd better swim back and help him," yelled Wormillian before he dove deep under the rapids and headed back. In the whitewater's torrent, it was a struggle for Wormillian to reach Roachard, and he couldn't free his RoACh friend, who was wedged in tight. Panicking that Roachard might drown, Wormillian tried to wriggle free the smaller obstacle. He was about to give up and surface for air when he noticed Wormella beside him shoving the larger mass, which broke free and tumbled down river along with Roachard. Wormillian raced after Roachard and drove him up to the surface for air.

As Wormillian held Roachard at the surface, Wormella swam up beside them. "How were you able to move that large rock?" asked Wormillian. "The smaller one wouldn't budge."

"That wasn't a rock but a waterlogged bough," snickered Wormella. "And although it was covered in moss, I could see its branch caught on the bottom. I wiggled a little at the snag, and it broke free."

Beetrix popped out between them, and Wormella whipped her tail around her before the BEE submerged again.

"Thanks, Wormella. I've been bobbing up and down like driftwood in powerful waves," sputtered Beetrix. "I don't know how much longer I could have taken it."

"No problem, girl. Have you seen Beebuzz?" Wormella asked.

"We were trying to hold on to each other at the surface,

but we got pulled apart by a strong vortex," Beetrix sputtered. "After that, I saw him trying to pull himself onto a rock. I hope he's okay."

"Mill, puff yourself up and grab my tail, and I'll hold yours, and we'll make a floating ring," suggested Wormella. "As long as Roachard and Beetrix can hang on, we can form a flotation device and catch the others as they go by."

"I'm feeling better now," responded Roachard. "I can hang on."

"Me too," added Beetrix. Hey, there's Wobbert and Wobbin, but they seem okay. "They're not even going under."

"Where are the others?" shouted Wormella.

"I saw Flynette and Flyapper bounce off some rocks and take flight. They're okay," replied Wobbert. "They offered to pluck us out of the water, but I told them to look for Anthiery and Antianna, since I knew they couldn't float like us."

"What about Beebuzz and Roachelia?" cried Beetrix.

"I haven't seen Roachelia, but I saw Beebuzz clinging to a rock upstream," answered Wobbin. "We were on the far side and couldn't help him, as he barely hung on."

Suddenly, Beebuzz shot out of the side of a whirlpool and ended upright between the two WoBBs, who grabbed him before he submerged again.

"Try to work your way over to us," yelled Wormella. "He might pull you two under."

The two WoBBs did their best to paddle their way over to the ring of WoRMs but struggled to hold the waterlogged Beebuzz. Roachard and Beetrix kicked, and the WoRMs wriggled the best they could while still forming the circle. Just as Wobbin neared the WoRMs, the two WoBBs and Beebuzz descended into an eddy.

"Oh no, we lost…" screamed Beetrix. But before she even gasped her last word, the three unwitting divers burst back to the surface right in the center of the WoRM ring.

"Super!" cried Wormella. "Now, we just need to find Anthiery, Antianna, and Roachelia."

The five rescued insectoids safely encircled by the WoRM ring floated down to a less turbulent section of the river while searching the fast water for their remaining friends. They did not know that the two ANTs and Roachelia were bouncing through the rapids on a tree bough. Fortunately, Flyapper and Flynette were already scouring for their missing friends.

"That was a close one," cried Flyapper as he and Flynette vaulted off the rocks into the air. "If we were deeper when we hit the rock, we might have never made it."

"You're right, Yaps," added Flynette. "But we best look for the others so they don't suffer a worse fate."

"Look down there," shouted Flyapper. "Is that the two ANTs and Roachelia clinging to a log?"

"Yes, and they're barely hanging on," gasped Flynette. "Let's fly down and steer them towards the shore."

"You bet!" responded Flyapper.

As the FLYs flew down, they realized that Anthiery and Antianna had a good grip on the bough with their three upper limbs. Roachelia, on the other claw, desperately struggled to hang on.

"You grab onto the log, and I'll get Roachelia," cried Flynette.

As Flyapper clutched onto the log and pulled it to shore, Roachelia slipped off and slid entirely into the water. Thinking swiftly, Flynette grabbed Roachelia before a swirling pool dragged her underwater. Flynette grasped her friend's legs and flipped her on her back. "Don't panic, Elia. You can float on your back while I tow you to shore," reassured Flynette. "Heck, I can haul trees—this will be like sailing a boat."

The WoRM ring flotilla of seven arrived just as Flyapper and Flynette were dragging their three friends to shore. And the twelve insectoids all crawled onto the sandy beach together.

"Wait, what about Bugbert and Bugabelle?" shrieked Wobbert. "Has anyone seen them?"

As everyone scanned the river for their BUG friends, Bugbert and Bugabelle came walking over a dune on the beach, holding claws and laughing.

"Wasn't that the greatest ride ever!" said Bugabelle, spouting a festal fragrance. "Buggy and I were just going to head up to the top to do it again." With their round balloon-like unibodies, the BUGs just bounced from crest to crest of the whitewater and barely even got wet.

⚘ ⚘ ⚘

After surviving the wormhole passage and the whitewater adventure, the first order of business for the Fabled Fourteen was to find food and shelter. The group was fortunate that the vegetation covered the moon with many fruits and vegetables. Flynette and Flyapper's rapid flying speed allowed them to scan much of the moon, searching for food sources. The two FLYs also helped Beetrix and Beebuzz transport nectar and pollen to their temporary encampment. Bugabelle and Bugbert's ability to spin up bins and Roachard and Roachelia's capability to transport items back to camp aided their efforts.

After finding ample food and water sources, they worked to ensure they had shelter. The two WoRMs helped to build burrows. Wormillian could dig like no other WoRM. Wormella was also an excellent digger and had an extraordinary mind for designing subterranean and above-ground structures. Before long, they all had large comfortable nests and an above-ground meeting hall that Wormella's mentor Archiant would have been proud to say he designed.

Before they entered the portal, Wormella and Wormillian shed their skin to wrap up the bodies of their dead heroes. The tight waterproof wrapping kept the bodies secure through their harrowing arrival on the moon. They buried Shebee and Flyhero on the shore close to the portal and placed a monument at the site to commemorate their lives and the brave way they died. They put the graves close to the wormhole to remember what they left behind—death and destruction. Inscribed on the monument was: *The mortal and cybernetic remains of Shebee and Flyhero lie underneath these pads. Two brave insectoids who gave their lives for us comrades.*

The Fabled Fourteen were political exiles fleeing Poo-ponic from a desire to escape the totalitarian dict*ant*orship of the cruel Antilla. The third order of business was to organize their new colony to avoid the political and economic pitfalls leading to the decline of society on Poo-ponic. Anthiery and Antianna brought all fourteen new colonists together in Wormella's meeting hall to plan how to rule the moon. Their first pronouncement was that all future decisions of the fourteen required unanimity, no matter how long it took. Next, they wrote a constitution and a bill of rights. They planned a Congress with a Hive of Representatives and Senate requiring equal male and female insectoids of all seven insect families. Their laws prohibited any executive branch or President, avoiding an *ant*ocracy or other *insect*ocracy. Congress also required representation from each cyborg family. The group also spelled out the responsibilities of each cyborg family, and all insectoids were to be taught from creation to respect all other cyborgs. These tasks mirrored the work-related chores each family had fulfilled on Poo-ponic, with ANTs still acting as supervisors of various work-related activities. Anthiery asserted, "No despot will ever crush our community, oppressing us with unwarranted impunity!"

They abolished the class system and banned the words alphas, betas, and chi. Antianna expounded, "Never again shall we allow any insect to be ranked or given no respect."

After fourteen ayes, Anthiery moved on to the next item on the agenda and tapped Antianna on the back.

"Anthiery and I approached the others, and together we agreed that all future cyborg WoRMs would have six tiny legs. We will induct them into the insectoid class, *Cybernetic Insecta*," announced Antianna.

"But we didn't tell you, Mill and Mella, that we wanted to have a special ceremony to present you with legs," added Anthiery. "On behalf of the rest of us, please accept these clip-on legs that I constructed." He handed them to the WoRMs.

"Oh, that means a lot to us." Wormella, who, like all WoRMs, had experienced her share of discrimination on Poo-ponic.

Wormillian helped Wormella clip hers on, then adjusted his own, and a fluffy fragrance flooded the hall. "Thank you, everyone. We'll cherish them and wear them always."

"I'll take that as a unanimous acclamation, and unless there are any objections, I'll close the session now," declared Anthiery.

The Fabled Fourteen met again after completing the Constitution and Bill of Rights drafts.

Beebuzz stood at attention, looked at the others, and shook his antennae to broadcast clearly. "Twelve of my colleagues and friends asked me to propose a clause to the Constitution, which I am delighted to do. The proposal is that Bilaluna should have a ceremonial queen. We agree that we should have a monarch that is a queen BEE, and we wish to anoint Princess Beetrix as our new Queen immediately." He turned, looked at Beetrix, and queried. "What do you say, Trix?"

Beetrix jolted and nearly slid out of her chair, discharging a shocking scent. "Indeed, I am a princess, but not yet a queen. I'm stunned and quite chilled. But if you want me to be your Queen, I am honored and thrilled." She had always dreamed of this day from the time she was a young pupa, but she was utterly astonished when it came.

Bugabelle elaborated, "This is a ceremonial position that each Queen keeps until the selection of another Queen. She will remain Queen until her death or her chosen time of abdication."

Anthiery explained further, "This post recognizes the essential role BEEs play in food production for the colony. It also reminds male ANTs that although they may be supervisors, a female BEE is the moon's figurehead."

Antianna added, "We realize that, in time, the public might idolize the Queen. Yet, she will have no more political power than any other insectoid."

Wormella chimed in, "The Queen's chief duty will be to organize formal events to uplift the spirits of all in the colony.

She will also ensure all members of Congress and the nation uphold the Constitution."

Beebuzz asked Beetrix to stand, pulled out a beautiful multi-colored robe Bugabelle and Bugbert had weaved, and draped it over Beetrix's shoulders. "And so, without further ado, fuss, or *theatrix*, on behalf of my esteemed colleagues, I anoint you, Queen Beetrix."

In response, Queen Beetrix buzzed her wings briefly and proclaimed, "I am honored to be your Queen, my friends. I will always do everything I can to uphold the Constitution and strive to raise the spirits of all insectoids on Bilaluna." She smiled at all her friends. "I recognize too, although I am named Queen, I have no more power than any other resident of this moon, whom I am only here to serve." In her state of shock, she forgot to use Antspearean speech or any rhymes at all.

Yet, moved by Beetrix's words, the others vowed to write them down as the pledge each future Queen would make at her coronation.

All the thirteen others had noticed Queen Beetrix had used no rhymes when she gave her address. Although it was unconventional for such a formal statement, it did not offend them. When the group discussed the speech later, they described it as refreshing. They immediately decided rhyming was no longer a required element of formal speech or written prose. They did not ban old Antspearean verse altogether, but it was neither required nor encouraged. Right then was born the concept of insectoid free speech, by which one could say whatever one wanted, whichever way they chose.

When someone suggested she needed a crown, the humble BEE said, "No crown, cause it will mess up my hair. A throne would be nice, though, as I have outgrown all the seats around here!"

They added provisions in the Constitution to guard against the government taking over the press as a propaganda machine, as happened on Poo-ponic. The addition reinforced their sound ideas about freedom of the press, and in honor of their heroic friend, they called it the *Shebee Clause*. The concepts of free speech and freedom of the press became the last two articles of the new constitution.

The Constitution also required fourteen male and fourteen female members, with two insectoids, one male and one female, elected from each cyborg family to the Hive of Representatives and the Senate. The law demanded *one insectoid, one vote,* and the ballots required each insectoid to vote for all seven families of cyborgs while ensuring equality of the sexes within each family. More important than political equality, the Constitution insisted on a principle of economic equality. They also abolished the concept of currency, and honey, deemed the root of all evil, was no longer produced.

❧ ❧ ❧

Beetrix and Anthiery had an exchange that ended the last session on the Constitution.

Queen Beetrix commented about honey, "Although we BEEs have always made honey, it shouldn't have been a currency or the evil idol it became. We can, and will, live on fortified nectar to reduce this temptation."

Anthiery spewed an abashing aroma. "Yes, Queen, as an ANT, I am ashamed of my phylogenetic family. Had we not been so greedy for honey, we would still be on Poo-ponic." *We must prevent that from ever happening again.*

Beetrix buzzed. "Although Antilla was greedy, I don't think it was only greed that drove him to such malevolence."

Anthiery put a claw to his head and pondered, "True, he had a lust for both honey and power. But more than that, he lacked empathy for his fellow insects and used whoever he could to achieve his selfish goals." *I remember my early teenage years when I realized Antilla's selfishness, and I could no longer be his friend.*

Beetrix raised her stinger. "And he found followers that echoed his uncaring views."

"Sometimes I think about Poo-ponic and how things are going," responded Anthiery. *It scares me to think about what Antilla will do next.*

"I can't see things getting better unless they depose Antilla," deduced Beetrix. "His party does not seem to stand up against him or for what is right."

"I guess that's true," added Anthiery. "Poo-ponic paid the price not only for the actions of one evil leader but also for those who enabled him." *It takes more than one ANT to exert tyranny. That Decadant is no choirboy, and Antrich is the worst.*

Beetrix bowed slightly toward Anthiery and Antianna. "You and Antianna have done Bilaluna proud. The ANT legacy here could not be stronger."

"Thank you, Trix," gushed Anthiery. "That means a lot to Antianna and me." After a brief pause, he scratched his head and continued, "Sometimes I feel like we didn't think things through too well with creating so many cyborgs on Poo-ponic. I suggest we limit the numbers on Bilaluna." *We'll do better here.*

"And with no Antilla and no honey, our future looks bright," concluded Beetrix.

All insectoids received equal amounts of fortified nectar

besides the free-access, unprocessed food sources that they foraged themselves. If times were good, they stored nectar for bad times. If times were bad, everyone in the colony suffered equally. The only trading allowed was recipes for different ways to spice up the nectar, which they encouraged if everyone kept their basic quota of raw nectar.

After writing the Constitution, the Fabled Fourteen simplified the document for the future public by writing the following summary about insectism, which was the basis for the Constitution:

The Six Principles of Insectism

1. *All insectoids are created equal and will respect each member of their own and other insectoid families, which will include WoRMs and BUGs.*

2. *All insectoids are entitled to liberty and the opportunity for success and happiness.*

3. *All insectoids will be served by a Congress of equal numbers of male and female peers from each insectoid family, elected by all insectoids (one insectoid, one vote).*

4. *Insectoids will respect the Queen BEE as a leader, but neither she nor any other insectoid or group shall rule with power exceeding the Congress of Insectoids.*

5. *No insectoid family will ever again be ranked, and the words alphas, betas, and chi are banned from use.*

6. *Insectoids will never have a currency, honey is banned, and all insectoids will receive equal amounts of nectar and the same comfortable accommodations.*

In a tribute to their rhyming ancestors, they also vowed to teach young insectoids the following song:

Every bug is equal, and no ranking is allowed.
We all strive to be happy and never to be cowed.
We will elect a Congress and love our precious Queen.
We'll neither worship honey nor forget the wrongs we've seen.

Because the moon was much smaller than Poo-ponic, Congress kept the colony population low, so it never exceeded 1,000 insectoids. With such a sparse population, all insectoids knew each other well. There was a family-like congeniality, where the cyborgs worked together and needed to take care of each other. Except for a few minor arguments, the society was the idyllic colony for which they had hoped.

One beautiful hexay, while on a short walk with Antianna, Queen Beetrix buoyed, "Bilaluna is a place you want to raise offspring. And the locale where you want to retire. Heck, it's a place you never want to leave, not that there's anywhere else to go." *I love being a queen BEE in a society that is so peaceful.*

"Yes, Queen, it is amazing how society achieves such harmony when you understand and apply the principles of a solid constitution." Antianna dribbled a vibrant bouquet.

Beetrix slid her robe off her shoulders to enjoy the rays of the solar star. "Oh, please call me Trix, like you used to. You, of all insectoids, have earned that privilege. And we went through some hard times to learn the lessons we did." *I'm so pleased our friendship has remained strong through good times and bad.*

"Sometimes, I wonder what Antuna would think about

this place," pondered Antianna. "Anthiery says she was the original proponent of insectism."

Beetrix stopped and stared at Antianna. "Yes, her and Beefirst." *She taught Antuna the rightful path.*

"Of course, Beefirst too. I guess that was very ANT-like of us to forget a bee," blushed Antianna.

"I'll forgive you this time. And Anthiery's not quite Antilla yet," joked Beetrix. *I'm glad we have an Antunite among us. His genes will ensure altruism exists among ANTs.*

Antianna laughed. "Now look who's dissing ANTs."

Beetrix tossed her robe over Antianna's head. "As long as our insults are in jest, our moon will continue to orbit." *And our society will survive intact.*

Antianna pulled the robe over her shoulders to try it on for size. "Antuna and Beefirst would be proud of our new orbit," concluded Antianna.

"Indeed," responded Beetrix, snatching back the robe.

The colony achieved harmony they never knew on Pooponic. There was no fighting, no killing, and insectoids lived in peace. Other than the equal amounts of nectar they received for nourishment and the identical comfortable lodgings they each had in their nests, they required nothing except the tools they used for work. Reports suggest there was no hunger, no greed, and they reached a genuine sense of sharing the moon, with unparalleled solidarity among cyborgs—imagine that!

When the colonists arrived, Bilaluna had beautiful rainforests, rivers, and old-growth forests dominating the woodlands. The Fabled Fourteen did not notice when they landed on Bilaluna that there were no tiny insects. Insects and many diverse plant seeds had passed through the wormhole after the original meteorite strike created the portal. The insects helped to create the conditions that developed the rainforest. Unknown, during the Great Small Insect War on Poo-ponic, some insects tried on three occasions to escape the planet by transiting through the wormhole. Unfortunately, each time they entered the wormhole, they allowed significant quantities of gases used as chemical warfare by the insectoids to pass through. Since insect life on Bilaluna was untouched by outside influences, exposure to these fumes was devastating. By the third passage through the portal, enough gases came along with the fleeing insects to extinguish all insect life on Bilaluna. Like Poo-ponic, Bilaluna had no fungi that broke down deadwood or plants. So, with no insects, the soil quality worsened. The forests remained but became more and more static. The existing trees continued to grow, but few new plants broke through.

Untouched by civilization for hexennia, many trees had become massive. Some sequoias were so gigantic that it took all the Fabled Fourteen holding claws with limbs stretched to span the circumference. Hit by lightning at some point, one tree had a large hole scorched in its trunk that three of the largest RoAChs walking side by side could traverse. Despite the lingering charcoal scent, the towering giant was as healthy as ever and did not topple.

These massive sky-scraping timbers had few offspring to replace them as they tumbled. Yet, the forests were robust enough to support themselves without logging. It was only when tree cutting began that the lands displayed resistance to any efforts for reforestation. As there were few insectoids on Bilaluna for the first few hexuries, the effects on the forests were not apparent since they did not need to cut many trees to make the nectar that fed them. But as the number of cyborgs increased, the forest showed the effects of over-logging. As on Poo-ponic, Bilaluna's spent land expanded and took over large swaths of forests and jungles. Yet, it took hexuries until the number of insectoids reached a level that had a significant impact.

～ ～ ～

Hearing that there were problems in the forests, the Queen BEE, who reigned about five hexuries after insectoids arrived on Bilaluna, toured the woodlands. Senant, a powerful voice in the Senate, escorted Queen Threebee on her excursion.

"Senant wasn't a crew supposed to replant this area," barked Threebee. "Where are all the saplings we cultivated?" *I can't believe our plans have failed so badly.*

"We can take seeds and grow them in greenhouses," explained Senant, "but they all die when we replant them in the wild."

"That makes no sense." Threebee radiated a fuming fragrance. "Why do they grow in greenhouses but not here?" *Spent land expansion is the direst problem facing our community.*

"It seems the seedlings like growing in pots, but not the forests," concluded Senant. "But no one knows why."

"Look, I think one survived," exclaimed Threebee. She reached down to feel the branches of the small sapling. "Oh no, I've killed it!" she cried as the needles trickled off the small tree.

"No, that's just what happens," described Senant. "They dry out, lose their needles, and die, no matter what we do."

"But why?" questioned the Queen. "The trees near the colony survive." *Why can't we solve this problem?*

"We haven't quite figured that out. Healthy trees seem to release chemicals that keep the soil in good enough condition to maintain the forest. But once we remove a tree, the soil quality quickly deteriorates."

"And why are the WoBBs taking down every tree?" shouted Threebee. "They're supposed to take every alternate one." *Their actions violate our Constitution, which I'm pledged to protect. This is unacceptable!*

"They did that for hexuries, but it didn't make a difference," explained Senant.

"What about trees that sprout new roots and twin themselves?" *I see even they don't survive!*

"Right, that process doesn't work," rued Senant. "It seems they're missing an important element we can't figure out."

Despite the civil harmony on Bilaluna, over the hexuries, the existing old-growth forests took a severe hit because reforestation was not possible. The one thing preventing a promised Utopian society was the same thing that had destroyed their mother planet—an environmental crisis. The leaders of the cyborg colony were not blind to the effects their nectar-producing activities were having on the environment; they were just at a loss on what to do about it. It was more vulnerable, with Bilaluna having a much smaller land mass than Poo-ponic.

Over the hexuries, with the growing population and increased nectar production needed to meet the greater demand, the spent lands expanded to 40% of the moon's surface. During Threebee's reign, an unusual incident utterly stunned the entire community on Bilaluna. They discovered three strange cyborgs, two ANTs, and a BUG, soaking wet, dazed, and distraught, close to the monument to Shebee and Flyhero. One ANT was elderly, and the other ANT and the BUG were post-pupal teens. On discovery that the three had come through the wormhole from Poo-ponic, Queen Threebee immediately granted them an audience.

Senant first met the Poo-ponic refugees and brought them before the Queen.

"Welcome, Poo-ponic friends. I have heard that you have had quite an ordeal," acknowledged Threebee.

Antoria bowed low before the Queen. "Thank you, your majesty. I am Antoria, and this is Gretant and Thunbug," she said. *We were cold and wet, but we survived.*

The Queen motioned for Antoria to straighten up. "Oh, please call me Threebee. Yes, I know, a history professor and two young activists. You sound like insectoids we need on Bilaluna."

Gretant curtsied. "Well, that's good, because I don't think we can go back."

Threebee patted Gretant on the shoulder. "No, I expect not. I heard you and Thunbug tried to fight Poo-ponic's climate crisis, but you were too late."

Thunbug kissed the Queen's claw when she extended it to him. "Yes, the atmosphere of Poo-ponic thinned in the last few hexths before we escaped. And we sensed its collapse as we transited through the portal."

Threebee put her front claws together. "I noticed that Poo-ponic darkened yester-hexay as it traversed our sky, and its gray-green hue changed to black. And I knew something terrible had happened."

"Yes, Antilla did his best to run Poo-ponic into the ground, and he finally succeeded," grieved Gretant.

"Antilla! You don't mean to say that tyrant is still the leader?" puzzled Senant.

"She meant Antilla III, Antilla's second clone," clarified Antoria. *To our dismay, he replicated himself.*

Threebee put her claws to her head. "He extended his rule."

"Yes, and each was as brutal as the other," added Antoria. *And together, they destroyed Poo-ponic.*

Threebee pointed to the beautiful lands all around them. "Well, I hope you'll find Bilaluna is much more hospitable. And our Congress works hard to protect our citizens," she contended.

"Congress?" wondered Gretant. "I thought you were the ruler."

Threebee grinned. "No, my position is only ceremonial, and the Congress rules our society," she explained.

"So is Senant here the President?" asked Thunbug.

"Oh, no." Senant laughed. "I am one of twenty-eight Senators, and together with another twenty-eight Representatives of the Hive, we rule together."

"That's wonderful," approved Antoria, sighing at the thought of a peaceful, democratic society. "We're going to love it here." *It sounds like Poo-ponic after our ancestors atoned for Antuna's demise.*

Threebee looked in the direction from where the visitors came. "For hexuries, we did our best to ensure no one approached the wormhole. We feared that someone might return to Poo-ponic and alert Antilla we are here."

"How did you manage that for so long?" posed Thunbug.

"It's next to our sacred gravesites," explained Senant. "And the exact area is adjacent to a gorge. But we also marked the shoreline as a toxic site containing carcinogenic materials, which keeps everyone away."

"Now, you don't have to worry about Antilla, but Poo-ponic itself may now be toxic," warned Gretant.

Threebee bowed down and emitted a faint azure aroma.

"I forgot you lost all your family and friends. I am so sorry for your loss."

"Yes, we are all devastated, and your sentiments are welcome," thanked Antoria. "But please give us a promise that you will do what you can to prevent such a tragedy from ever happening here," she pleaded. *History often repeats itself.*

"We will, I promise," attested Threebee. "Now, get some nectar and some rest." Threebee pointed to the dining hall next to the burrows.

"What no honey?" enquired a famished Thunbug.

"Don't worry, you'll love our fortified nectar," said the Queen with a wink over her compound eye.

CHAPTER 11

UNEXPECTED GUESTS

As the celestial ball of fire scorches the veneer,

'tis the sage that strips to the silvery undercoat
and allows the broth to season.

And though the unripe may be green,

like copper mixed with soupy air, their
hue may early stew with reason.

AFTER MAKING HER promise to Antoria, Queen Threebee requested to make an address at the next session of Congress.

She urged the members, "We must do something about the spent lands. Our world depends on it. I have seen first-claw how our forests are declining, and I have also learned about the utter devastation that has stricken Poo-ponic, and I made a solemn promise it will not happen here." *I dislike many things about our moon's environmental conditions, but I'm hopeful we can reverse the trend.*

Senant expressed his agreement, "Yes, Antoria mentioned we should bring together our sharpest minds to figure this out. I know several self-taught scientists and educators that have been keen to create an institute of higher learning, as they had on Poo-ponic."

Threebee clapped her claws together. "I agree. Gretant told us how courageous the scientists were that tried to save Poo-ponic. This plan is a wonderful idea, as long as we ensure no insectoid can corrupt any discoveries for an evil purpose." *I am mindful of the potential political pitfalls that science and industry sometimes trigger.*

In response, Congress voted to open an all-insectoid insti-tute for advanced study of environmental issues, called BITE for Bilaluna's Institute of Technology for the Environment. They hoped that BITE would have the teeth to solve the spent land problem to accomplish their goals. Antoria became the first Chancellor of BITE and acquired the resources she needed to write the thesis she planned. She wrote her manuscript on pre-cyborg history and a detailed account of the last hexuries on Poo-ponic. Gretant helped by writing a foreword about ancient Poo-ponic history recounting the details of Antuna's story, with specifics passed down to her by her relatives. Both she and Thunbug continued to study environmental issues and later became professors at BITE. They brought awareness to the public about the dangers of climate change, and they trained the next generation of environmental scientists and activists.

❦ ❦ ❦

Soon after BITE hired them, Gretant met Thunbug in his new office.

Gretant checked out his new digs and the view from his

window. "Thunbug, we have to step up our efforts to reduce forest degradation and spent lands." *I am depressed and fear the spent land problem on Bilaluna could mushroom into the disastrous proportions seen on Poo-ponic. And Antoria's recent death also has me down.*

Thunbug reached out to her. "I see you have been extra troubled since Antoria died."

Gretant held Thunbug's claw, wafting indigo incense. "Yes, she gave me the final draft of her manuscript on pre-cyborg history on her deathbed, and I just read it." A tear came to her eye. *I can't believe she's gone!*

Thunbug looked down. "It is a tragic story."

Gretant nodded. "But I feel she didn't quite finish it." *It seemed to me the ending was too abrupt.*

"Why do you say that?" questioned Thunbug.

Gretant raised her claws. "I don't know, she was getting to their key contributions to society, but she didn't finish." *I guess it died with her.*

"She was a historian, and she likely wanted to make a point about the importance of the continuity of society. And how tragically this entire branch of our history ended," Thunbug supposed.

"You might be right. But there was something else I can't get my claws around," Gretant pondered. *It makes me think about Bilaluna's poor soil.*

"But you started by talking about doing more for the environment," noted Thunbug.

Gretant smiled. "Yes, while reading Antoria's thesis, I had a feeling that we should make more efforts to work the soil to improve forest health." *She inspires me so much.*

Thunbug made a digging motion with his claws. "You mean having the WoBBs and WoRMs dig it up and turn it over?"

"Exactly, and the seedlings will have a better chance of surviving," explained Gretant. "My research also supports this idea." *Something in Antoria's book has made me understand my recent research could have critical applications.*

"So, your studies of soil chemistry are paying off?" asked Thunbug.

"Well, you know Bilaluna scientists had to start from scratch when the colonists arrived here, and BITE only opened when we arrived," said Gretant. "My lab research in environmental chemistry is very new." *But I think it may help in time.*

"So, what in the soil is so important?" asked Thunbug. "My research shows that nitrogen is important for plant photosynthesis."

"I determined that it's not nitrogen that is critical for plants, but the nitrates it produces." Gretant smiled. *This guy seems to read my mind. We're such a great team.*

"That's interesting," said Thunbug, "but what does it have to do with working the soil?"

"I found that infertile soil was full of nitrogen and toxic nitrites," explained Gretant. *I so enjoy our brainstorming.*

"But you said nitrates were important for plants," puzzled Thunbug.

"Yes, turning over the soil exposes it to oxygen that converts toxic nitrites to nitrates." *I think that may be key.*

Thunbug paused for a moment. "Is that why the gardeners found seedlings do well in pots?"

Gretant, excited that Thunbug had zeroed in on her main conclusion, said, "Yes, digging up soil and putting it in pots exposes the soil to more oxygen from the air and produces nitrates." *We just need to do the same in the forests.*

"That's great, but I think we should also do something about essence extraction. It kills too many plants," proposed Thunbug. "My research shows that essence is critical for bringing amino acids, sugars, and nutrients throughout the plant."

"What if the BEEs could take less essence from the plants, say half? Then more might survive, and you could use them again and again," suggested Gretant. *We can beat this thing.*

"Yes, the forests and jungles would be healthier, and you would get more nectar in the long run," concluded Thunbug.

Gretant smiled and headed for the door. "We should meet with Threebee as soon as possible and make these recommendations. By the way, come check out my office later. I got a much better view than you."

❀ ❀ ❀

The Queen loved Gretant and Thunbug's ideas. She encouraged Congress to mandate soil turning and recyclable nectar extraction, with new teams of WoBBs and WoRMs working on the former and the BEEs on the latter. The programs were successful within the unspent lands and improved the vegetation in the jungles and forests. Like the bamboo stocks and fan palms, ferns, lilies, hostas, and begonias flourished. In time, the old-growth forests looked more diverse and healthier, with new growth filling in spaces and replacing old plants and trees. It happened at a rate that beautified the jungles and forests and stopped spreading unspent lands for generations. It seemed Gretant, Thunbug, and the late Antoria saved the moon from its path to destruction. The WoBBs and WoRMs could not do much in the spent lands. The soil was too hard and resistant to any efforts for rejuvenation. It was like using shovels and augers to break through well-cured cement, and nothing they tried worked.

⁂

Gretant and Thunbug continued to encourage more sustainable forestry practices and efficient energy methods during their lifetimes. They introduced conservation techniques like mulching of unused tree branches that helped improve soil quality and constructing terraces to prevent water erosion. They kept seed banks to ensure plant species' survival. They also encouraged the engineers to develop high-efficiency double-burning furnaces to reduce tree destruction. These efforts continued to maintain and improve the unspent lands. Society was so grateful for their actions that the two of them received a special environmental award when they retired from BITE.

An aged Threebee invited the two retired professors to the Grand Hall for a special ceremony.

Threebee stood up from her throne. "Gretant and Thunbug, it is my privilege to bestow upon you Bilaluna's highest honor, the 'Best Luminaries of Bilaluna' award. In receiving this award, you will join our most illustrious insectoids. This distinguished list includes your friend Antoria, the Fabled Fourteen, and their fallen heroes. With this award, all will remember you forever as insectoid BLOBs," she proclaimed.

Gretant bowed before her monarch, oozing a puffy perfume. "Queen, you don't know how much this means to us. As we aged, it never occurred to us we would become BLOBs. Thunbug and I lived through adversity and crawled through the darkest of tunnels." She spread her arms wide. "But on Bilaluna, we found the light. It has been our lives' work to make that light even brighter. We helped Bilaluna, and we are all the better for it." *I believe we will avoid Poo-ponic's fate.*

Thunbug bowed and tipped the hat he found for the occasion. "We are grateful for this award, and we wish to thank everyone for the tribute. We have helped halt the spread of spent lands and have lent a claw or two towards making the unspent lands even more beautiful." He pointed towards the spent lands. "But there is much more to do. Both Gretant and I will continue to train future generations of Bilalunans to do the same."

Gretant looked up at Thunbug, admiring how distinguished he looked in his new hat. "My good friend has forever been both a gentle-BUG and a scholar and my inspiration. This recognition is long overdue." *I'd be nowhere without him.*

Thunbug blushed and smiled back at Gretant. "There would not be Thunbug without Gretant, or Gretant without Thunbug," he added. "We are a team, lifelong friends, and partners in protest and action. And now we are BLOBs, joined in adulation so that we will stick together forever."

～ ～ ～

Beemajor was the principal of BITE about the 9th hexury after cyborg insects arrived on Bilaluna. Despite the innovations made by Gretant and Thunbug in retaining the spent lands at about 40%, there was still much to be done to reverse deforestation and soil degradation. Beemajor was pleased to hire Natbug, the great-granddaughter of Thunbug, who was a rising star in environmental science. Eager to learn about the young scientist's research, Beemajor joined her on one of her field study excursions to the spent lands.

"Natbug, I am so glad that you continued in academia and joined us at BITE," shared Beemajor.

"Thank you for hiring me," said Natbug. "It's been my life's goal to follow in the pod steps of my great grandfather, and I only hope I can have half the impact he and Gretant had." *I am excited to do what I can to help save our beautiful moon.*

"I'm sure you will," assured Beemajor. "It is obvious from your record that you are a brilliant young scientist."

"I have some ideas...." Natbug began, but a loud explosion interrupted her. "What was that!" she cried.

"Quickly cover yourself," exclaimed Beemajor.

Natbug grabbed a large tarp that she had just unpacked and pulled it over herself and Beemajor. No sooner than they sheltered themselves, several feet of dirt rained down. Luckily, Natbug had her lab equipment nearby, which with the tarp created a tent-like air pocket, allowing the submerged pair to breathe.

"We've been buried alive," surmised Beemajor, shaking from the panic.

"Well, we have enough air for now," muttered Natbug. "And there are two shovels in my lab pack. I always knew this stuff supported my livelihood, but now more than ever." *My mom always said I was levelheaded and resourceful. Let's see how much it helps during a disaster.*

"Wow, you come prepared," complimented Beemajor, but with certain doom still on his mind, he asked, "But I'm worried about how long this air will hold out and how deep we are."

"We'd better shovel, or we'll be digging our graves," joked Natbug. *Not funny, I guess. Humor is not my strong suit.*

"I'm already finding it difficult to breathe." Beemajor

coughed. "Quick, pass me a shovel.," he urged, puffing a bal-
looned bouquet.

"Don't dig too fast, sir," advised Natbug. "We need to con-
serve air." *Don't panic. I've got this.*

"But we gotta get out of here!" Beemajor panicked. "I can't
breathe. I'm feeling faint."

"Wait, I have some soil sample tubes," said Natbug. "I'll
push one up towards the surface. It'll tell us how deep we are,
and if it's long enough, it will provide us some air." *A scientist
needs to have creative solutions to the problems at hand, no matter
how dire.*

Beemajor gasped for air. "But won't it just fill with dirt
when you shove it up?"

"No, I'll cap it first and then push the top off with my tape
measure," responded Natbug, one step ahead. *I wish he'd relax.*

As she pulled the tube out of her pack, Beemajor collapsed.

"Don't worry, Principal. I'll get us out of here," Natbug
cried, gasping as she pushed the tube skyward. *Now, where is my
tape measure?* She felt around in her pack. *Darn it. I already put
the tape measure on my work belt.*

Although the tube was in place and fully extended, she
staggered as she pulled on the tape measure. She took one last
deep breath and poked the tape measure into the tube. She collapsed on her back, gasping as she pushed the button that auto-
matically extended the tape measure 12 feet. Within a hexond,
the end breached the top of the sample tube, and air rushed
into their makeshift tent. Natbug gulped air with her spiracles, regained her composure, and began administering CPR
to Beemajor. She dragged him close to the tube and continued
to compress his thorax. Natbug was exhausted and about to

give up when Beemajor coughed, puffed, and inhaled deeply on his own.

"Welcome back, Principal Beemajor." *Now let me dig.*

She hastily dug them out from underground. They later learned that the soil that covered them was a tsunami of dirt that spewed out of a crater formed by a large meteorite strike several hundred miles away. The impact occurred near the center of the spent lands, so the blast injured no one. Yet, the soil debris spread for hundreds of miles in every direction and destroyed extensive forests in the unspent lands. Flying dust caused thick clouds in the atmosphere, worsening vegetation throughout the moon.

~ ~ ~

After returning from his excursion with Natbug, Beemajor met with the Queen to report on the catastrophe. "Although most insectoids escaped injury, the large meteorite has marred Bilaluna's surface and demolished a good chunk of our remaining forest," he said. *I'm sorry to report bad news.*

"I am so glad the meteorite strike did not harm you," stated Beewise, the new Queen of Bilaluna.

"Yes, I owe my life to Natbug," replied Beemajor thankfully. "With her quick thinking and fast actions, she saved us both." *I am humbled and highly gratified to have been saved by our young female recruit to BITE.*

"But much of the forest was not so fortunate," noted Beewise. "I urge you and BITE scientists to do everything you can. We've lost so much forest when we had so little, to begin with."

Beemajor lowered his head, secreting a spindly scent. "It now appears the spent lands have expanded to cover half of our moon," he agreed. He was distraught at this news and doubly motivated to reverse the trend. *Don't worry. We'll solve this.*

"This is unacceptable. We need to do something, but what?" implored Beewise.

Beemajor defended, "We are working on it, your Majesty. Luckily, the forests in the unspent lands are still quite robust." *I'm sure Natbug will figure it out.*

"That's good to hear. But we need to expand the woodlands," beseeched Beewise. "Last night, Antuna's spirit came to me in my dreams. She was with her friends and insects from all families, even termites and spiders. Three enormous beings, the likes of which I had never seen, surrounded them. I thought the giants would squash them, but they released them into the forest."

"What does it mean?" asked Beemajor. *It seems odd to me that Antuna came to a BEE.*

"I'm not sure, but I felt that we all must work together to save our forests."

Leaving, Beemajor bowed more deeply. "We will do our utmost to solve this problem, Queen," he promised. "And with Natbug on our team, I am very hopeful."

Unbeknownst to the inhabitants of Bilaluna, the meteorite strike also created a new wormhole—it opened a portal to Planet Earth. The impact was so violent it disrupted the ancient wormhole to Earth and split its path from Poo-Ponic with a branch extending towards the moon. No one knew the wormhole existed, so it surprised them when hexades later, three unassuming young Earthling humans appeared from the wormhole and changed life on Bilaluna forever.

Although the BITE institute concentrated on environmental studies, it allowed considerable academic freedom and pockets of expertise developed in other areas. Ironically, studies in the diverse areas of astronomy and linguistics, not the environment, played critical roles in turning around their moon's fortune.

Beemajor arranged a meeting with Queen Beewise to discuss new programs at BITE. "Your majesty, I would like to suggest that we open another faculty within BITE," posed Beemajor. *I've never been so nervous about a proposal.*

Beewise rubbed her claws together. "Oh, is it something that will help with our environmental problems?"

"Not exactly," replied Beemajor, releasing a fluttering fragrance. *I hope she supports this!*

"What is it then?" demanded Beewise.

Beemajor looked skyward. "Well, we now have a clever group of investigators interested in astronomy and extraterrestrial life. Their research will be critical if Bilaluna's environmental crisis becomes so dire the inhabitants might have to leave Bilaluna," he explained. *It's our last chance option.*

"I hope you're not giving up on the environment?" questioned Beewise.

"No, we continue to work hard on that," Beemajor defended. "Only we have had little success. So, we need to think about alternatives," he justified. *Please don't say no. We need this!*

Beewise shook Beemajor's claw. "I like the idea, and I've always enjoyed studying the stars. I will recommend it to Congress for approval."

Even though it occurred long ago, everyone on Bilaluna was very conscious of the devastation on Poo-ponic. They were all descendants of the few defectors that had escaped the planet. They also received frequent reminders of Poo-ponic's demise as the dark orb traversed from the Western to the Eastern horizon on each hexay. The ebony spherical wasteland cast an enormous shadow on the small moon. Although Poo-ponic's dark image blotted the noon sky, Bilaluna's celestial dome was ablaze with starlight at night. Since the insectoids could see in the dark, they did not need artificial light. There was no light pollution to mask the night sky. Poo-ponic and Bilaluna were near the tail end of a spiral galaxy at the apex of a funnel of stars that fanned out in all directions above them. A multi-layered halo of celestial rings surrounded Poo-ponic and gave a fuzzy glow to the stars. They also changed hues, with the component gases acting as prisms that diffracted the light emitted through them into a rainbow of colors. Their night sky was like a giant, decorated fir tree on its end, adorned by spiraling multi-colored lights that twinkled every night.

After twilight, with the backdrop of the Aurora Borealis-like sky, Beewise and Beemajor inaugurated the opening of FAST, the Faculty of Astronomic Sciences and Technology.

As she cut the ribbon, the Queen quipped, "I know this place will work FAST to discover the secrets of our universe!"

"As we stand out here under the night sky and take in its splendid beauty, we hope there might be intelligent life out there," posed Beemajor, relieved that Beewise and Congress appreciated astronomical sciences.

Beewise stared up at the heavens and effused a shimmering

smell. "Our night sky is brilliant and magnificent, as are the scientists BITE hired to run FAST. I urge them to learn as much as possible and scan our universe for signs of life. I am sure there is more out there than a breath-taking sight."

A key goal of FAST was to find another world with an atmosphere that could sustain insectoid life. Although they never observed another suitable nearby planet and had no way to get there if they did, they soon made another exciting discovery. Hexs after the massive meteorite impact, a small group of ANT astronomers picked up a faint bleep from a satellite deep in space. After trying to enhance the signal and focus on the correct frequencies of the beacon's transmission, they zoomed in on the message. Soon after, they deciphered the message. The signal conveyed a digital communication made up of zeros and ones, standard human digital computer code.

Beemajor streamed a festive fragrance, "We have received a message from deep space that likely comes from a far-away planet. Our team is working non-stop to decode the message so that we can learn from other intelligent life in the universe." *I am so proud I pushed to establish FAST.*

Queen Beewise rejoiced. "I knew there had to be intelligent life out there. The universe is so vast, and we can't be the only civilization that advanced."

Besides astronomy, BITE also had a group of investigators studying linguistics. An intersection of these two studies became critical to Bilaluna's future. Language, and the study of it, was an essential aspect of life on Bilaluna. Despite sharing a common pheromonal insectoid language, members within a single insectoid family also interacted using their own communication methods. Some dialects were close, like for WoBBs and RoAChs, who used beetle speech, one of the leg-clicking and chirping languages. But there was a more significant difference between the communication of BEEs and WoRMs. BEEs conversed with high-frequency wing flaps or buzzing when not using waggle dance movements. In contrast, WoRMs communicated using low-frequency, full-body wriggling vibrations.

Linguists at the UNIT had spent many hexs studying the similarities and differences between the syntax and grammatical structures of these languages, intending to improve the common insectoid language. Folklore and humor were challenging to translate, so comprehending each other's family dialect enriched the understanding of others in the colony. When the astronomers found the correct wavelength of the satellite message, they realized it contained communications in an alien language. So, they teamed up with the linguists to learn from their expertise in this area.

It took a long time, but the unlikely pairing of scientists deciphered the message, which told them the signal came from Earth. The astronomers discovered the satellite, but the linguists helped the astronomers interpret the communications emitted by the space probe. It excited them to learn the satellite came from the same planet where Antuna's stories said they'd originated. They were even more excited to realize that intelligent life had evolved on the old world about which they only had a slight collective memory. After cracking the coded message, they taught themselves the major Earth human languages the communication had sent with their rudimentary letters and syntax.

Beemajor held up a claw. "Our FAST astronomers and the linguists at BITE have figured it out. The alien's common language appears to be a 'digital' dialect, and it seems they use a finger to communicate, either showing it—1 or not—0," he surmised. *I think that's what they meant.*

Beewise added, "Our linguists say all they could see in their message was zeros and ones, but they finally cracked the code determining what the digits meant."

"We know from the stories of Antuna that we originally came from Earth, but then no species had developed the way we have. Yet it appears this message comes from another species on Earth that subsequently evolved to be highly intelligent," added Beemajor. *Our team is the best!*

Beemajor explained they determined the syntax of Earth's primary human spoken languages from the digital code. The team also concluded that, like Poo-ponic and Bilaluna, the intelligent beings on Earth had a common language. They figured it was the one the humans called English, as most decoded communication used it.

Although they weren't sure if they would ever use it, the scientists constructed a translation device that they called a syntax generator. This machine translated the common insectoid language into Earth's major languages and vice versa. They prepared it in the unlikely event they ever had to communicate with aliens from Earth.

Beemajor announced with a flapping fragrance, "We're ready if Earthlings come to visit. We'll understand when they show us the finger!"

Beewise mused, "Beemajor, you are joking. Right? Did you know that digits the linguists talked about referred to numbers and not fingers?"

"Oh, yes, of course," squirmed Beemajor. *Crap! I'm better than that.*

They did not know whether they would ever meet the human species from Earth. Yet, they did what they could to prepare for an encounter should it ever happen. It amazed them that the space probe had come from the same planet their ancestors had left so long ago. Common insectoids didn't realize that they came from Earth, as the tales of Antuna were now more like fables to them.

⁂

After Beemajor announced BITE's discovery, insectoids across the moon became obsessed with the possibility Earthlings might come to visit. Since they learned the satellite from which they received the message was a flying spacecraft, the cyborgs expected visitors to come from the sky. Many clubs searched the skies for NIFOs or Non-Insectoid Flying Objects, and astronomy became the most popular class at BITE. The lay insectoid population did not have any expectation of Earthlings' characteristics. As the message they received was peaceful, they did not expect Earthlings to come and conquer them. Yet, some insectoids feared the aliens may not be friendly and assumed the pacifist message was a trick.

The Senator and Commander of the RoAChs, Roachboss, argued, "Never trust alien intelligent life—these Earthlings may be too smart for their shells. So, we'll reinforce our armor if Earthlings think they can come and squash us."

Queen Beewise was much more optimistic and emanated a flashy fragrance. "I expect the humans on Earth will enjoy meeting us, and all from the two worlds will become great friends." *We must always think positively. I foresee good things coming from this.*

"Remember, the odds of humans coming to Bilaluna are slim," Beemajor noted, trying to redeem himself from earlier gaffs.

They determined what humans looked like from the digital photos and descriptions of the message, but they were not sure how big they were. Signs appeared showing a giant human foot stepping on scurrying insectoids, with a line crossing through it, as if to say, do not let this happen. Opposing signs showed sociable Earthlings reaching out to cyborgs with a single finger extended to state: *yes, we're friendly*. Although some pushed the authorities to develop a space force to defend against hostile Earthlings, even the youngest insectoids knew the idea was silly, so they dropped the plan.

"Carry a syntax generator and some weapons in case you ever come across an Earthling alien." Queen Beewise advised scouts that canvassed both the unspent and spent lands. *We should be friendly but also careful.*

One of the diplomatic ANTs, Antwell, raised his claw and asked, "Do you expect we'll need to use weapons?"

"It's unlikely, but better to be safe," cautioned Beewise. "Make sure they see them, but only use them in defense." *Why would they send a probe if they wanted to attack us?*

"Of course, we wouldn't want to kill innocent visitors," reassured Roachian, the guard on the team with Antwell.

"Set your syntax generator to Analyze," instructed Beemajor. "When it determines the language, it will switch to Translation mode."

About four hexades after the great meteorite strike, the unbelievable happened. While on a routine expedition deep into the spent territory, a scouting party with Antwell, Gofly (a FLY messenger), and Roachian, stumbled on three Earthling aliens who arrived on Bilaluna. They came not by spacecraft but through the wormhole, providing a portal from Earth to Bilaluna.

Roachian took charge of the situation, warning the others to be cautious.

"These are alien visitors in our midst. Stay on your guard until we determine they have no ill intent." *We should be cautious, but I don't want any rash actions.*

"One of them is moving," cried Gofly. "Maybe it has a weapon. Should I shoot?"

"Don't shoot!" shouted Antwell. "Our mission is to bring aliens back alive."

"Antwell is right," piped in Roachian. "We are scouts, not soldiers. Use your weapons only if attacked." *I don't want any mistakes on my watch.*

"How did they get here?" twitched Gofly. "We're in the middle of the spent land, and they don't have a spacecraft unless it's invisible." He looked all around.

"Let's ask them. I'll activate the syntax generator," replied Antwell, with a broad bouquet. "They seem stunned and helpless, and I don't think they're a threat."

Gofly smiled. "I expect they're children. You know how young ones always look so cute. Look, they're talking to each other."

Although the insectoid scouts drew their weapons, it was

clear they did not need them. After raising them from the crater with telekinesis, they contacted the humans.

"Earthlings, welcome to Bilaluna, Poo-ponic's moon," Antwell released a greeting translated by the syntax generator. "How did you get here? Where is your spacecraft?"

Hawk, one of the male humans, responded, "We, we came through a wormhole. We don't have a spaceship."

"How come we understand you?" the other male asked.

"We're using a syntax generator," responded Antwell. "It determined you were speaking English, and it translates from our language to yours and back to us. This place is Bilaluna, the moon where we live, and I believe it is many million light-hexs from your planet."

"Oh no, the female collapsed," exclaimed Gofly. "Maybe our air is toxic to Earthlings. Give them the oxygen masks."

"Is the girl okay?" asked Roachian. "Do we need to resuscitate her?" *We must bring them to the queen alive.*

The male named Matt spoke, "I think she fainted. She'll be fine in a moment."

Hawk shook his friend lightly. "Celeste, wake up. It's okay; they're friendly."

Celeste opened her eyes and groaned. "What's happening?" she cried. "I can't breathe very well. Those guys look like giant bugs!"

"The air is thin here in the spent lands," explained Antwell. "We'll take you to our colony, where the air is better. Wear these masks to help you breathe. I'll explain to you about our community on our way." Antwell turned and looked towards his fellow scouts. "Gofly, tell the Queen that we are coming with some guests from Earth."

The scouting party knew the aliens were human, as they'd

seen pictures from the space probe. The insectoids assumed they were young, as they did not communicate or interact in a way that conveyed a maturity expected from adult humans.

⁂

The scouting team brought the children before the Queen BEE when they reached the colony. Queen Beewise was a stunning figure, almost twice the size of all the other bees and twice as large as most adult humans.

Beewise addressed the three children, "Welcome to Bilaluna. I assume Antwell has told you about all the members of our society. How we got here, and how we evolved." *I am so thrilled to meet you.*

"Yes, Queen," answered Hawk. "It's an amazing story."

Beewise pointed towards the spent lands, "And you came here through a wormhole as our ancestors did long ago." *My gigantic size must intimidate them, so I must try my best to put them at ease.*

"It was kinda cool," replied Matt. "One second we're on Earth, and the next second we're here. Bam."

"Celeste. Is that your name? You are quite quiet." *I appreciate adventurous girls.*

"I'm a little overwhelmed. I have never met royalty before, your majesty. And you are so big. You all are much bigger than our insects on Earth."

"Please call me Beewise." The Queen laughed and gushed a vivacious vapor. "I am told you are a smart pupa and know a lot about insects." *And I'm even more impressed by female intellect.*

"Yes, I love bugs," replied Celeste. "I mean, I like to study insects, and I even have an ant farm."

"Antwell says you three know much about environmental

issues on Earth," continued Beewise. "Are children responsible for the environment on Earth? Or is it more that you are the ones most affected by any problems?"

"We have many problems on Earth," interjected Hawk. "We call it a climate crisis, and we have studied it at school."

"Our top scientist, Beemajor, tells me you have unique perspectives that might help us with the problems facing Bilaluna." *I'll do my best to make the children feel important. We need their help.*

Beemajor stepped forward. "I assume that since you are Earthlings, you may have some knowledge about how to restore our barren earth. I expect you picked that name for your planet for some reason."

"We'd be happy to help," replied Matt. "But we hope you can help us get back home."

"It shouldn't be difficult. You came through a wormhole, so you just need to return there," responded Beemajor. "We can bring you there once you learn more about us and teach us what you know." *You help us, and we'll take care of you.*

"We're not sure how we got here," added Celeste. "We accidentally entered the wormhole." *It's just so crazy!*

"I don't know about Earth's side of the wormhole," responded Beemajor. "but I expect a meteorite impact on Bilaluna recently created the portal."

CHAPTER 12

NEED TO NURTURE NATURE

Naivety is oft the seed of youthful exuberance.

*Yet, as naivety germinates, it is fodder for
fear, obstruction, and consternation.*

*But we call it worldly when the pureness
of our nature becomes adulterated.*

TO BE A gracious host and recognizing the young visitors' youthful exuberance, Beewise organized an educational excursion for the kids. The expedition, guided by Antwell, allowed them to see the nectar production operations in a fun yet informative way.

Antwell described each part of the tour to the kids. "Here we have WoRMs at work tunneling a new wing of nests." *My Queen trained me to do these kinds of tours, but I never expected I'd be entertaining children, little alone aliens.*

"Whoa, look at those giant worms go! What if they come across rocks?" asked Hawk.

Antwell quivered and replied, "They use vibrations to loosen it and push it out of the tunnel. They are mighty." *I imitate the WoRMs wriggling for the kids' benefit.*

In the main square, they saw many BEEs dancing.

"The BEEs are doing a ceremonial waggle dance. They don't always do it since they can talk pheromonally too, but they are doing it in your honor," explained Antwell. *I hope this impresses the kids.*

"I read about this," exclaimed Celeste. "By their wiggles and the direction they move, they tell other BEEs where the best flowers are. It's amazing to see it up close and magnified!"

"That's right. The number of waggles tells the distance, and the line they take points in the direction they need to go," responded Antwell. *How does she know so much about us?*

"That's so cool," commented Matt. He and Hawk then danced around, mimicking the BEEs.

"Okay, now we will follow the departing BEEs to see them extract essence," Antwell continued. *They need to see the critical activities of our society.*

Hawk shrugged, "What's essence?"

"It's the phloem sap from plants, like chunky fortified nectar," explained Antwell. *I love my job, and I'm always pleased to show my knowledge.*

Celeste licked her lips. "Do you use it to make honey?"

"No, we don't make honey anymore. We eat pressed, fortified nectar," replied Antwell. *I'll let the Queen explain to them why.*

Matt walked forward to get a better look. "They are so efficient, and they don't even disturb the pollen," he remarked.

"Now I'll take you to a tree removal site," continued

Antwell, emitting a steadfast smell. *It's our most impressive work, although destructive.*

"This is so cool. It's like a busy bug town!" exclaimed Hawk.

As they arrived at the tree extraction operation, Antwell continued the commentary. He pointed at some WoBBs popping out of holes in the trees, pushing out sawdust as they came. "Here, the ANT supervisors are directing the WoBBs as to the correct number and angle of boreholes needed to cut down the trees," described Antwell, proud of the work of his ANT family members. *Isn't our teamwork great?*

"Are you cutting the trees for building?" pondered Matt.

"No, we burn them to heat tree sap and generate steam that runs our presses. You'll see that after the FLYs carry you across the forest to the furnaces. There'll be some beautiful waterfalls, gorges, and streams along the way," replied Antwell. *I deflect away from tree burning to a fun aspect of the tour.*

Celeste jumped up and down. "Wait, did you say carried by FLYs? I can't believe it."

When they arrived at the processing center, Antwell continued, "Here are the large furnaces I told you about."

Hawk coughed. "Boy, that's lots of smoke. How many trees do they burn?"

Antwell frowned. "It takes a lot to run the presses." *I don't want to get into details on this matter, so please ask me something else.*

"What do they press?" quizzed Matt.

"They squeeze the nectar from the essence taken from the flowers and plants," responded Antwell. *These kids are so curious. But I must tell them the truth. They need to know so they can help.*

"Does it hurt the plants to take out the essence?" asked Celeste.

Antwell paused, then replied, "It used to, but we reduced how much we take, and they survive now. It's much more efficient than taking a little raw nectar, and we get much more food this way." *But it's a topic I don't want to delve into too deeply.*

"I guess that's why the unspent lands are so beautiful," surmised Hawk, admiring the rainforest jungle behind them.

Antwell pointed to the far side of the presses. "Please walk this way, and you'll see BUGs loading bins of the nectar into RoACHs." *I am glad to discuss our less troubling tasks.*

"Into roaches! Why would they do that?" Matt said, laughing.

"You'll see," he answered.

Celeste stared in awe. "That's a beautiful weave. How do you make those bins?"

"The BUGs make them from their spinning fiber," replied Antwell. "It's like sticky spider web thread that hardens." *They ask me so many questions! I guess that's good.*

Matt spread his arms wide apart. "Now I see why they use RoACHs. They can carry a lot."

"Yes, and they have armored shells to prevent thefts," noted Antwell.

"Do you have to worry about nectar getting stolen?" asked Celeste.

"No, everyone has been friendly on Bilaluna," replied Antwell. "But we employ the designs first used on Poo-ponic, where such worries were well-founded." *I find the depth of their probing so surprising. I thought kids were supposed to be naïve.*

"How fast can they go?" quizzed Hawk.

"You can find out for yourselves," replied Antwell. "Hop on, everyone." *They're going to love this.*

"This is outstanding!" exclaimed Matt, running up to one of them.

The kids encouraged the RoAChs to race through the jungle from stream to stream, which the hosts reported was both a fast and close race. Enthralled by the experience, the young Earthlings conveyed they enjoyed the excursion very much. They noticed a large group of insectoids assembling in the main square outside the burrow as they returned to the colony. As he took them around to the back entrance, Antwell explained the crowd was probably a group of curious onlookers since no one on the moon had ever seen an alien before.

⁂

After the tour, all observed Beewise's astute ability to establish a constructive interaction with the Earthlings. Their meetings resulted in very productive discussions about Bilaluna's current environmental dilemma and ways to overcome it. All those taking part in the consultations acknowledged the young humans' non-judgmental understanding of the difficulties Bilaluna faced. They also appreciated the children's concerted efforts to provide helpful potential remedies. The youngsters understood their deep concern for the looming environmental crisis, mentioning that the people on Earth had some problems that they must solve. They spoke of their clear-cutting in the Amazon Jungle and shared their deep desire to find solutions.

Celeste sighed and remarked to Queen Beewise, "When we arrived in the spent lands, we thought this moon could not support life. But when we reached the unspent lands, we saw how splendid the rainforests and jungles were. It was like you transported us from a desert to the most beautiful oasis in the universe."

Young Hawk also bemoaned about Poo-ponic, "I can't believe that black spot in the sky was ever your home planet.

You say it was more beautiful than these unspent lands. Yet now it looks as barren as our moon."

Beewise and Antwell described two crucial discussions with the young humans that resulted in very positive suggestions. Both their engineers and BITE scientists saw the ideas embodied significant recommendations that they should implement immediately.

Antwell explained, "The brainstorming during the first meeting identified three positive approaches that might aid in our efforts for reforestation." He continued, "These included two novel suggestions from the young Earthling Matt. He first proposed that spent lands could receive needed moisture by digging irrigation ditches to bring water from our large river."

Beemajor, who also attended the conference, added: "He suggested we increase seed production and vegetative spread by cross-pollinating flowering plants and trees."

Matt spent some time on a farm, where he learned about these processes. He recommended that while extracting the essence, the BEEs should not be too efficient and allow pollen to spread from blossom to blossom.

Beewise explained, "He mentioned that cross-pollination would produce additional seeds to generate more trees and plants and that irrigation would soften the spent lands." *I hoped the tour would help the kids relax and encourage them to talk freely about Bilaluna's environmental issues.*

Beemajor continued, "The other young male Earthling named Hawk recommended we dismantle our steam turbines and generate power with impellers turned by moving water from our many waterfalls and turbulent streams."

Antwell noted, "Hawk suggested that by harnessing the power of moving water, we could reduce the burning of trees."

Beewise shivered. "I guess our innate fear of fast-moving water prevented us from considering this unique approach." *I am a little embarrassed by our oversights, but I'm delighted the children can identify them without reservations.*

The first meeting was beneficial, and the engineers and scientists confirmed that each of these ideas could work and improve conditions to a large degree.

It particularly encouraged Beemajor, who released a stirring scent. "Our scientists and engineers are up to the task, and we will make up for our oversights and carry out these original plans as soon as possible."

There was some resistance at first, realizing these humans were young. Still, everyone agreed that their naïve perspectives and heartfelt ideas might help overcome the insectoids' obstructed thinking on these issues.

Beewise held her claws low and declared, "I know these are youngsters, but it appears young Earthlings understand environmental issues and have learned from their own planet's problems. They also care deeply, as if they know the consequences of inaction!" *They see our potential peril.*

※ ※ ※

Near the completion of their first meeting, Beewise discretely asked Antwell to take his team outside into the central square to determine what was going on. Although the human children heard nothing, the Queen could sense a commotion outside the burrow.

"Let me go out first," insisted Roachian. "And bring your weapons. I detect an intense incense."

"The crowd sounds angry, everyone on your guard," said

Antwell, "but please don't be trigger-happy. These are our fellow citizens."

"Roachboss," yelled Roachian. "What's going on here?"

"We do not trust human aliens," replied Roachboss. "We are here to save the Queen from those evil beings that may have a plan to kill her."

"Yes, kill them all," yelled one insectoid in the crowd.

The crowd responded and pushed Roachian, Antwell, and his team against the doors to the burrow. Antwell heard the crowd chanting, "Exoskeletons trump endoskeletons" and "Six legs good, two legs bad." There was an engorged essence in the air.

Before the crowd got any more violent, Antwell jumped up and stood on Roachian's back. "Insectoids of Bilaluna, friends, neighbors, we do not fight on our moon. You know me, and you know Roachian and our team. We are one of you. Trust us!" *I've spent a lot of time with the children, and I know they have no ill intentions. But I must communicate that to all the insectoids. Everyone should just calm down!*

The crowd stopped chanting, and Roachboss spoke again, "But how do we know these evil aliens are not deceiving you?"

"Roachboss, my friends, these are not evil aliens," Roachian responded. "They are children. They came here by accident, and they have provided us with some ideas that might save our spent lands. They did not come to harm us, and they want to help."

Roachboss assumed a stilt stance. "Roachian, you and I have been friends all of our lives, and I have no reason to mistrust you. And Antwell, you are a pillar of the ANT community; I know you are honest and true. But bring out the aliens to show they are no threat."

"Roachboss, you are a leader among all insectoids, and I

know your intentions are good," replied Antwell. *I must show my best diplomatic skills.* "Please, calm the crowd, and I will bring your request to the Queen."

Roachboss maintained his stance, turned to the crowd, and raised his forelimbs to hush them. "We will peacefully await your return."

⁂

The news incensed her when Antwell reported back to the Queen, but she did not show it to the human children or others in the hall. "Friends, human guests, a crowd outside is eager to meet our visitors, and I don't want to disappoint them." *I do not want to alert anyone about a potential conflict.*

"But will the children be safe?" whispered Antwell.

"Of course, everyone will adore these beautiful children. But they will have to hang on tight." Beewise hinted at her clever plan. *We must shock them to turn them!*

"What do you mean, Queen?" asked Celeste.

"I want us to make a splashy entrance," replied Beewise. "My citizens have never seen me take to the air. They will be astonished to see me flying you around the square, and it will make a statement no one will ignore. Hop on, children!" *I am ever mindful of appearances, and I know the power of surprise. This flight will divert the crowd from their unwarranted concerns.*

Everyone in the crowd hushed as Beewise exited the burrow, spread her massive wings, and sailed above them around the square. Hawk, Matt, and Celeste laughed and giggled as Beewise soared up and glided down.

Beewise looked back at the kids. "Hold on tight! We are going to make a loop." *I know this will win them over.*

The crowd gasped as the Queen flew in a loop over the

square. Then there was a ringing reek as one FLY noticed Celeste lost her grip when Beewise reached the top of her arc. The mob gasped as Celeste tumbled. But within less than a hexond, Beewise rounded her loop and flew under Celeste, who Hawk and Matt caught. The three children laughed and urged the Queen to go around again. That moment of fear for Celeste's life made the crowd realize the children did not even understand their peril, and they softened their view of the aliens. They erupted into a loud cheer as Hawk and Matt grasped Celeste. They clapped and cheered, with an electrifying essence emanating from the crowd as Beewise landed.

After the Queen lowered the children off her back, she stood on her outdoor throne and addressed the crowd, "Roachboss, I am so happy you assembled the crowd to meet our young guests. And my fellow citizens, I could not be more pleased with that round of applause."

I expect that will do it.

In the evening, after meeting the crowd, the Queen introduced the three human children to a group of post-pupal cyborgs who expressed an interest in playing a game.

"I know. Let's play hide-and-seek," suggested Matt. "You baby bugs, close your eyes and count to ten. While you're counting, Hawk, Celeste, and I will hide. Then, when you reach ten, you come to search for us."

The young insectoids giggled and nodded their approval, broadcasting a babbling bouquet. Then, they all closed their eyes and started clicking and chirping when the three humans ran off to hide. Most of the tunnels in the burrow had low-level lighting, but the children found one much darker one.

"Let's go down here," suggested Hawk.

"No, it's creepy," replied Celeste. She stopped dead in her tracks. *There's something sinister in this tunnel. He's got to be kidding!*

"But it's darker," explained Hawk. "It'll be harder to find us."

Hawk linked arms with Celeste, and she linked arms with Matt, and the three cautiously headed down the jet-black tunnel.

"What's that awful stench?" questioned Matt, holding his nose.

Celeste sniffed the air. "I don't know." She then turned as if to leave the foul tunnel and hide somewhere else. *We're not supposed to be here.*

"Smells like there's some evil monster down here that stores its rotting prey," snickered Matt. "Maybe it's a giant spider."

"Stop kidding around, Matt," scolded Celeste. "They said spiders are extinct."

"Well, something's rotten," Hawk said.

"Let's get out of here," cried Celeste. *It's not safe!*

"Just a little further. What's that down there?" replied Hawk.

"God, it reeks so bad!" Matt coughed and pulled his shirt over his mouth and nose.

Celeste buckled over as if she might vomit. "We should leave." *I'm going to be sick.*

"What's that?" asked Hawk, pointing to a dimly lit gelatinous mass that plugged up the tunnel ahead of them.

"I don't know, but I can't breathe, and the stench is making me faint," said Matt. "We'd better scram!"

Wait, what is that? I got to check this out. Celeste shook her arms free of Hawk and Matt and slowly crept towards the gooey pile. "Let me look."

"Celeste, don't get any closer," cried Hawk. "It might swallow you up!"

Celeste ignored Hawk and skulked further forward. Then, while she stared at the jelly-like mound in the dark tunnel, she tripped on a rock hidden in the shadows and tumbled towards the steaming heap. With her face only inches from the sweltering mass, she screamed, "I know what this is. It's rotting insect eggs. They look like the eggs in my ant farm at home." *Nothing to fear here, I'm sure.*

Hawk reached down to help Celeste up. "Are you sure? And no nasty monster spider is hiding behind?"

"I don't care what it is. I'm getting out of here." Matt turned to head for the tunnel opening.

Just as Matt bolted, the young cyborg insects found them and picked up the three kids, laughing and clicking back to the main hall where they started.

As the young cyborgs set them down, Celeste turned to Hawk and Matt and asked, "Did you ever see any tiny insects in the jungle or anywhere on the moon?" *I haven't, and it's very odd.*

Hawk looked solemnly at Celeste. "No, I never did."

"Me neither," added Matt.

"I think they destroy all the insect eggs they don't use for cyborgs and throw them in that tunnel," Celeste surmised.

❦ ❦ ❦

All the insectoid leaders concurred; a quintessential moment came during the second brainstorming session with the humans when the young female, Celeste, advised the insectoids that small non-cyborg insects were critical for soil rejuvenation. She suggested they hatch their eggs instead of exterminating them. She described facts she had learned about the tons of soil that beetles and ants produced on Earth by chewing up deadwood and how worms turned over the new soil and aerated the old earth. This suggestion was an idea the insectoids never entertained. Yet once they heard it, everyone agreed it made perfect sense.

Beewise was beside herself when she said, "How did we not think of that? Celeste, you are as brilliant as the stars in the cosmos from which your name originates." *This is what we've been missing all along.*

There was a universal feeling among scientists and engineers that their historical perspective and teachings about the Great Small Insect War had colored their objectivity on this matter. There was a sprightly stench in the air.

Beemajor reported, "I expect we were afraid that the insects would multiply, devour vegetation, and cut our yields."

On hearing this novel solution from an outsider, though, it made perfect sense. Small insect soil rejuvenation was the missing part of the puzzle they needed to reclaim the rest of their moon.

Beewise raised her claws and reiterated, "We can't turn back time, but we can dial up our efforts to rectify our past transgressions and rebuild our forests again." *I'm ecstatic that the children have provided us with the keys to solving our environmental problems.* "Our land is not bequeathed to us from our forebears—we lease it from our heirs."

🐜 🐜 🐜

On Congress' instructions, the engineers implemented the environmentally-conscious recommendations of the young

Earthlings, and within hexths, various advances in forest health occurred. WoRMs dug irrigation ditches, ANTs constructed water impellers, and BEEs transferred some pollen from flower to flower, producing expected improvements. Especially critical were the significant advances in soil restoration after the rapid breeding of small insects. Of course, this was the easiest of the innovations since it only required them to hatch non-cyborg-destined eggs. With thousands of eggs laid every hexth, and no predators to hunt them, the insect breeding program took off in a flash. The hardest part was distributing them around the moon. At first, they concentrated on freshly harvested lands. The non-cyborg insects worked their magic on soil rejuvenation in the unspent land for immediate reforestation. Gradually, they ventured into the spent land, bringing it back to health.

Beewise squeezed her claws together and emanated a shimmering scent. "Our small cousins are busy as BEEs, breaking down dead plants and turning them into precious soil." *I cannot be prouder of our innovations. It's simply incredible!*

"Who knew that alien children would help us with our problems?" exclaimed Beemajor.

Beewise shrugged and responded, "Even though the ANT corps of engineers chief was resistant, he knew we needed a fresh perspective." *I'm delighted all insectoids are buying into the children's ideas. We can do this together.*

Cyborg WoRMs turned over the rocks and hard soil in the spent land, which was easier after digging the irrigation ditches to bring water from the great river. WoBBs helped break down the deadwood from fallen trees and branches.

⁂

In time, the non-cyborg insect population flourished, and the unspent lands increased. BITE's environmental scientists studied insect behavior to help understand the unfolding process. There was a growing recognition that nature was the best teacher in these matters. They had forgotten this lesson with their earlier attempts to over-produce honey on Poo-ponic and nectar on Bilaluna.

Beewise met with Beemajor and a prominent environmental sciences professor at BITE to discuss what they had learned about the tiny insects' contribution to soil health.

Beewise sighed, "On Poo-ponic, all they cared about was honey. Having spent their intellectual capital on it, they also spent their lands. On Bilaluna, with a much smaller landmass, we didn't have enough trees." *But now we can reverse the spent lands.*

Beemajor added, "We simply needed to study our history to realize spent lands began when we eradicated our tiny insects."

"I hear our scientists have been figuring out how small insects improve soil," noted Beewise. *And to think we just discarded their eggs.*

"Yes, and I want to introduce you to the rising star of environmental science, Natbug, the great-granddaughter of Thunbug. She's the resourceful one that saved me when the meteorite struck. She has discovered several ways tiny insects help," said Beemajor, introducing the cyborg next to him.

"Nice to meet you, Natbug," said Beewise. "Can you share your findings?" *I am eager to learn all I can.*

"I've determined that tiny insects do more than we thought to improve soil health," responded Natbug, happy to convey her knowledge to the Queen, who she knew would follow her explanations. "As well as producing a nitrogen source when they break down dead plants and aerating the soil, their feces are also important."

"Please go on. This is fascinating," said Beewise, leaning closer. *I can tell this girl is brilliant.*

"I discovered that our small relatives have bacteria in their gut that they release in their feces. These bacteria are critical for the final breakdown of organic materials. We need this step to produce important mineral nutrients in the soil that prevent soil degradation." Natbug smiled, delighted to report her discovery to Beewise.

"That is a major piece of the solution. I'll repeat it: Our small ancestors are more important than we thought," exclaimed Beewise. "I know the work of Gretant and your great-grandfather Thunbug. Gretant's Antunite ideals rubbed off on Thunbug and have passed down through his genes to you. Your keen scientific mind may have taken it to a new level." *You are the cream of our scientific minds.*

Natbug beamed at the mention of her idols. "Well, if my scientific discoveries attain only half the level of your wisdom and Gretant and Thunbug's conviction, they will make a stellar impact."

Beewise smiled widely, proud of the accomplishments of a female BUG. "Girl, your flattery matches your wit, and your inspired discoveries do your family and your gender proud." *Girl, you do our moon proud.*

The insects played an essential role in the mineralization of soil, which was critical since on Bilaluna, like Poo-Ponic, plant-decomposing fungi, did not survive.

❧ ❧ ❧

Although the insects were helping reduce the spent land, as their numbers grew, they were also eating plants in the unspent land at a worrying rate. Some feared that their heavy consumption of plants might cause problems outweighing the benefits.

Natbug took an interest in insect history before the Great Small Insect War on Poo-ponic. She came across an old manuscript by Antoria, one of the last three insectoids who escaped from Poo-ponic right before the planet's atmosphere collapsed. Natbug showed the manuscript to Beemajor. "Antoria points to the same ideas about non-cyborg insects the Earthlings had taught us. But according to the biography of Antoria, written by her fellow escapees, Gretant and Thunbug, she died before she could finish her thesis." She got even more animated, knowing the best part was yet to come. "Her manuscript missed a final revealing chapter about how tiny insects promote soil rejuvenation." *I'm sure that's what she missed.*

Beemajor grimaced, "That's unfortunate. Had she finished, we may have solved our problems hexuries ago."

Natbug flipped through the pages. "But she wrote a chapter about the insect population explosion, which triggered the Great Small Insect War. She concluded the infestation was because the insects had no predators after their battles with termites, and spiders had killed off all their foes." She tapped hard on the book. "This effect was not a serious problem until the insectoids took over and non-cyborg insects moved into the wilds and began a campaign to increase their numbers dramatically." *I know this is critical.*

"That's interesting," noted Beemajor.

Natbug pointed to the page. "With no natural enemies, there was no predation to offset insect breeding and overpopulation." *This fact provides the solution to all our problems.*

"Are you saying the insects were intelligent enough to

develop chemical warfare but not smart enough to prevent the population explosion?" posed Beemajor. "Which led to their destruction when insectoids turned the chemical warfare on them."

"Exactly, at least after the insectoids drove them out of the colonies. Combine Antoria's conclusions about overpopulation with human ideas on tiny insects' soil rejuvenation, and together they may solve Bilaluna's long-sustained environmental problems," explained Natbug. *We finally have it!*

Beemajor put his claw on his forehead. "Natbug, that is genius."

"When our ancestors killed off the termites and spiders, they also threw off the delicate balance of our ecosystem. The non-cyborg insects rejuvenate the soil, and their enemies keep them from over-populating the lands and eating all the plants," Natbug elaborated with a shiny scent. *We now have all the pieces to the puzzle.*

Beemajor smiled, "That proves the point that knowledge builds over time with great minds standing on the shells of those before them."

"This time, we also need to throw in the bones of our Earthling friends," added Natbug. *We need to give credit to whom it is due.*

"Let's go talk to the Queen," suggested Beemajor. "She will be excited to hear this."

Natbug held up Antoria's manuscript and concluded, "Antoria has opened our compound eyes to understanding that nature is our most distinguished teacher!" *It's a lesson we forgot as we put technology before the environment.*

"And kudos to you too for opening your eyes at the right time," congratulated Beemajor.

Although Antoria was old when she arrived on Bilaluna, her detailed accounting of the plague on Poo-ponic, and the planet's ultimate demise, afforded her a famous historical figure status. She was one of few insectoid BLOBs ever selected. So, when Natbug revealed the details of her long-lost treatise, they made quite a splash. All BITE scientists were excited about the discovery. There was once again an 'aha' moment in insectoid intellectual thinking.

The insectoid scientists at BITE immediately started developing cloning techniques to reanimate the termite family.

In a meeting with Beewise, Beemajor held up a phylogenetic chart and explained, "Termites are closely related to roaches, so genetic manipulation and cloning of this insect family was quite simple." *I love relaying new findings to my Queen.*

"I'm happy to hear this. It was so tragic how Malevolant destroyed them. And now we will bring them back," gushed Beewise.

"Although termites do not eat other insects, they compete with ants, beetles, and roaches for food and kill some in battles over territory," Beemajor explained. *She'll love this.*

Soon later, they genetically engineered some of the BUG eggs to recreate the spiders of the arachnid phylogenetic class, allowing both termites and spiders to join the ecosystem.

"Queen, I am happy to report we have re-animated the extinct arachnid family," beamed Beemajor. *I don't hold back with our Queen. I know she understands it all.*

Beewise cowered but grinned, exuding a sludgy scent. "I never thought I'd say this about spiders, but I welcome their kind if it helps."

Beemajor replied, "Yes, they are the crucial element missing from our environment. The hungry spiders will now join termites in keeping our small insects in check." *We've figured it out.*

"Once thought of as our mortal enemies, the spiders and termites will now be our partners in this grand experiment called nature," gleamed Beewise.

Beemajor added, "Termites will also help recycle deadwood into fertile earth. Natbug told me that the material in their abandoned mounds helps rejuvenate the soil." *We learned nature is fantastic.*

In time, the rainforest insect ecosystem redeveloped the balance it had before the Great Small Insect War, and the forests were healthier for it.

～ ～ ～

Hexuries passed, and insects reduced the spent lands and allowed a small logging industry that eluded forest degradation. Replacing steam turbines with waterwheels reduced logging to a large degree, and massive tree replanting programs reforested the moon.

As the reforestation program reached near 100% completion around the 14th hexury after insectoids first arrived on Bilaluna, the new Queen BEE, Beehappy, declared with a sunny stench: "Mission accomplished, trees have once again spread throughout the moon. This struggle is one battle where winning is when we are completely taken over. Long live our tall forest friends!"

Once the colony replenished the forests on Bilaluna and life was again idyllic, the insectoids turned their attention to Poo-ponic. But unfortunately, BITE scientists learned from the loss of the first investigative team sent through the wormhole that the devastation on Poo-ponic was worse than they thought.

Beehappy announced the news about the disastrous expedition with a sapphire smell, "Our astronauts traversed the wormhole to Poo-ponic, as we received emissions from their transponders after the transit. But we regret we received no communicative transmissions, and the exploration party did not return through the wormhole at the predetermined rendezvous time. We extend our condolences to the families and friends of our lost colleagues." *This is not news that I cherish relaying.*

Expecting the atmosphere had collapsed, later teams to visit the planet wore pressurized suits and carried oxygen. When they returned, they confirmed Poo-ponic could not sustain life in its current condition. However, they scattered plant seeds as an experiment.

Beehappy reported once again, this time more optimistically, "Our exploration party returned and brought back our lost team for burial on Bilaluna. But their studies on Poo-ponic suggest the atmosphere cannot sustain life at present. On the bright side, the ozone layer was not obliterated and has largely recovered, and algae appeared to be growing in the marshes again. There are signs that the ozonosphere might re-establish itself to an atmosphere-sustaining level in time." She oozed a pleasant aroma and clapped at her own speech. *I'm so thrilled.*

Ever optimistic, insectoids on Bilaluna did not give up hope on their lost planet.

Beehappy danced and inspired her subjects. "Bilaluna is now as magnificent as ever. And we will not rest until we restore Poo-ponic to its former natural glory!" *This is a promise I fully intend to keep.*

Indeed, the insectoids were unsure whether they could ever reverse the devastation that occurred on Poo-ponic. Yet they had restored the forests on Bilaluna and saved their moon.

Beehappy continued with a steadfast scent, "We pray no planet will ever again have to learn the hard lessons we did. With a political, economic, and ecological plague of our own making—the Poo-ponic plague!"

❧ ❧ ❧

Be the species big or small,
there is neither vice so insipient as willful ignorance,
nor virtue so percipient as witting intendance.

CLOSING PODCAST [*TRANSCRIPT*]

Vive: As promised, we're back for a final interview with Narrant so he can sum things up for us, and we'll have live audio chat questions from our listeners.

Narrant: Hello, Vive. I'm happy to answer your listeners' questions.

Vive: The final epoch was about Bilaluna, which sounds so idyllic. If only your leaders on Poo-ponic had been so insightful, you wouldn't live now on a small moon, however beautiful. And your ancestors had to work hard to save Bilaluna.

Narrant: Yes, our moon is a paradise now, however small. [00:32] We must limit the number of cyborgs we produce to maintain our ecosystem.

Vive: And you have no honey, no currency, that's hard to believe.

Narrant: Well, it may not work in a larger world, but with the society we have, it functions well. We have achieved our constitutional goal of pursuing happiness. All Bilalunans are very content. I named our last queen Beehappy for a reason.

Vive: Two last questions from me, Narrant. Where does your name come from, and what is your real name? [01:00]

Narrant: Narrator ANT, of course, and the first part of my real name is written chemically as *n-cis*-3, *cis*-6, *trans*-8-dodecatrien-1-ol; methyl 4-methylpyrrole-2-carboxylate.

Vive: Okay, that explains why you made up names, but I recognize those chemicals as pheromones from my organic chemistry studies.

Narrant: You're right! The first is a sexual attractant, and the second marks an ant trail. So, I translate my first name as Attractive Trailblazer, and the rest of the title gets quite complicated, so I'll leave it out. [01:31]

Vive: Yes, let's not go there. I will say goodbye now because I want our podcast to finish with Narrant answering questions from our listeners. I want to thank Narrant for sharing his fabulous book and giving us his valuable time.

Narrant: Thank you, Vive. I hope your listeners enjoyed the book.

Vive: Now I want to get to our live audio chat because many people have clamored to ask you about Bilaluna. Okay, we have our first live audio chat with Buster from the shores of Boston Bay. [02:03] Take it away, Buster.

Buster: Hello, Narrant. I don't want to be disrespectful, but I don't trust your government on Bilaluna. It sounds like some evil communist plot. Won't your queen take all the nectar for herself and act like Marie-Antoinette or Stalin or Chairman Mao?

Narrant: Welcome, Buster. I must commend you on your knowledge of history, but I hope to convince you that our government is not evil. Our system promotes insectism, which parallels what you might call humanism. [02:34] Both insectism and humanism stress virtues, such as understanding, benevolence, compassion, and mercy. When you combine these ideals with the tenets of democracy and ensure there are strict guard rails against racism, sexism, self-indulgence, and autocracy, you can achieve Utopia.

Buster: But all attempts at communism in our world have failed. Why is yours different?

Narrant: Buster, I beg your pardon. You conflate socialism and communism. [03:00] Despite the failures of communism, socialism is a healthy component of many countries in your world. Your Scandinavian countries, New Zealand and Canada, have governments that healthily practice socialism. Surveys show people in these countries are among the happiest on your planet.

Buster: In my book, socialism equals communism.

Narrant: The key is the practice of social democracy. Democracy that cares about the society it serves. [03:27] Perhaps because we have gone through so much tragedy, we have designed our democracy to put our community first. We have a system that ensures common insects regulate the government rather than the government ruling the insects. We had a democracy that failed, so we learned how to ensure it wouldn't happen again.

Buster: I think your queen will take over and oppress the people like many monarchies have?

Narrant: Our Queen is like King William V of Great Britain—her title is only ceremonial. [03:59]

Buster: But will your president, chairman, or supreme leader become power-hungry and turn into a dictator?

Narrant: We have no president, chairman, or leader. We split power between fifty-six members of Congress. Having a dictator destroy our planet encouraged us to make sure we'll never have one again.

Buster: That may be well and good, but it still sounds like communism. I can't stand for that, and you shouldn't either.

Narrant: I respect your opinion, although I disagree. All in your world, my world, [04:30] and across the universe need to learn that it is impossible to achieve Utopia without practicing the first five letters. Remember that society works best when all can say U-top-I. That is, your fellow citizen comes first.

Vive: If we could only follow our own golden rule.

Narrant: You will never need to deal with a golden ruler if everyone follows the golden rule. And if we don't crave gold too much, be it coins or honey, we will enjoy our golden sunshine forever.

Vive: We have a final live audio chat with Bao in Xinghua, China. [04:58] Ask away, Bao.

Bao: Thank you, Narrant, for your book. I like it. Do your leaders approve of it?

Narrant: You're welcome, Bao, and that's a good question. I am sure Antilla, the long-time leader of Poo-ponic, would have hated it and had me thrown in jail or executed. But our current leaders on Bilaluna are much more tolerant. Like in your country, our leaders drastically changed how they led our people. You can see we moved away from capitalism, but we did it in a way that not only retained yet enhanced democracy. [05:32]

Bao: My leaders say that too, but is it true? Many millions in my country have lost their land. We had to move west when the tsunamis came, and the last one never left. And what about your environment? Did it improve enough so you won't have problems again, or is that only what your government says?

Narrant: Well, we had to lose our planet first, but our moon has political and social harmony, and now our climate crisis has receded, I assure you. But we must be vigilant. Both politics and the environment need constant care. [06:03] When someone asked one of the founding fathers of the United States, Ben Franklin, about the nature and sustainability of the colony's new government, he said: 'A republic,

if you can keep it.' On Bilaluna, one of our most esteemed queens, Queen Beewise, said something similar and stated it in verse to make a strong point. When asked whether Bilaluna's Congress was doing a good job, she said, 'Our republic is strong, our democracy is robust, but what are political vigor and social justice if we reduce our world to dust?'"
[06:30]

The End

AUTHOR'S NOTE

As a reader, I have always enjoyed allegorical, anthropomorphic fiction stories, particularly those with a political message. Although I have written this story about insect and insectoid societies on a faraway planet and moon, I did not intend it as a young children's book. Its societal, political, and environmental themes and its satirical approach appeal to a more mature young adult or adult audience. However, a youthful sense of humor might enhance its enjoyment. Ironically, a young children's story spawned this book and book I of The Antunite Chronicles—Antuna's Story. The two novels are the backstory or full story preceding and following the events in the children's chapter book—*Blackhole Radio: Bilaluna*, written by my wife, Ann Birdgenaw. The two stories are each completely stand-alone, targeting different audiences. Having your young relatives read that book while you read this one, though, might generate some interesting age-spanning discussions about the environment and the climate crisis. Years after reading the children's story, older kids or adults may enjoy finding this book. If you appreciate this book, you might also enjoy reading the children's book with your younger siblings, children, or grandchildren.

APPENDICES

APPENDIX 1

Insect time units using heximal counting system as compared to human time

Insects count using a heximal system (i.e., base 6), and insect time reflects this counting. One hex is approximately equivalent to an Earth year and reflects one orbit of Poo-ponic around its solar star. Other time units use hex as a base and endings similar to a decade, century, and millennium, except the rise, which is based on the power of 6 rather than 10. Thus, six times a hex is a hexade, 6X6 or 36 times a hex is a hexury, and 6X6X6 or 216 times a hex is a hexennium. We use similar terms for months, weeks and days; except that a hexth is one-sixth of a hex (about two months), a hexek is one-sixth of a hexth (or about ten days), and a hexay is one-sixth of a hexek (or 10/6 days = 40 hours). The terms hex-hexay (1/6 hexay), hexour, hex-hexour (1/6 hexour), hexute, hexond, and hex-hexond (1/6 hexond) are roughly equivalent to 6.67 hours, 1.1 hours, 11 minutes, 1.8 minutes, 18 seconds, and 3 seconds in human time.

Appendix 2

Pheromonic-English dictionary of insect emotions/non-verbal speech

    abashing aroma: humiliation

    abrasive aroma: annoyance

    achy aroma: regret

    acidic aroma: sarcasm

    acrid aroma: hatred

    affable aroma: contentedness

    airy aroma: carefree

    alluring aroma: attractive, sexy

    anorexic aroma: saying nothing

    antsy aroma: disturbed

    appalling aroma: cruel

    azure aroma: sad

    babbling bouquet: gossipy

    baked bouquet: conviction

    ballooning bouquet: egotism

    balmy bouquet: positivity

    beaming bouquet: admiration

    beefy bouquet: resistance

    biting bouquet: sarcasm

    bitter bouquet: ill-will, badness

    blaring bouquet: angry crowd noise

    blazing bouquet: hatred

    blinding bouquet: overwhelmed

    blistering bouquet: very upset

    bloated bouquet: intense pride

    blubbery bouquet: big lie, bold lie

blustery bouquet: argumentative
bold bouquet: defiance
booming bouquet: yelling
bouncy bouquet: excitement, happy
brassy bouquet: arrogance
brawny bouquet: strength
breezy bouquet: cheerfulness
bright bouquet: happiness
brilliant bouquet: optimism
brisk bouquet: petulance, crabbiness
bristly bouquet: grumpy, cranky
broad bouquet: confidence
broken bouquet: verklempt
bubbly bouquet: excitement, happy
buffed bouquet: strength, leadership
bulged bouquet: gratified, proud
bulky bouquet: hardy, resilient
buoyant bouquet: optimism
burly bouquet: overzealous
buxom bouquet: greedy
delicate fragrance: soft voice
dim perfume: uncertainty
earthy essence: grounded
eased essence: targeted speech
echoing essence: stuttering
effervescent essence: optimism
electrifying essence: excited crowd
engorged essence: yelling by a crowd
enticing essence: alluring
explosive essence: deafening noise
fat fragrance: obvious message

feathery fragrance: whisper

festal fragrance: merriment

festive fragrance: cheer, optimism

fiery fragrance: anger

firm fragrance: confidence

fishy fragrance: mysterious, devious

fizzing fragrance: uncertainty

flabby fragrance: stretch the truth

flaky fragrance: desperation

flapping fragrance: uncertainty

flashy fragrance: optimism, flare

flat fragrance: no emotion, monotone

flickering fragrance: idea

flimsy fragrance: fragile, weak

flowing fragrance: verbose, talkative

fluffy fragrance: gratefulness

fluttering fragrance: nervousness

foggy fragrance: confusion

foul fragrance: rotten, obscene

fragile fragrance: soft speech

freezing fragrance: fear

fresh fragrance: naïve, truthful

frigid fragrance: cold message

frosty fragrance: cold, unfeeling

fluid fragrance: articulate

fuming fragrance: angry

funky fragrance: strange

fuzzy fragrance: uncertainty

icy incense: cold fear

indigo incense: depression

inflamed incense: anger

inflated incense: egotism
intense incense: tension
intense perfume: insistence
ion-charged incense: excitement
itchy incense: eager, anxiety
odious odor: revolting
ominous odor: menacing
onerous odor: burdensome
padded perfume: guarded speech
pale perfume: soft speech
pealing perfume: screaming
piercing perfume: sudden loud noise
plaintive perfume: pleading speech
pleasant aroma: thrilled, happy
pleasant scent: sociable
plump perfume: arrogance, haughty
poignant perfume: dejected
pointed perfume: coherent message
polished perfume: eloquent speech
popping perfume: inspiration
portly perfume: pompous
prickly perfume: bristling speech
pudgy perfume: pushy
puffy perfume: pride
pulsating perfume: fearful
pungent perfume: irritation
puttering perfume: mumbling
radiant bouquet: enthusiastic
radiant reek: overjoyed, proud
ragged reek: cranky, disheveled
raging reek: anger

rambling reek: gossip

rasping reek: needling speech

ratty reek: annoyed

raw reek: naivety

rickety reek: anxiety, nervousness

ringing reek: scream

ripe reek: wisdom

roaring reek: loud, boisterous

robust reek: captivating

rocky reek: hard message

ruffled reek: panic

rumpled reek: alarm, terror

rutted reek: cringing, uncertainty

sapphire scent: sad

sapphire smell: gloomy

sapphire stench: suicidal

sapphire stink: depression

scalding scent: anger

scalding stench: evil, intense anger

scalding stink: angry response

scorching scent: hatred

scorching smell: anger, hatred

scorching stench: burning anger

scratchy stink: annoyed

scrawny scent: meek, guilty

screaming scent: obvious message

screaming smell: urgency

screaming stench: obvious deceit

screeching smell: urgent talk

screeching stink: urgency

scruffy scent: disheveled

 Terry Birdgenaw

searing scent: anger
seasoned scent: wisdom
seasoned smell: well-developed idea
seasoned stench: evil plan
seasoned stink: devious plan
secretive scent: whisper
seething stench: anger
seething stink: rage
shabby scent: upset
shabby smell: distressed
shabby stench: panicked
shabby stink: desperate
shadowy stench: deceit
shaky scent: uncertain
sharp scent: come back, rebuff
sharp smell: panic
sharp stink: sarcasm
shifty smell: deviousness
shifty stink: scheming
shimmering scent: happiness
shimmering smell: overjoyed
shimmering stink: ecstatic
shining scent: joy, contentment
shiny scent: happiness, joy
shiny smell: pride for others
shocking scent: surprise
shrill smell: alarming talk
shrill stink: alarmed
silken scent: smarmy
silky scent: romantic speech
sinewy scent: tough talk

sizzling scent: sexy
sizzling stench: anger, hatred
skinny, slim scent: shy
skinny, slim smell: cautious
skinny, slim stench: wary
skinny, slim stink: vigilant
slender scent: submissive
slender smell: gentle
slender stench: acquiescence
slender stink: compliance
slight scent: whisper
slimy scent: an obvious lie
slimy stench: deceitful plan
sludgy scent: unsure
smarmy scent: pleading
smarmy smell: beseeching
smarmy stink: evil plan
smooth scent: reassurance
smothering scent: frustrated, trapped
smoldering scent: passion
smoldering stench: lasting deceit
smoldering stink: growing deceit
sneaky stink: devious plan
snug scent: friendly
soft scent: caring speech
soggy scent: disinterested
soggy smell: unsure
solid scent: simple message
solid smell: rule
solid stench: evil rule
solid stink: unfair rule

     Terry Birdgenaw

soothing scent: reassurance
sour scent: resentful, bitter
sour stench: hostile
sour stink: sullen
sparkling scent: pride, joyfulness
sparkly scent: excitement
spiky scent: scheming
spiky smell: deceitful scheme
spiky stench: evil scheme
spiky stink: devious scheme
spindly scent: embarrassed, humbled
spiny scent: bullying
spiny smell: offensive
spiny stench: evil
spiny stink: cruel
sprightly scent: happiness
sprightly stench: ecstatic
squeaking stink: bothersome
squealing scent: screaming
stabbing stink: harsh insult
stale scent: dull, boring
stale smell: tedious
stalwart scent: brave
stanch scent: confidence
stanch smell: authoritative
steadfast scent: conviction
steamy scent: passion, sexy
steely stench: hard advice
steely stink: insistence
sticky scent: worry
sticky smell: anxiety, worried

sticky stench: devious
sticky stench: trickery
sticky stink: deception
stifling scent: oppression
stifling stench: overbearing
stinging scent: insult
stinging stench: sarcasm
stinging stink: insult
stirring scent: energized
stocky scent: unconvinced
stout scent: honest
stout smell: frank
stout stench: moral superiority
strangling stink: deep oppression
strapping scent: defiance
strapping stench: rebellious
stringy scent: tough talk
strong fragrance: pride
stroppy smell: awkward, obstinate
stroppy stink: belligerent
stuffy scent: arrogance
stuffy smell: conceit
suffocating scent: worries, anxiety
suffocating stink: cringeworthy
sulking smell: brooding
sultry scent: sexy
sunny scent: cheerful
sunny smell: overjoyed
sunny stench: ecstatic
sweet scent: nice
sweet smell: enjoyment

sweet stench: greedy

sweet stink: overindulgent

sweltering stink/stench: domineering

swollen scent: pride

swollen stench: megalomaniacal

syrupy scent: sentimental

syrupy smell: tricky

syrupy stench: devious

syrupy stink: cunning

thorny stink: devious scheme

vague vapor: uncertainty, hesitation

vacillating vapor: unsure, frightened

vexing vapor: confusion, upset

vibrant bouquet: proud

vibrant scent: ecstatic

vibrating vapor: trembling

vigorous reek: with authority

vigorous vapor: energized

vile vapor: evil

vinegary aroma: acidy smell

vinegary vapor: sarcasm

viscid vapor: sticky feeling

vivacious vapor: lively, excited

volatile vapor: aggression

waffling whiff: uncertainty

wafting whiff: uncertainty

wailing whiff: soft cry

warm whiff: tenderness, hope

wee whiff: whisper, quiet talk

wet whiff: rebuff

whining whiff: complaining

whispering whiff: subtle

wispy whiff: whisper

whistling whiff: brief shrill speech

wily whiff: cunning, tricky

withered whiff: muttering

APPENDIX 3

Quotations from Famous Persons and References to Movies, Books or Indigenous Lore

p. 15 "An ounce of good measure spares a pound of displeasure." From a Benjamin Franklin quote: "An ounce of prevention is worth a pound of cure."

p. 15 "If there's a way to do it better—find it—do not quit till you can say you designed it." From a Thomas Edison quote: "There's a way to do it better—find it."

p. 15 "You may delay, but time will not. Turn back your clock with a robot." From a Benjamin Franklin quote: "You may delay, but time will not."

p. 52 "That all insects are equal is self-evident, but denying ants their due is improvident." From the second paragraph of the United States Declaration of Independence: "We hold these truths to be self-evident, that all men are created equal …."

p. 53 "You know my favorite saying: Nectar is our sustenance, we're told, but don't forget honey is gold!" From a John Pierpont Morgan quote: "Money is gold and nothing else."

p. 53 "Indeed, plants may keep us fed and sound, but *honey* makes the world go round." From 'The Money Song' by John Kander and Fred Ebb, sung in Cabaret by Joel Grey and Liza Minnelli "Money Makes the World Go Round."

p. 57 "One small step for cyborg insects. Is a giant leap for insect-kind." Referring to astronaut Neil Armstrong's statement as he stepped onto the moon, "That's one small step for man. One a giant leap for mankind."

p. 59 "The program wanted us to think big with a plus. Soon, you big brothers and sisters will take care of all of us." Reference to '1984' by George Orwell, "Big brother is watching you."

p. 94 "Antuna once said, 'Insects did not weave the web of life; we are but strands that fray with strife. We must mend the discord we sew and allow nature's lattice to grow.' All life on Poo-ponic is interconnected, and any harm we bring to others we bring upon ourselves." From a quote by Chief Seattle: "Man did not weave the web of life. He is merely a strand in it. Whatever he does to the web, he does to himself."

p. 95 "The cyborgs are coming! The cyborgs are coming! We'd better get our defenses a-humming," From a text by William H. Sumner incorrectly attributed as a quote by Paul Revere: "The British are coming! The British are coming!"

p. 99 "And the *Battle of Lily Valley* humiliated us with those loser cyborg troops." From a quote attributed to President Donald Trump, "Why should I go to that cemetery? It's filled with losers."

p. 102 "Nations, like each insect, are punished for their transgressions. In the long run, Antilla's crew will pay for these aggressions."

From a quote by Ulysses S. Grant: "Nations, like individuals, are punished for their transgressions."

p. 104 "Or you could make up *new rules* for the game." From quotes by President Donald Trump: "Rules and regulations are really meant to be broken." and "Sometimes by losing a battle, you find a new way to win the war."

p. 116 "All leakers are traitors who use fame as a crutch. They are treasonous and must be treated as such." From a President Donald Trump tweet: "Leakers are traitors and cowards, and we will find out who they are!" and quote: "We're going to find the leakers, and they're going to pay a high price."

p. 117 "Leakers are like spies and spying on the President is a big deal. I expect there was spying. And when we find the spy, we'll make him squeal." From a William Barr quote: "Yes, I think spying did occur, and I think spying on a political campaign is a big deal."

p. 117 "She is a traitor who should go to the morgues. It's clear she's an enemy of us cyborgs," From a President Donald Trump tweet: "They are truly the ENEMY OF THE PEOPLE!"

p. 118 "Though my reply on this matter may give you woe, it relies on the alternative truths that I know." Reference to a Kelly Anne Conway quote, "You're saying it's a falsehood. And they're giving Sean Spicer, our press secretary, gave alternative facts...."

p. 119 "Antilla says we should jail or exterminate the leaders of the protests. These betas and chi are treasonous traitors, you see, and Antilla knows what to do to such treacherous scree!" From President Donald Trump's quote: "You know what we used to do

     Terry Birdgenaw

in the old days when we were smart? Right? With spies and treason, right?

p. 139 "Our history has shown us there is nothing we can't do.
If we put all our heads and thoraxes into the stew." From a Rick
Hansen quote: "There is nothing you can't do if you set your mind
to it."

p. 188 "I want you to act as if your nest is on fire—because it is!
And believe me, our prospects are dire." From a Greta Thunberg
quote: "I want you to act as if the house was on fire. Because it is."

p. 188 "Antilla and his thugs have robbed young cyborgs of our
dreams. We must act before Poo-ponic comes apart at the seams."
From a Greta Thunberg quote: "You have stolen my dreams and
my childhood."

p. 191 "It is as if an illness has infected our colonies and compels
us to destroy what we have contrived. This evil malady knows
if we fail to stop our careless actions, insectoids will perish, and
Poo-ponic will revert to the state before we arrived." Reference to
the indigenous lore known as the Cannibal Giant as described in
the film 'Dancing with the Cannibal Giant,' narrated by Sherri
Mitchell and produced by Chris Wood.

p. 192 "An ANT who can make insectoids believe in absurdities
can make us all commit gross atrocities." From a Voltaire quote:
"Anyone who can make you believe absurdities can make you
commit atrocities."

p. 196 "Enough with their ranting poems. Let them eat honeycombs!" From a quote attributed to Marie Antoinette: "Let them
eat cake" or "Qu'ils mangent de la brioche."

p. 203 "To be a BEE or not a BEE, that was the question. I tried to stop them, and they ignored my suggestion." Reference to William Shakespeare's 'Hamlet': "To be, or not to be, that is the question."

p. 231 Paragraph ending "Imagine that!" Reference to the lyrics of the John Lennon song 'Imagine.'

p. 233 "Oh no, I've killed it!" Reference to a line in 'A Charlie Brown Christmas' by Charles M. Schulz: "I've killed it. Oh! Everything I touch gets ruined."

p. 267 "Six legs good, two legs bad." Reference to 'Animal Farm' by George Orwell "Four legs good, two legs bad."

p. 272 "Our land is not bequeathed to us from our forebears—we lease it from our heirs." From a Chief Seattle quote: "We do not inherit the earth from our ancestors; we borrow it from our children."

p. 283 "*n-cis*-3, *cis*-6, *trans*-8-dodecatrien-1-ol; methyl 4-methylpyrrole-2-carboxylate." Reference to the chemical structures of two pheromones described in a paper by Blum MS & Brand JM. Social insect pheromones: Their chemistry and function. Am. Zoologist, 12:553-576 (1972).

p. 287 "A republic, if you can keep it." Reference to a quote attributed to U.S. founding father Benjamin Franklin.

ACKNOWLEDGMENTS

The author wishes to acknowledge a few individuals who played a vital role in completing this novel. Foremost, I want to thank my wife, Ann Birdgenaw, for I would not have written this book without her inspiration. She also played an essential role as a reading partner and proofreader. I also want to thank my book coach and developmental editor Nina Munteanu, a fellow author and scientist, and a creative writing instructor. Nina inspired me to expand my work from a novella to a trilogy, and her suggestions taught me the essentials of fiction writing. Additional thanks to the author and editor Erin Bledsoe, who helped with the finishing touches. Thanks to my kids, Kelly, Sophie, and Justin, for their encouragement and comments. Famous quotes or indigenous lore inspired many of the insect rhymes.

ABOUT THE AUTHOR

The author, Terry Birdgenaw, is a Metis of Oji-Cree, English, Scottish, Dutch and French-Canadian heritage, whose mother's first cousin is a long-time lead elder of the Metis Nation of Canada. However, Terry would argue that by moving away from the Oji-Cree territory a few generations ago, his family became assimilated by European Canadian culture. Yet, Terry has long been fascinated by the story of his ancestor, Mistigoose, the indigenous Canadian woman who was the first to welcome a European into his family line.

Mistigoose was both a tragic figure and an inspiration for parts of this novel and series. Her tragedy was that she drowned herself while distraught over the loss of her first son William, whom her British husband Robert had taken permanently to England. Against her will, the author's fifth great grandfather wanted to ensure their son would be eligible to receive a handsome inheritance promised to his heir. Ironically, as British law prohibited Metis from owning property, William never received his rightful inheritance, so his translocation and mother's death were both in vain.

The translation of Mistigoose, an Oji-Cree word, inspired parts of the story told in *The Antunites Chronicles*. In English, Mistigoose means little branch or twig. The series' first character, Antuna, whose own mother drowned, used a twig to save her newfound friend Dinomite in *Antuna's Story*. The resolution of *The Rise and Fall of Antocracy* also depended on the insectoids' realization that they needed tiny insects to break down little branches to generate the new soil required to rehabilitate their spent lands.

Visit Terry at:
TerryBirdgenaw.WordPress.com
https://twitter.com/TerryBirdgenaw
https://www.instagram.com/authorterrybirdgenaw/
https://www.facebook.com/TerryBirdgenawWriter

ABOUT THE SERIES

Antuna's Story is the first book in *The Antunite Chronicles.* It follows the lives of Earth insects transported through a wormhole to a far-off planet they call Poo-ponic. Young Antuna encouraged the settlers to work together, but hexs later, conflicts resumed. Despite her convictions, Antuna could not save herself or her diverse friends from the devastation of war. Still, surviving stories told how Antuna fought discrimination, saved the colony from starvation, reversed gender roles, became a scholar, and led the resistance effort. And though just a tiny ant, Antuna's actions changed society forever.

The Rise and Fall of Antocracy is the second book in *The Antunite Chronicles.* This *Animal Farm*-like story tracks the insects' evolution to cyborg insects, the growth and decline of a fledgling democracy, and the destruction of life on the planet caused by a long-ignored climate crisis. It also follows the utopian society created by a group of cyborg insects that escape to Poo-ponic's moon Bilaluna before Poo-ponic's atmosphere collapses.

Look out soon for *The Antunite Chronicles'* third book, released later this year. The novel *Antunites Unite* begins several generations after insectoids from Bilaluna recolonize their old planet with its rejuvenated atmosphere, which they rename Intopia. Despite their optimism, an authoritarian leader takes control of the colony and designs genetic modifications of ANTs to replace unwanted insect cyborgs and uses biological alterations and sociological rules to dominate its inhabitants. It is an allegory reminiscent of *1984* and *Brave New World,* where rebel spies must overcome a dystopian regime that uses histrionics, bionics, and socionics to subjugate its citizens. It's a brave new world that's out of this world!

www.ingramcontent.com/pod-product-compliance
Lightning Source LLC
Chambersburg PA
CBHW061316190726
48288CB00002B/532